To a bright and satisfying future.

Donovan

Julia recognized the label. An expensive and uncommon bottle. She hadn't needed to read the card attached to know it was all Donovan. All class. Attraction flared. Which showed just how long she'd been without a boyfriend, that a bottle of wine, even if it did cost more than most people's weekly paychecks, was enough to get her all heated up.

Well, that might be so, but she didn't have to act on it. *Couldn't* act on it. Her focus needed to be on the restaurant. She didn't have time for anything else. Maybe in a few years when her name was on the deed, when La Petite Bouchée was spoken about in the same breath as other great Vancouver restaurants, she could ease off a little. But until then, she'd accept the gift at face value, a way of welcoming her and her team to the company. Nothing more.

Dear Reader,

As much as I love to cook (and oddly enough, it's one of my great joys to slave over a hot stove—no, this isn't sarcasm), I also love eating in restaurants. And I love Paris. And siblings who support and snark in the same breath. So I put them all together in *Tempting Donovan Ford* and whipped up what I hope is a tasty treat. As an added bonus, no calories will be consumed during the reading of this book. Unless you add chocolate. Because everything is better with chocolate.

If you're curious about the music I played and the actors I pictured while writing the book, visit my website, jennifermckenzie.com.

Happy reading,

Jennifer McKenzie

JENNIFER McKENZIE

———

Tempting Donovan Ford

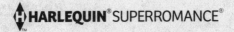
HARLEQUIN®SUPERROMANCE®

Recycling programs
for this product may
not exist in your area.

ISBN-13: 978-0-373-60893-5

Tempting Donovan Ford

Copyright © 2015 by Jennifer McKenzie

HARLEQUIN®
™ www.Harlequin.com

Printed in U.S.A.

Jennifer McKenzie lives in Vancouver, Canada, where she enjoys being able to ski and surf in the same day—not that she ever does either of those things. She spends her days writing emails, text messages, newsletters and books. When she's not writing, she's reading, eating chocolate, trying to talk herself into working off said chocolate on the treadmill or spending time with her husband.

Books by Jennifer McKenzie

HARLEQUIN SUPERROMANCE

That Weekend...
Not Another Wedding
This Just In...

Visit the Author Profile page
at Harlequin.com for more titles

This is for my aunts who were the first to buy my books, tell me how proud they were and brag about knowing me in grocery stores. Shelley, Bonnie, Anna, Kathy and Pam. (No, you were not listed in order of importance. Or age.)

CHAPTER ONE

JULIA LAURENT HAD always liked traditions. Turkey at Thanksgiving, cinnamon rolls on Christmas morning, strawberry pie in the summer. Classics. Things that stood the test of time.

She hummed as she stepped out of the cold, midmorning January air and into the back entrance of her restaurant, La Petite Bouchée. Though her name wasn't on the deed, in every other way the space was hers. As executive chef, she'd lovingly tweaked the menu, hung some of her own personal photos on the walls and trained the staff. She'd spent the past two years building traditions and trust, taking the routines her mother had started in the kitchen and making them better. In time, she was certain her name would be listed on the deed, too.

Assuming she could ever get Jean-Paul, current owner and massive pain in her ass, to agree to terms.

Still, she was satisfied. Jean-Paul had no interest in the restaurant. He'd inherited the Vancouver property six months ago and had been looking to sell it ever since. And she had financial backers and an offer on the table. As soon as they could come to an agreement, La Petite Bouchée would be hers.

Julia unwound her scarf as she passed through the delivery bay and into the long hallway that led to the staff rooms and her office. The kitchen would already be buzzing. Prep chefs would be chopping, dicing and julienning the mise en place for tonight's service. Stocks and sauces would be simmering on the burners. Veggies tourneed, beans soaking.

And Sasha, her closest friend and sous chef, flying out of the swinging doors toward her. "Julia."

Julia stopped and stared. Sasha looked harried and not the normal busy-kitchen harried. More like the sky was falling. Or they'd run out of chicken.

"Where have you been? Why aren't you answering your phone?" There was a spatter of brown sauce on Sasha's chef coat and a dusting of flour on her cheek.

"My phone?" Julia frowned and pulled the device out of her bag. A black screen looked back at her even when she tapped the power button. Obviously, she'd forgotten to plug it in last night. Again. Which was why people rarely called her on it. Something Sasha well knew. "It's out of juice. Why?"

"Never mind." Sasha waved away the concerns of the dead phone. "You haven't heard."

"Heard what?" Julia felt a trickle of unease run down her spine, but she kept her expression cool. Sasha might be one of the few people she felt close to, but at the restaurant, Julia needed to appear in charge at all times. It was key to the authority structure of the kitchen.

"Jean-Paul sold the restaurant."

Julia's stomach dropped. Actually it took a sky-dive off a skyscraper and splatted on the concrete sidewalk. But she didn't even flinch. She'd trained in some of the toughest kitchens in Paris. She'd mislabeled food in the walk-in and had her chef throw it all over her and the floor before insisting that she clean the cooler and relabel everything. She'd fired salmon too early and put the entire kitchen in the weeds on a night when they were serving the prime minister and other heads of state. And she'd made it through without losing her job or her cool. She knew how to hide fear. "He sold the restaurant."

"Yes." Sasha's huge green eyes looked worried. "And the new owner is here." Sasha's gaze darted back toward the kitchen door. "I tried to call you."

Julia dropped her phone back into the depths

of her bag, where she'd probably forget to charge it again tonight. "I see."

But she didn't see. Jean-Paul had sold? And not to her?

"Where is the new owner?" Julia fought back the rise of terror. She had no information, nothing to make an informed decision with.

"I set him up in the dining room. He's been waiting there about twenty minutes. He's a Ford."

Julia knew the name. The restaurant industry was a small one and everyone either knew or knew of each other. The Fords ran a string of well-respected, well-run wine bars that populated Vancouver's hot spots. She'd been to one last month and been pleased with the friendly service, decent selection of wines and small plates that could be ordered à la carte or in pairs with the wine. But running a bar was nothing like running a restaurant. Nothing at all.

Oh, God. Her restaurant.

La Petite Bouchée had a great location on Granville Island, which was actually a peninsula not an island, located on False Creek across from the downtown core. Once a premier eating spot, over the past couple of decades it had fallen out of favor with local foodies and been replaced by hipper establishments that catered to the city's adventurous palates. But Julia thought—no, *knew*—she could turn that around, given the necessary time and money.

The restaurant didn't need a complete overhaul. It was full of old-world charm and she'd put her food up against anyone else's. But… A chilly dread crept over her. Was it possible that the Fords had bought the place simply to turn it into another wine bar? Was the owner here now to tell her to pack her things and get out?

Julia swallowed the sick feeling that was trying to rise. She wouldn't, couldn't, show weakness. "I'll go speak with him."

She used her chef voice, the one that accepted nothing but absolute obedience. The deference of cooks to those above them in the line of command was key. One person who didn't follow orders could lead to a complete breakdown. An entire table's meal needing to be remade because someone didn't fire the steak on time or the veggies weren't ready. And that didn't just affect one table—it was a domino effect, rippling through the restaurant as other orders backed up. Julia's biggest job was ensuring that this happened. Every service. Every night.

But she wished she'd worn something nicer today. Of course, she hadn't expected to meet a new owner. Up until two minutes ago, she'd thought she would be the next owner of the restaurant. At least her jeans were clean and her sweater was cashmere. Julia didn't have closets full of clothing, but the pieces she owned were expensive and classic. Something she'd picked up from living in France for six years before returning to Vancouver.

Julia took the time to open her office and remove her scarf and coat, to check her teeth and smooth her hair. Then she steeled her spine and headed out to face whatever might be waiting for her. She had no clue what the Fords intended to do with the restaurant or with her. But if she was going to get fired, she'd do it in style, looking as cool and chic as any Parisienne.

The sounds of the kitchen washed over her as she walked toward the dining room. Noises that normally relaxed her, the clink of spoons and pots, the hiss of sauces reducing on gas burners, the whir of sharp knives hitting cutting boards, served only to highlight that she couldn't join her staff, at least not yet.

She pushed open the doors that led to the dining room. The space was cool and dim, as though it was sleeping in preparation for service tonight. Julia strode down the middle of the tables, most with the chairs still upended, toward the one in the center. Her eyes locked on the man sitting there.

He glanced up at her and smiled. A nice smile that made her stomach do a slow turn. Of course, that might also be the fear of the unknown. Julia shook off both thoughts. Her apprehension and the man's attractiveness needed to remain on the back burner until she uncovered exactly why he'd chosen to drop in without notice.

She smiled back, a slightly haughty one learned at the elbow of France's best, and held out her hand. "Mr. Ford."

He rose, clasping her hand in his larger one. "Donovan."

The oldest son. The one who'd been groomed to take over the family business. Julia had heard the stories about all three of the Ford children. The youngest, a daughter who was off in Jamaica or somewhere running a restaurant with her boyfriend; the middle son, Owen, who was a regular in the social pages; and the oldest, Donovan, who, while not exactly like his brother, was no social slouch himself. "Donovan, then." She inclined her head. "Julia Laurent. Executive chef."

Might as well put it out there now. If she was about to get canned, she didn't want to waste the next ten minutes on the niceties. She felt the ball of dread in her stomach grow.

She eyeballed him up and down, taking everything in. His steel-gray wool pants. No doubt made by Armani or some other expensive designer. The immaculate white shirt left open at the collar and leather shoes so shiny that she could see the reflection of her kitchen in the toes. Black, polished, Italian, expensive.

Oh, yes, even if she hadn't already heard of

him, she would have known everything about him from his clothes. Even his hair looked pricey. Dark and styled off his face so she could get the full brunt of his brown eyes.

She realized they were still holding hands though they'd stopped shaking long ago, and carefully disentangled her fingers. Polite and professional was the order of the day. She needed to know what his plans were and how—or if—she fit into them. Until she'd established that, nothing else mattered.

So Julia took a seat, allowing him to assist her into the chair as if he was serving her and waited until he'd sat back down across from her. She noted a briefcase on the floor by his chair and the intense look in his eyes. This was no ordinary, getting-to-know-you meeting. No quick visit to introduce himself and explain that he had no intention of making any big changes.

Then she took a deep breath and said, "So what is it you have in mind for my restaurant?"

DONOVAN WATCHED THE woman across the table from him. Julia Laurent's dark hair fell over her shoulders in smooth waves and her eyes had that sleepy look, like a woman who'd just rolled out of bed. And she wanted to know his plans for *her* restaurant?

As far as he was concerned, she could have it. La Petite Bouchée had been overpriced and, though the location was excellent, it didn't break even. Which was just one of the reasons he'd argued against the purchase. He thought that was reason enough. But if not? He had another trust fund's worth of motives to spend the company's money elsewhere. Top of them being that an investment in a restaurant was the reason he no longer had much of a trust fund to speak of. But despite his clear and concise arguments, his father had made up his mind. He wanted this restaurant and they were buying it. And even a heart attack two months ago hadn't been enough to change Gus Ford's decision on the matter.

Donovan exhaled around the twist in his gut that formed whenever he thought of that afternoon. His loud, gregarious father gray-faced and gasping as the paramedics wheeled him from his office into an ambulance and off to the hospital.

They'd been lucky. Gus had survived and according to the doctor would go on to lead a full life with only some changes to his diet and exercise routine. But the difference in lifestyle and the inability to go into the office every day had been hard on him. The entire family had felt Gus needed something, a distraction or a reminder of the way he'd been before the heart attack. Which was why Donovan now sat in the dining room of the Ford Group's newest acquisition.

He focused on the pretty chef again, his gaze

drinking her up. Her clothes were simple but well made and showed off a curvy figure. She watched him with keen eyes that he suspected missed very little and he felt a tingle of interest. "Maybe I should ask you what you have in mind."

She narrowed her eyes at him. "Is this the part where you thank me for my hard work and show me the door?"

He blinked. She thought he was going to fire her? As far as he could tell, Julia Laurent was one of the few good things about the restaurant. And since he still believed he could convince his father that the Fords were wine-bar owners and should be expanding into the gastropub market, not restaurants, he wanted to make as few waves and spend as little money as he could before selling it to the highest bidder. Ensuring that he didn't have to go hunting for a new chef was a key part of that plan. "No. I have no intention of firing you."

Julia didn't smile at his statement, didn't even blink, just continued to watch him with those sleepy eyes and folded her hands in front of her. "I see."

Donovan frowned. Shouldn't she be showing some signs of interest here? He'd just made it explicitly clear that he was keeping her on as executive chef. Something that didn't always happen when a restaurant changed owners. He pushed the thought aside. "I reviewed your contract with the previous owner."

Her fingers tightened, the knuckles turning white, but Julia didn't say anything.

Donovan pulled a new contract out of his leather briefcase. The contract was standard, a customary agreement of employment that all employees of the Ford Group signed, including the executive chef for all of their wine bars. Donovan opened the folder and slid it across the table to her. "I think you'll see that compensation is fair and on par with other restaurants in the city."

Julia didn't even read the large print, let alone the small, before pushing it back at him. "I'm not signing that."

Donovan felt the growing inklings of irritation. It had cost a small fortune to have their lawyer draw up the contract over the holidays, but that was what happened when your father insisted on buying a property in the second week of January. He studied her, leaving the papers there in the middle of the table. "Are you intending to leave the restaurant?"

A part of him was elated by the idea. If Julia left, it might be the impetus he needed to convince his father that the Ford Group had no place in the restaurant industry. But even as anticipation skirted through him, guilt overtook it.

"Absolutely not." Julia looked shocked, as though

the thought had never crossed her mind. So if she wanted to be here, why wouldn't she sign the papers? Her old contract had been lousy. Even if his offer had been under market value, it still would have provided more.

Donovan pushed the papers back toward her. "Then I think you should read over our offer. It's a standard term of employment."

"I'm not signing." She leaned back in her chair. "And I'm not a standard anything." She raised a dark eyebrow at him as though daring him to disagree.

That flicker of attraction returned. He was used to people who agreed with him, who nodded and did as he requested. There was something about her confidence, the innate conviction that she could turn him down cold and be okay, that intrigued him. "Perhaps you want to read the contract before refusing."

"Perhaps." But she still didn't pull the papers toward her or bother to even grace them with a glance. "Are shares included in the terms?"

"No." Of the many things he'd learned about business, keeping control of the company was the one he considered most necessary. Maybe if he'd been sole proprietor of the last restaurant he'd bought, he'd have been able to save it. Maybe not, but allowing little bits of the business to be sold off here and there, permitting other voices to share the leadership, inevitably led to disaster and eventually dissolution. He'd seen it happen not only to himself, but to thousands of once-strong companies. All fooled into believing that trading a few shares and board votes for money and expansion would be the boost needed to turn a floundering enterprise into a successful one. They were rarely correct.

Julia folded her arms over her chest. "Then I won't sign."

Donovan brushed some nonexistent lint from his knee and gathered the cool facade he was known for closely around him. "I don't think you understand how this business works."

"Terms are negotiable."

"Terms are. Ownership and shares are not."

Julia chewed her lip, the first sign that maybe she wasn't quite as confident as she appeared. "I'm not working for nothing."

"I'm not expecting you to work for nothing, but the Ford Group is family-owned and will remain that way." Feeling that they were back on solid ground, or at least ground he was comfortable on, Donovan slid the papers back toward her. "As I said, the compensation is more than adequate." He took a pen from his briefcase, a silver Montblanc that his parents had bought him for his graduation from an Ivy League school with a master's of management in hospitality, and clicked it open.

"As you can see here and here." He pointed with the nib of his pen.

Julia didn't even bother to read the salary and bonus structure, which he knew were better than fair. "I'm sure your terms are perfectly *adequate* in your eyes. I'm still not signing. I want shares."

Donovan clicked the pen closed with a forceful snap of his thumb. Great. Just great. He could already feel a tension headache starting behind his left eye. "Shares are not on the table."

"Then neither is my signature."

He pondered that. And her. She stared back, chin lifted, a crackle of heat in her eyes. "And if we can't agree?" His voice was soft. "Then what?"

"I guess that depends what you offer." She leaned forward. "What else do you have?"

Donovan knew he needed to keep the upper hand during negotiations. He studied her, looking for a crack. Instead, he found his gaze running over those lush curves again.

He was used to beautiful women and had dated plenty of them. And yet, there was a spark here, a flame that could easily be fanned into fire with the lightest breath. He put the pen down on the table. "Since you're the one making all the demands, I think you should fire the first salvo. Aside from ownership."

Julia tapped a finger to her lips, drawing his attention to how soft they looked. Soft and warm, as though they could eat a man up. He dragged his eyes away. He was supposed to be negotiating, not picturing those lips pressed against him.

"Can I be honest?"

He looked back at her. At least she was no longer tapping. "I hope you will."

"And you won't fire me?"

"Ms. Laurent, let me assure you that firing you is the last thing I plan for this restaurant."

She stared at him for another few seconds. Assessing. Donovan could see the moment she decided to trust him, the loosening of her jawline, the relaxing of her shoulders. "It's Julia."

Donovan ignored the warm surge of pleasure. It was only her name, not an invitation to her bed.

"I'm going to be completely honest with you. I want to own this restaurant."

Her candor surprised him, as did the information. "I'll be honest with you." He decided to lay it out on the table. Sharing confidences with her should go a long way toward moving forward as a team. "I don't want to own this restaurant."

He'd surprised her. Her eyes widened and her eyebrows lifted, but she didn't say anything.

"My father is the one who wanted to purchase it. I hope that I can convince him to sell." Once they'd brought La Petite Bouchée back up to its former glory and could demand a higher price than they'd paid. Maybe even to her. He tilted his head. "If you want the restaurant, why didn't you buy it from Jean-Paul?"

A small wrinkling of her nose. "I tried, but we couldn't come to an agreement."

Probably because her investors had recognized that the price was too high. A fact that his father had stubbornly ignored no matter how many times Donovan had brought it to his attention. He shoved the disloyal thought aside. His father was a good man, perhaps a little sentimental, but he wasn't an idiot. And if he believed La Petite Bouchée could be a success, then it was up to Donovan and his sister, Mal, to prove him right.

He nudged the contract back toward her, which earned him a sharp look. "We're going to have to have some sort of contract."

"Not this one."

"Maybe not. You don't have to sign now. Take it home. Have your lawyer look it over."

She laughed, a light, bright sound. "You think I have a lawyer?"

He eyed her steadily. "You should. I recommend one to anyone signing a contract."

She glanced down at the pages, then carefully closed the folder. "Well, you're either shockingly honest or this is your attempt at reverse psychology."

He didn't see the need to argue. He simply wanted to get the job done and was looking for the shortest and easiest path. "I'd like to get this settled as soon as possible."

"I would, too." She clutched the folder to her chest.

"A week?"

"A week." She smiled and Donovan felt something warm bloom in his chest.

No, that was a lie. It was a bullet of heat that shot straight to his groin. And despite his best attempts to shake it loose, including a ten-minute drive back to the office, it remained with him.

Or she did.

Donovan parked on the street in front of the three-level building in the heart of Yaletown, which not only housed the Ford Group's offices but also their first and most popular bar, Elephants, which served wine from around the world and paired food to suit it. The bar took up the first two floors and even now was filled with people. Primarily office workers who'd popped in for a tasty lunch.

They'd debated opening for lunch since it wasn't a particularly profitable time, but they'd discovered that customers often came back after work and stayed through the evening. And it looked good to anyone wandering by. Here was a place that was busy and vibrant, a place they should consider patronizing. And often, they did.

Donovan chose the stairs over the elevator to

reach the third-floor offices. He greeted Bailey, their young receptionist, briefly as he headed down the hall to his office.

He had the second-largest space on the floor. His father's currently dark office was larger, but Donovan thought his own was actually nicer. His father had a stunning view of the mountains, but Donovan had that *and* a peek of the ocean. More important, he could keep an eye on the sidewalk in front of the bar. See who was entering and exiting.

He hung his coat on the rack in the corner of his distinguished office. The space was decorated in high-gloss whites and ivories. Glass-topped desks and Lucite chairs. Everything open and transparent with elegant accents of silver and gold. It was a wealthy look and one that fit the jet-set lifestyle their company tried to sell.

La Petite Bouchée looked like a poor country cousin. But that would be simple to change. He made a note to call his designer this week and start discussing the renovation. Something simple and quick. Donovan saw no reason to dump a whack of money into a project when it wasn't necessary.

The restaurant needed updating, but there was nothing wrong with the space that some freshening up wouldn't fix. The room was open, there was a bar that could be easily extended to add visual interest and more seating, and a wall of windows that looked out onto False Creek, the inlet that separated downtown from the rest of the city.

He moved to his heavy glass desk and checked his email. He really did have plenty to keep him busy today and tonight and tomorrow. But his mind kept wandering back to Julia. Her sleepy eyes and slow smile. A man could lose his head to a smile like that.

"How did it go?" Mal, his younger sister—his only sister—stuck her head in, interrupting his thoughts. She was wearing the wireless earpiece that kept her in constant contact with her cell phone and meant she was liable to spin away midsentence to start a new conversation. But right now she simply watched him with knowing brown eyes. "Oh, my God." She plopped down in one of the low-slung visitor's chairs, kicking up her needle-thin heels. "Are you smiling? After that fit you threw when Dad insisted on going through with the purchase?"

He brought out his best older-brother I'm-in-charge-here expression. "It wasn't a fit." It had been a well-reasoned, logical attempt to change Gus's mind. Donovan hadn't even stomped his foot. "We had a discussion."

"Right." He never had managed much success in pulling anything over on his younger sister, but that didn't stop him from trying. "So what happened?"

Donovan shook off thoughts of rosebud lips and sexy curves. "Nothing I can't handle."

"Not what I asked." Mal raised an eyebrow at him. "You don't have to do everything yourself. I'm here now. I can help."

"I'm not doing everything myself." He wasn't. Hell, he didn't even have a signed contract. "I'm just letting you know that I have everything under control." Including his libido. Good thing he was seeing Tatiana tonight. The tall platinum blonde would be the perfect antidote to the discomforting feelings coursing through him.

Mal rolled her eyes in the same way she'd been doing since she was ten. "Whatever, Donovan."

"I'm not trying to keep you out of the loop." Or he was learning not to. Over the past couple of years, he'd gotten used to being the only Ford child heavily involved in the family business and the one their father relied on. Owen had never shown any interest beyond doing enough to collect a paycheck and, until their father's heart attack, Mal had been living in Aruba with her fiancé, Travis, running a beach bistro. But Mal had flown home immediately after getting the call and had stayed, taking on the role of marketing and media-relations director for the company. And there had been plenty of times since then that Donovan had been grateful for her support. Not only was she a whiz at the job, but she was also someone he could count on to make good business decisions. "I'll ask if I need help."

"No, you won't. You always think you need to do everything yourself." Mal pulled out her smartphone, tapping something on the screen. An email pinged on Donovan's computer in response. "The projections for Dad's little restaurant and my media plan when we're ready to relaunch."

He and Mal had discussed the plan in depth last night. Her plan was three step. First, the announcement of the sale. Followed by a short article highlighting the new look and extolling the exciting new path La Petite Bouchée was on. Finished with a personalized interview showcasing their chef. Donovan felt another flicker of attraction as Julia's face flashed through his mind.

"When will we be ready to go?"

Donovan shoved Julia's dark eyes out of his mind. They wouldn't be ready to go until they had said chef's signature on a contract. "I'll let you know."

But rather than nodding and accepting his information as gospel, Mal frowned. "No, I'm going to need more than that. Dates, decisions." She ticked them off on her fingers. "We can't hold off indefinitely. No one is going to write about the purchase two months after the fact."

He knew she was right. He also knew that they couldn't move forward without Julia's consent. "Then we come up with a new strategy."

She stared at him with that skewering glare she was so good at. "You thought this was a great plan this morning. What happened?"

"Nothing." Which was the truth. No signed contract. No verbal one. Just a promise that they'd meet in a week and that sizzle of attraction.

Mal scowled, her earlier good humor disappearing. But she'd been like that lately. Quick to grow irritated over small details. About the same time she'd returned from a visit to Aruba no longer wearing the sapphire ring Travis had given her. "Then what am I supposed to do? Sit around and wait for you to dole out information? When, Donovan? I need to know when to start contacting my people, dropping hints about an exclusive and setting up other events."

He rubbed his temple. "I know. Let's discuss later."

"When?"

He knew Mal wouldn't leave until she'd pinned him down. It was just one of the many reasons she was so good at her job. He made a decision. "First thing tomorrow morning. You and me." They could pick some hard dates and make decisions based on the assumption that Julia would have signed the contract by next week. He didn't want to consider the fact that Julia might turn him down.

"You and me and coffee," Mal agreed. She tapped on her phone again. "Should we invite Owen?"

"Why?" Donovan loved his brother even though he was regularly annoyed by him, but Owen was not a businessman. "What's he going to do? Offer to sleep with the reporter?"

Mal smirked, some of her earlier good mood returning. "Oh, I don't think you should be throwing any stones, brother."

"Me?" Donovan enjoyed the company of women. A lot. But he was hardly the Romeo his brother was. Donovan doubted Owen had ever gone out with the same woman twice in a row and he regularly juggled multiple lady friends. Donovan was a one-woman-at-a-time guy. It was just that he hadn't met a woman who made him want to give up all others forever. Nothing wrong with that.

"Yes, you." Mal shrugged. "Hey, maybe you'd find the reporter so appealing that you wouldn't be able to help yourself, and the great story with excellent placement on the front page would just be a bonus."

"You would pimp me out for the family business?"

Mal considered that and then shook her head. "You're right. It would be wrong of me."

"Exactly." Now, if she wanted to pimp him out to convince the new chef to sign…

"I'd pimp out Owen. He's much prettier."

Donovan snorted.

CHAPTER TWO

"I STILL CAN'T believe you refused to sign." Sasha stared at her with wide green eyes, looking impossibly innocent though Julia knew that to be far from true. Still, Sasha's innocence or lack thereof wasn't the point here.

They were holed up in a corner booth at Elephants, a destination Julia hadn't chosen and wasn't comfortable with. But when she'd mentioned to Sasha that perhaps they should find another place to have a bite to eat and a drink to unwind, Sasha had overruled her since they were now part of the Ford family group of establishments.

Julia didn't know about that, but she was keeping an eye out for the family in question. Or for one particular member. "Of course I refused to sign." It was probably ridiculous to think that Donovan would be down here in the wine bar. He worked in the offices. He didn't get down and dirty in the trenches. "No doubt it was full of legal ropes that would bind me to a lifetime of servitude."

The interior of the bar was gorgeous. Not Julia's style, but stunning. Although the lighting was low, everything sparkled and gleamed, like the inside of a snowflake. A long white glass bar and crystal lights that gave off just enough illumination to see without ruining the cool ambience.

"Exaggerate much? I hardly think he's trying to trick you into indentured servitude. Although I have to say, if I was going to be tied up, he would definitely make the list." Sasha tapped a finger against the stem of her wineglass. "And I thought he seemed nice."

Julia rolled her eyes and turned her attention to the food on the table. It was a little boring but tasty. Not something she'd serve, but then, this wasn't her restaurant. She swallowed the sudden lump in her throat. Ignoring the fact that she didn't have a restaurant to call her own. Not really.

"He had a nice body. Or are you going to tell me you didn't notice that, either?" Sasha wasn't giving up.

Oh, she'd noticed, and filed it away as a wasted observance. Because the only thing Donovan Ford had that she wanted was La Petite Bouchée.

Julia noted the lascivious glint in Sasha's eye, obvious even in the dim interior of the wine bar. She didn't like it. "Not that it matters, but he's off-limits." She wasn't going to get into a session about the rest of Donovan Ford's obvious attributes. Danger and distraction lay that way. And really, she didn't care who or what he did in his spare time, so long as her staff weren't involved.

"Oh, is he?"

Julia ignored the teasing tone and questioning look. "I told him I wanted him to pay me in shares."

The diversion appeared to work, since Sasha frowned and asked, "For the restaurant?"

"Yes. Like the deal I had with Alain." The original owner, the one who'd loved the restaurant as much as she did. The deal she'd never bothered to get in writing because she'd trusted Alain. Julia sighed. It was her own fault.

When she'd returned to Vancouver, she'd been thinking only about caring for her ailing mother, not her career. But Suzanne had wanted Julia to take the role of executive chef at La Petite Bouchée, a role Suzanne had held for a decade. Julia had agreed, noting that it was only temporary, just until her mother recovered and could return to the kitchen. Except Suzanne had never recovered, the cancer metastasizing through her body, leaving Julia with no family and a temporary job.

When Alain had offered her the position permanently, she'd agreed. There had been comfort in working at the same place as her mother, working with the staff who had loved Suzanne as much as she had. And she found consolation working in a space imbued with her mother's presence. Due to the restaurant's struggling fortunes, Alain had been unable to pay her the salary she knew she deserved, but he'd offered something better. The promise that when he retired the following year, he'd sell her La Petite Bouchée at a discounted price.

Except Alain had passed away before retirement, and when his nephew and sole heir, Jean-Paul, claimed no knowledge of the deal, Julia found herself with no legal recourse. Just a nearly empty bank account. But she could learn from her mistakes. This time, she'd get everything on paper. And notarized. Assuming she could talk Donovan Ford into it.

"And what did he say?"

"He wasn't amenable to the idea." Which was putting it mildly. He'd been painfully, stridently clear that he wouldn't offer shares. On the other hand, he'd admitted he wanted to sell, which provided her with opportunity. If she could find a way to merge the two, they might have a deal.

"And will you sign without them?"

That was the question that had been rolling around in her head since the meeting. Without some sort of ownership promise from the Fords, she was merely an employee and replaceable. After all, there were plenty of fantastic cooks in the city.

The thought of leaving the restaurant made her stomach twist. A strong, visceral gut reaction of

JENNIFER McKENZIE   35

no. No way. No how. No dice. La Petite Bouchée
was hers. No matter if her name was on the deed
or not.

"I don't know," she told Sasha, not willing to
go into her thoughts until she had some of them
sorted out.

Julia had spent too much time thinking about
it. She hadn't been able to stop thinking about it
all day. Not when she chopped vegetables, oversaw the evening service or assisted with cleanup
after closing. But she was still no closer to figuring out what she would do if she and Donovan
couldn't come to an agreement.

She did know one thing. "I won't be underval-
ued." Julia didn't think it was bragging to say that
the only reason La Petite Bouchée hadn't gone
completely under when Jean-Paul took over and
decided to cut her budget in half was that she'd
made it work. Unwilling to see the once-grand
restaurant where her mother had been head chef
declare bankruptcy, she'd worked around his ridiculous decisions, always with an eye on the
final prize of buying it from him.

Of course, that hadn't gone according to plan.

Julia's throat tightened. She lifted her wineglass to her lips and then put it down without sipping. Wine wasn't going to ease the rigidity there.
The restaurant, her mother, family had all gotten

twisted together and she didn't know how to separate them. She sniffed and dabbed at her eyelashes.

"Your mom?" Sasha asked, her voice quiet but
still audible under the hubbub of other conversa-
tions, most patrons half-corked by this time of
the night. One of the benefits of being such close
friends and spending so much time together meant
she didn't have to explain why she was feeling
emotional.

Julia nodded. Her mom had been gone for just
over eighteen months, but it still felt so close.
There were mornings she woke up and couldn't
believe she was gone. She wondered if that place
in her heart would ever be filled or, at least, not
feel so big.

She had no other family. An only child of an
only child. Her grandparents had died when she
was little and she'd never known her father. All
her mother would tell her was that he was a Parisian she'd met while apprenticing as a chef in the
City of Light. No name, no background, not even
a photo, though Julia could surmise he'd been lithe
and dark like her. Her mother had been short and
round, the years of butter and heavy cream she featured in her dishes showing on her round cheeks
and rounder hips. Suzanne had also been much
fairer than Julia.

"I miss her."

"Of course you do." Sasha hugged her. Julia

absorbed her friend's comfort. The kindness and sympathy offered without judgment or expectation of payment. Sometimes Sasha reminded her of her mom. The welcoming way they invited others into their lives so easily.

When she'd gone to Paris for staging—working in high-end kitchens for a pittance, the real salary being the opportunity to train under a highly respected chef—she'd looked for her father, checking the eyes of every man of the right age to see if they looked like hers.

Her direct appraisal had gotten her hit on a few times, but no closer to finding her father. She'd finally come to accept that she would probably never know. Her mother claimed not to have even told the man she was pregnant. Julia suspected he might have been married. Maybe she had an entire family in France, half brothers and sisters, a stepmother who would make those clucking French noises when she didn't like something and a father who shared her eyes. But she wasn't going to find them.

She sighed. Instead, it was just her against the world.

"I want to buy the restaurant."

She didn't need to tell Sasha. Her best friend was well aware of her plans.

"I know." Sasha rocked her for a moment. "But what if you can't?"

Julia didn't like thinking about that. Not tonight. Not when she was already physically and emotionally drained from the long day on her feet and the surprise of the sale.

So she didn't. She shoved it out of her mind and sat up, picking at the food in front of them. She knew that although Sasha was empathetic, she couldn't really understand.

Their dreams were as different as their upbringings. Sasha had come from a nice suburban childhood with a big backyard and parents who were still married. Julia had grown up in a two-bedroom apartment in the city. A beautiful top-floor apartment, but far from the picket fence Sasha had known. Sasha's mom thought gravy from a bag was an acceptable choice, while Julia's mother had made everything from scratch, even bread. And Sasha had zero interest in owning her own place and had once told Julia that she wasn't sure she wanted to even become an executive chef. The one night a week she ran the kitchen was enough for her.

It was as foreign an idea to Julia as growing up with two parents in the suburbs.

"Can we talk about something else? Who's your latest boyfriend?" Sasha always had a new beau, claiming that she'd yet to find one who could hold her interest for more than a few weeks. It amused Julia to see the way she cut a swath through them, somehow always managing to have an amicable breakup.

And because she was a good friend, Sasha went along with the subject change, telling a humorous story about a man she'd met last week and how he already wanted to take her away for a tropical vacation.

But Julia couldn't keep her mind on the story or on anything but the dilemma now facing her. She was going to have to figure something out. Luckily, she had a week and she planned to take every minute of it.

"Uh, Jules?"

"Yes?" Julia blinked, mentally rewinding their conversation to see if there was something she'd missed. Some particularly outrageous comment or a question that she hadn't responded to, but she didn't recall anything. Sasha's eyes seemed to take up half her face. "What is it?"

But Sasha was busy fluffing her hair and pouting her lips.

"Okay, *who* is it?" Julia asked, smiling as she turned to see what fine specimen of man had caught her friend's attention. And right there, having just come through the entrance in a tux that he no doubt owned, was Donovan Ford. With a beautiful blonde on his arm.

Julia swiveled back and reminded herself that she didn't care who was on Donovan's arm. But she turned her body just enough that she could sneak another peek.

The blonde's dress flowed around her, rippling like waves, and was a blue so pale that it almost appeared white. There was virtually no color to her. Skin like the glow of the moon, platinum hair of a shade not found in nature and eyes an even paler blue than the dress. She looked like part of the bar's design. The perfect woman in the perfect room, and her fingers were wrapped around Donovan's forearm, a clear announcement that he was spoken for.

Julia hoped he got frostbite.

"Damn. There's someone with him." Sasha sighed heavily. "Guess that means he's off-limits."

"I already told you that." Julia rarely got involved in the love lives of her staff. As long as they showed up for work on time and didn't bring their personal issues to the kitchen, they could sleep with whomever they wanted. Even Jean-Paul.

But not Donovan.

"Yes, I remember that." Sasha raised a strawberry-blond eyebrow in her direction. "Care to explain?"

Julia raised an eyebrow back. "Not really."

Sasha smiled, a broad, bright smile that had won and then broken the hearts of plenty of men in the city. "Please, please, tell me it's because you want him for yourself."

"I don't want him," Julia said, but her stomach

twisted. She ate another dull bite from her plate and washed it down with a sip of wine.

"Right. You just want his shares."

"I don't want his anything. And even if I did…" Her fingers fluttered up to her hair. "Oh, God. Stop talking. He saw us. He's coming over." She tucked a stray lock behind her ear though she didn't know why she cared. So what if her hair was a bit messy because she'd only pulled it out of her bun and done a quick finger comb? That was life. Not shellacking her coif into a helmet that could break someone's nose like the ice queen over there.

At least her clothing was nothing to sniff at. She straightened the hem of her nutty-colored tweed blazer, an investment piece she'd splurged on when she lived in Paris, and reknotted the leopard-print scarf around her neck. Paired with an army-green tee and black skinny pants, she looked chic and casual.

Keeping a spare change of clothes in her office was a necessity of being friends with Sasha. Sasha liked to go out after work and Julia liked to go with her. She loved cooking, but the industry could be hard on a person's social life. She worked while others were out and having fun. When she was off work, most people were in bed. Now Julia wished she'd begged off after work and gone home to bed, too.

She could feel Donovan's eyes on her, homed

in, noting everything about her. A shiver passed through her. She hid it under a small smile and picked up her wineglass, raising it toward him as if in toast. A statement that she saw and acknowledged him but no further contact was necessary.

He didn't take the hint.

"Sasha." Donovan strode up to their table looking very dashing and debonair and just the slightest bit mussed. His bow tie was angled as though he'd stuck his fingers beneath it to loosen the knot and his cuffs weren't perfectly even. A man who knew who he was and didn't have to put on a show for the little people.

He bent to kiss Sasha on the cheek, and Julia inhaled his scent. Basil. Fresh and just a little spicy, like the scent of summer. Another shiver rocked through her, rocked harder when he turned toward her.

"Julia." He bent to kiss her cheek. Cool air radiated off his skin, highlighted the warmth of his lips.

The shiver didn't come back, but that was because Julia was swamped with a wave of them. She swallowed and tried to act like his kiss, his nearness, didn't affect her in the least.

"Who's your date?" Sasha wanted to know.

Julia kicked her. Asking Donovan about his love life was not appropriate. Even if she wanted to know, as well.

Sasha pinched her under the table but didn't redact her question.

To his credit, Donovan didn't look flustered or flushed at being interrogated by a pair of women he barely knew. "Tatiana Ivanova."

Julia eyed the blonde. Her name suited her, cool and exotic and glamorous. Tatiana had stopped at a table of well-dressed people near the middle of the room, clearly friends, judging by the way she helped herself to a sip of wine from one of the goblets.

"Is she your girlfriend?"

This time, Julia didn't kick Sasha but she did listen keenly for Donovan's answer. Not that she cared what he said. Girlfriend, fiancée, wife, it didn't matter to her and didn't affect her life in any way. And yet, there were her ears, so finely tuned to any nuance that they were practically swiveling.

His eyes strayed to Julia and locked there. "I wouldn't say that."

She sipped her wine, feeling his gaze like a touch. It warmed her to the core. She sensed rather than saw Sasha sit back, knew she was going to have to answer a ton of questions later, but suddenly she didn't care. She met Donovan's dark gaze. "Oh? Then what would you say?"

Heat flared in his look, reached out to curl around her. Even with the limited lighting, Julia saw his eyes darken, the small curve of his mouth and the opening of his body as he angled himself more fully toward her. Signs of attraction. Her breath caught and held. She forgot Sasha was sitting right there, watching and listening to everything.

Donovan ran a hand through his hair, leaving lines through the dark waves. "She's an old friend that I should get back to." But he didn't turn to look at the woman in question.

"Of course." Julia tried to swallow the spark of attraction as easily as the wine. It was nothing she would act on anyway. "Enjoy your evening."

He didn't say anything, just watched her for a few seconds longer and then excused himself with a polite nod.

Julia watched him walk back, the easy way his hand slid around his date's waist and the familiar look she gave him, leaning back just slightly so their bodies were touching from chest to thigh. A different kind of pulse coursed through her. Hot and envious. Which was ridiculous.

"You want to tell me what that was about?" Sasha asked.

"What what was about?" Julia feigned ignorance, swirling her wine in her glass without sipping.

"About the fact that I'm sitting over here with

my eyebrows practically singed off." Sasha fanned herself.

"You exaggerate." Julia swirled again, watching the legs of the wine run down the inside of the glass, and willed her eyes to stay there and not where they wanted to go, which was to see what Donovan was doing with his blonde date.

"Really? Then why can't he stop staring at you?"

"He's not." But she looked because she couldn't help herself. It was instinctual. Anyone would look. And found Donovan's dark eyes on her. Heat flamed in her cheeks. He shouldn't be looking at her like that when he had his hand on another woman. Except he didn't anymore. He'd taken a step away from the lovely Tatiana, his hand resting by his side.

Julia reminded herself that he was her de facto boss. That he'd bought the restaurant out from under her. That she needed to focus on her career if she wanted to reach her goals.

And wondered what that hand would feel like on her waist.

CHAPTER THREE

JULIA SLID HER arms into the sleeves of her charcoal suit jacket and eyed herself in her bedroom mirror. It had been a week since Donovan Ford had barged into her restaurant and her life. And although she'd realized almost immediately that her options were limited, she'd felt obligated to take the full seven days just to ensure he knew he wasn't calling all the shots. He might sign the checks and be the one with his name on the deed, but the kitchen and everyone in it were hers.

She ran a lint brush over her jacket, making sure there were no extraneous pieces of fluff on the dark wool, before fixing the collar of her crisp white dress shirt. Paired with a matching pencil skirt, her mother's pearls and a pair of simple black heels, she knew she looked stylish and in control. Exactly the look she was going for in her meeting with Donovan Ford about the contract she still hadn't signed. She grabbed her purse, did one last check in the mirror and headed out the door.

The day was cool, one that brought color to her cheeks and made her glad she kept a pair of leather gloves in the pocket of her winter coat. She slipped them on, covering up her short nails, nicked hands—the badges of honor every chef had—and caught a cab from her downtown West End apartment to Yaletown, where the Ford Group had their administrative offices.

She'd done her research and knew they owned the entire building. She peeked through the windows of Elephants, cheeks flushing as she recalled the flash of jealousy that had accosted her there when she'd seen Donovan walk in with his date. But that was a week ago, and in the interim, Julia had come to realize that she was over it. Over him.

She was surprised to see how full the wine bar was for a Monday at lunchtime. Tables of business professionals with bottles of sparkling water instead of wine. It was as full as La Petite Bouchée had been on Saturday night, a sobering realization, but not one she needed to analyze now.

Julia continued past the wine bar's entrance to a smaller, less ostentatious door that had the company name written on it in gold font and opened into a tiny entry with an elevator and stairwell.

After a quick debate, she took the stairs. She appreciated the echo of her heels off the concrete walls. Strong, powerful, just as she was. She'd worked with some of the toughest chefs in Europe. A meeting with her new owner wouldn't rattle her. Even if she did find herself thinking of him at the most inopportune times. Though she blamed much of that on Sasha, who'd somehow gotten the crazy idea that Julia liked Donovan.

Julia shook her head. Of course she didn't like him. For one thing, he was thwarting her plans to buy the restaurant herself. For another, he wasn't her type. She liked creative types who worked with their hands and weren't afraid to get dirty. Plus, she barely knew him.

So no, she didn't like Donovan so much as she knew they needed to have a good working relationship. Nothing more, nothing less.

She reached the top of the stairwell and rolled her shoulders. Breathed in and out. No reason to linger even if she did have a bit of time before the kitchen expected her. She affected her best moue—the French expression that indicated boredom or a desire to get this over and done with—and opened the stairwell door.

A young woman with the kind of smooth skin that came from good genetics sat behind a long wooden desk that shared the same glossy effect as the bar downstairs. Clearly, this was their brand. All sparkle and flash. Julia swallowed. She hoped there was some substance beneath the sheen.

There was a handsome man leaning up against the desk. Julia recognized him as a Ford immediately. The younger son, Owen. He looked like

Donovan, but sweeter or maybe just more relaxed. Whatever he'd been saying to the receptionist made her laugh.

She stopped midgiggle and cleared her throat
when she noticed Julia. "Good afternoon."

"Hello. I'm Julia Laurent." She glanced at Owen,
who appeared to have perked up at the mention
of her name. Great. Exactly what had Donovan
been telling his family about her? She decided to
ignore the question. No need to borrow trouble.
Maybe it was nothing, just human interest at putting a face to a name. "I have an appointment with
Donovan Ford."

The woman nodded. "Yes, Ms. Laurent. If you'd
like to take a seat, I'll let Mr. Ford know you've
arrived." She gestured to a long white leather Bar-
celona couch. It looked custom-made, the tufted
seat and back running the length of the entryway.

Julia remained standing while the woman picked
up the phone and pressed a few buttons. A small
ploy to show that she was on the same level as
Donovan Ford when he appeared. But she hoped
he wouldn't be too long. Her feet hurt in these
shoes. Though she was used to standing all night,
she never did so in heels.

Instead, she stripped off her gloves, stuffing
them in the pocket of her coat, and then slid out of
the heavy wool. The offices weren't overly warm,
but they felt that way after the brisk outdoor air

and her brisker climb up the stairs. She folded the coat over her arm, keeping her practiced pout in place.

"The lovely Julia Laurent." Owen pushed away from the desk and held out a hand. "Owen Ford."

Julia shook his hand politely, perfunctorily. Was it just coincidence that he was out here prior to her meeting with Donovan? Or had he been planted here? Some sort of gatekeeper to soften her up or throw her off her game? "Hello."

She searched for something, anything, that might hint why Owen just happened to be in the reception area when she arrived, but the only thing she noticed were the laugh lines that radiated from his eyes. She liked them. They made him look like the kind of person who knew how to have a good time and included everyone around him in the fun. He moved that way, too, a smooth, laid-back roll to his motions that indicated a man who enjoyed living and didn't always have a set goal.

For just a second, Julia wondered what that was like. How it would feel to simply take life as it came and not worry about the things she couldn't control. "It's nice to meet you," she said.

She'd done some research on the family over the past few days. Elephants was their first purchase and had been a swanky lounge back in the '80s. One of those of the time monuments to shoulder pads and three-martini lunches that had become a city staple during that decade. But, unlike La Petite Bouchée, it hadn't stagnated. Instead, it had been renovated in line with the times, shifting from bright neon to flashy lasers and disco balls to its current clean look. And it had been successful enough to allow the family to buy the building that housed it and expand to three other locations in the city. All shared the same styling and nod to excess.

Owen wasn't listed on the company website. In fact, the only place Julia had seen his photo was on the city's social pages. Always with his arm around one beautiful woman or two. Maybe he didn't have the cutthroat instincts necessary for business.

His smile certainly didn't indicate a cold, shark-like nature. "The pleasure is all mine." And somehow, when he said it, the words came off as charming and self-effacing rather than smarmy. All in the delivery, she suspected. He took her hand and bent to buss a kiss along the back. "I love your food."

Julia decided she liked him. The pout slipped off her face, more easily than it had slipped on, replaced by her real, natural smile. "You've been to the restaurant?" She hadn't planned to talk about food. Today was about numbers and contracts, budgets and projections. The back-end things that needed to be done properly to allow her to focus her attention where it belonged. In the kitchen.

"A few times. The coq au vin blanc is amazing."

Since the coq au vin blanc happened to be one of Julia's favorite dishes, she couldn't knock his taste. She inclined her head. "Thank you."

"And the fact that you're not making life easy for my brother is just one more reason to like you."

No, she decided, eyeing Owen Ford. She didn't like him—she *loved* him.

Owen's smile deepened, showing off his dimples. "He's used to getting his own way. Being the boss. Always has. It's good that you're standing up to him."

Julia opened her mouth to tell him that she wasn't standing up to Donovan so much as standing up for herself, but another voice spoke first.

"Owen, what are you doing here?"

Julia turned to see Donovan behind her, arms crossed over his chest. She hadn't realized quite how broad his shoulders were. Not that she should be noticing now.

Owen's tone remained easy, a noticeable difference from the tightness that edged Donovan's. "Just checking in."

Donovan frowned and looked from his brother to the pretty receptionist and back again. "Well, if you're all done checking in, perhaps you could do some work."

Julia felt a twinge of sympathy, but the loaded statement appeared not to bother Owen. "Sure thing, boss. Bailey." He nodded at the receptionist. "Julia." He kissed her on the cheek and then exited the offices.

Julia watched him go, wondering what all that was about. She hadn't been kissed goodbye by someone she'd just met since her time in France, but somehow Owen pulled it off. Maybe because it felt genuine. He was the kind of person who liked people and was comfortable sharing easy affection. She liked it. She liked him.

"Julia." There was a low growl in Donovan's voice. She turned and took his outstretched hand, noting that it wasn't nearly as warm or friendly as his brother's handshake, and yet unlike Owen's handshake or kiss, Donovan's touch sent an arc of attraction through her.

Why? Why, after all these months of being perfectly content to focus on the restaurant and her staff, being satisfied with the occasional night of flirting when out with Sasha, was she suddenly finding her hormones waking up? And why were they waking up for him?

Seriously, she was going to kill Sasha for ever mentioning the attraction and planting that seed in her head. Because, yeah, she totally wouldn't be attracted to Donovan at all if Sasha hadn't brought it up.

Julia batted away the thought. Even if she were interested in pursuing the lure of Donovan Ford, now was not the time. She followed him as he led her down the hall, decorated with a few discreet black-and-white photos and a flashy starburst mirror, and into an equally glossy office with a wall of glass overlooking the city street.

"Can I get you something? Water? Coffee?" He turned to look at her and the attraction flared again.

"Water, please." Something to cool the fire within her. She needed to focus—and not on Donovan Ford.

He nodded and procured a bottle from a small fridge built into the mirrored sideboard along one wall. The glass he handed her was heavy crystal. Julia recognized the style as Baccarat tumblers. No plain or inexpensive glassware for the Fords.

She took a seat in the visitor's chair across the desk. No cheap imitation leather or rough, scratched wood, either. The seat looked like glass, but despite its cold and unbending appearance, was surprisingly comfortable. She'd bet it cost more than anything in her apartment except her chef knives.

Donovan lowered himself into the chair across from her and put down his tumbler without taking a sip. "I've had my lawyer look over your suggested changes."

Julia had taken his advice and contacted a lawyer to look over the original offer. Actually, he'd been a former boyfriend of Sasha's who had agreed to do it as a favor. Probably because he hoped Sasha would give him a second chance if he did. He'd been thorough and proactive, determining what it was that Julia wanted and then figuring out how she might get it. He'd had some excellent suggestions, including the addition of a codicil that would provide her rights of first purchase should the Fords decide to put the property on the market.

It wasn't shares or ownership of any kind, but it was something. And since Donovan had, both in person and again through his own lawyer, made it clear that shares were not on the table, it was the best she was going to get.

Of course, she'd asked for a hefty raise for herself and the staff, too. Judging from what they'd paid for the location, the Fords had money to throw around. She saw no reason why her team shouldn't share in it.

"You'll see here—" Donovan used the same silver pen he'd had at the restaurant to point to the term in question "—we've dealt with your request regarding ownership."

Julia scanned the words, parsing the legal jargon to understand the actual meaning. She looked up at him. "Just to be clear here, you're agreeing that I'll be given rights of first purchase?"

Everything else was flexible to Julia. Her salary, hours, benefits and other perks were things she could compromise on, but pushing forward for ownership was not.

"Yes. Should we decide to sell the property, you'll be given the right to meet the asking price first."

Julia nodded. "And I'll have six weeks from that time?"

"Four." He angled the pen toward her, a subtle hint to take hold of the instrument and put her name on the page. "We have to consider that a third party may withdraw their offer if they have to wait too long."

She accepted the proffered pen. The metal was warm from his hand and smooth to the touch but impersonal. So different from her kitchen knives, which seemed to absorb a piece of her whenever she used them. They were all sharpened a certain way, worn down in a certain spot. It was one reason all serious cooks had their own set, which they were loath to share. Julia didn't even let other people clean hers.

She pressed the nib of the pen to the page. This was it. She either signed now or forever held her peace. Her lungs felt swollen, as though she'd sucked in a huge breath and forgotten to let it go. Yes, this was it, and in her opinion, there was really only one option.

Julia signed quickly and handed the pen back. Donovan's fingers brushed against hers, hotter than the metal. Suddenly, that metal didn't feel quite so impersonal. Her eyes darted up to meet his. He smiled and she felt a flicker of interest rise up, tamped it back down and looked at his hands instead.

Hands were safe. They told a person's story without words.

Donovan gripped the pen, lightly but firmly. In perfect control. And made a series of long, artful swoops as he added his name to the document. A man who wasn't afraid to be noticed, a man who wasn't afraid to demand it as his due. He wouldn't be the type to hide in the back, away from the lights, wouldn't be afraid to ask for what he wanted and expect to get it.

She took note of the scar on one knuckle and the thickness of his fingers. Donovan's hands weren't sleek and buffed, not polished within an inch of their lives. They didn't look long and elegant like those of a pianist or a doctor. They were manly hands. Ones that looked as if they'd be just as confident swinging a hammer or using a saw as signing a life-altering contract. And strong. And sexy.

Julia looked away and tried to pretend that wasn't her stomach doing a long, slow flip-flop and her brain wondering if those hands could hold a woman's body just as easily.

SASHA MET HER at the door when she walked into the kitchen, a splotch of sauce on the shoulder of her white chef's jacket. "So? Everything go okay?"

Julia nodded. Everything except the lingering attraction that had followed her all the way to the restaurant. She'd decided against taking a cab, hoping a walk in the cold afternoon would chase the feeling away, but the chill outside had only highlighted the heat building within her and the certain knowledge of one thing.

She liked his hands.

Julia had always liked hands. Even when she was small, she could remember watching her mother as she stood over the stove, stirring with one hand, dipping a finger into whatever she was making with a practiced swirl. Twisting the top off a piping bag and then squeezing the first drops of frosting into Julia's waiting mouth, using her thumb to wipe away any that might get on Julia's face.

Julia had chosen her first boyfriend because of his hands. Chris Wright had been tall and thin with glasses and a quiet way in class. His father owned a successful construction company and Chris spent his summer working for him. His hands were thick and muscled, a working man's hands. Julia had found them fascinating, and when he'd asked her out she'd agreed.

Hands were a calling card. Chris's scarred knuckles and rough edges told her he wasn't afraid of hard work. What they didn't tell her was that he was also capable of creating the most delicate wooden animals. Woodland creatures he whittled from leftover pieces at the work site.

She'd expected Donovan's hands to be soft and manicured like those of the other men she'd met who'd been born to families where trust funds were the norm. But she seriously doubted he'd ever seen the inside of a nail salon. She wondered what other secrets he hid.

"It was fine."

"You were there a long time." Sasha's eyes swept over her, halting on her hair, which was still pulled back in an elegant twist.

Julia's hands rose to touch it. "We negotiated." Which was one way of putting it. In fact, Donovan had explained the marketing plan that was to be implemented over the next two months and the role she would play in it. While her first instinct was to refuse—to explain that she was a chef, not a celebrity—she'd held her tongue.

The truth was that chefs today were more than creators of food. They were arbiters of style and taste. Name and face recognition were a considerable asset in the industry. As much of a draw as the food and decor. And the Fords wanted to use her.

Better yet, the Fords wanted to tie her to La Petite Bouchée and to tie her so intrinsically that there could be no separation. When she'd asked why, Donovan had explained it was all part of the branding push they needed to do to bring the restaurant out of the shadows. "We need to show everyone that it's not the same old restaurant. It's young and fresh and headed by a beautiful chef." Then she'd had to remind herself not to get all twisted up simply because he'd called her beautiful.

It was probably all part of his ploy to make her agree. It worked.

Julia knew that if the plan succeeded, it would raise the value of the restaurant. The deal she and her investors had put together wouldn't be enough anymore. But it should also mean that she'd find it easier to get financial backing. Maybe even swing it herself with the bank since she'd be able to prove her own worth.

A wave of pleasure crested through her at the thought. No, she didn't have shares in her pocket, but she had the promise of a future. Something to work toward. The heady feeling made her smile.

"And?" Sasha asked.

"And we came to a mutually agreeable solution." One that Julia hoped would see her vision of the restaurant become a reality. She saw no reason it wouldn't, since Donovan had confirmed that he hoped to sell the restaurant in the near future. But she popped the bubble of excitement that threatened to rise. They still had a long way to go before then. "Is the prep done?" Because no matter what else had happened today, she still had a service to run tonight. With a newly signed contract, it now felt more important than ever that things go well.

"Almost." Sasha turned back to her station, checking the sauces and stocks simmering on the burners.

Julia didn't need to look in the pots to know what was there. Variations on the five master sauces that were the basis of French cooking, stocks that would be used in the sauces and reduced to glaze certain dishes.

She inhaled the scent of tarragon and basil, parsley and chervil being chopped as she headed to her office to check on the delivery and change into her chef whites. Tonight would be a good night in the kitchen. No specter hanging over her head, no worry that she was going to be bounced out of the kitchen and restaurant. Nothing but cooking.

"Did you see the delivery in your office?" Sasha called from the kitchen a few minutes later. "I put it on the chair by the door."

Julia hadn't noticed anything, but then, she hadn't looked, either. She'd been thinking and swapping her business suit and heels for her comfy pants, T-shirt, chef jacket and Converse runners. "Anything important?" She received plenty of deliveries during the week. Invoices for food, bills for their linen service, samples from suppliers.

"I don't know. A bottle of wine with a gold bow around the neck sound important?"

"What?" Julia's head whipped up to look at Sasha, who was smirking in the doorway.

"I sense you haven't told me everything about the meeting." Sasha gestured to the chair with her head. "Well, go look at it and then come back to the kitchen and tell me everything."

Julia almost didn't. She didn't even know whom the bottle was from. But the excitement bubbling inside her did. An instinct confirmed when she pulled the note from the envelope attached by the ribbon.

To a bright and satisfying future.
Donovan

She recognized the label. An expensive and uncommon bottle. She hadn't needed to read the card to know it was all Donovan. All class. Attraction flared. Which showed just how long she'd been without a boyfriend, if a bottle of wine, even one that cost more than most people's weekly paychecks, was enough to get her all heated up.

Well, that may be so, but she didn't have to act on it. Couldn't act on it. Her focus needed to be on the restaurant. She didn't have time for anything else. Maybe in a few years when her name was on the deed, when La Petite Bouchée was spoken about in the same breath as other great Vancouver restaurants, she could ease off a little. But until then, she'd accept the gift at face value, a way of welcoming her and her team to the company. Nothing more. Then she went out to tell the staff they were going to have a treat with family meal tonight, the meal she cooked and served before the start of service to make sure everyone was fueled for the long night ahead.

Because what was the point of having such a fantastic bottle of wine if not to share it with the ones you loved?

DONOVAN LOOKED AROUND La Petite Bouchée with a discerning eye. In the glow of the lights, without the sharp, exposing brightness of the sun, the space looked better. Not good but better.

The walls were plain but clean, as were the tables and chairs. The bar was too small and should extend another couple of feet to make full use of the space. They could easily fit in three or four more stools at a longer bar, which would mean three or four more people eating and drinking and adding to their profits.

The parquet flooring was worn and scuffed, and even if it was salvageable, Donovan had no plans to keep it. It was just a dated look that added nothing to the space. He was bringing in the designer next week to look the place over and discuss some potential changes. Hopefully, it could be done quickly and cheaply.

"Stop working," Mal said, shooting him a withering stare. "Enjoy your meal and the fine company of your siblings."

Donovan hadn't wanted to bring them along when he'd decided to pop in for dinner tonight. Well, not entirely true. He never minded Mal tagging along, not even when he'd been twelve and she an annoying seven-year-old, but he could have done without Owen, who had already hit on both the server and the hostess and was even now eyeing up the bartender.

But he supposed they provided a better cover story than the one he'd come up with on his own. That he just happened to be in the neighborhood when what he really wanted was to see Julia.

He'd debated sending the wine. It was a vintage bottle, one from his private collection. Not the sort of thing he generally sent to staff no matter their level in the company hierarchy. But there was something different about Julia. A fact he'd been forced to acknowledge that night at Elephants when, instead of going home and enjoying an athletic and gratifying bout of sex with Tatiana, he'd sent her off with the clear disclosure that while he'd enjoyed dating her, he didn't see it going any further and saw no point in continuing.

"I'm not working," he said and forked up another bite of his meal. He'd selected the steak frites despite Owen's advice that if he was going to be stubborn and not get the coq au vin blanc, he should choose the boeuf bourguignon. And he was perfectly satisfied with his meal. "I'm just looking around."

"You're making mental notes. And, Owen," Mal said, turning her attention to him, "stop flirting with the staff and pay attention. Maybe if you thought about business once in a while instead of your sex life, you'd be able to convince Donovan to give you that promotion you want."

Donovan blinked at his brother. "You want a promotion?"

A flash of panic tightened Owen's face before it smoothed out into his usual laissez-faire expression. "Of course not. I don't know what Mal's talking about."

But Donovan wasn't sure he believed him. Still, he didn't chase his brother down. Owen had shown little interest in the business. While Donovan and Mal had worked summers in the office and gone to university to learn skills that would help them one day take over the business, Owen had preferred to spend his time lounging at the beach and had flunked out of university after two semesters.

Even now, while Donovan and Mal held management positions that helped shape the future of the company as a whole, Owen seemed content to manage Elephants. It was a mind-set that Donovan simply couldn't understand, and he'd long since given up trying.

He understood that Owen might not be interested in the food-and-wine industry. He might not even be interested in business. But Owen didn't seem to be interested in anything else, either. He flicked from hobby to hobby and woman to woman like a butterfly. Barely settling anywhere long enough to get a feel for the surface, let alone mine the depths. But that wasn't Donovan's problem. So long as Owen managed to keep Elephants running, he would leave him be.

They talked about other things. How their father was doing, the local sports teams, a ski vacation Owen was planning on taking next weekend. "And then maybe somewhere tropical." Owen looked at Mal. "I thought I might go and visit Travis." Owen and Travis had always gotten along well, far better than Owen and Donovan.

Donovan saw the way his sister seized up at the mention of Travis's name, though she covered it well, smoothing her napkin and picking up her wineglass without the slightest shake. Yes, there was definitely something going on, but she didn't seem inclined to talk about it, and Donovan wasn't about to bring it up here. He changed the subject, noting the release of his sister's shoulders.

The conversation meandered after that, and Donovan was grateful when their server came by to ask if they'd like anything else.

"Yes," Owen said. "Could you ask the chef to come out? I'd like to give her my compliments personally."

Donovan felt something strange and sharp bite through him. Owen shouldn't be asking for Julia, implying that he was the one who knew her. He glared at his brother. Kept glaring when Julia came out, looking warm and sexy, and allowed Owen to kiss her on the cheek and then kissed him in return.

"Julia, I'd like to introduce you to my sister, Mallory." The two women greeted each other with a friendly smile and murmured pleasantries. "And you know Donovan."

Julia's gaze barely flicked to him, fluttered over like nothing. It cut. He wasn't used to being passed over and he decided he didn't care for it.

"How was your meal?" Julia didn't even mention the bottle of wine, which surprised him. Unless she hadn't received it?

No, he knew it had arrived. He'd insisted on a signature upon delivery and recognized Sasha's name. While Donovan didn't know her well, he found it highly unlikely that Sasha would have forgotten to give Julia the bottle or kept it for herself, which meant Julia didn't want to acknowledge it. Or him.

His brother was practically falling all over himself and Julia, praising the excellence of the meal. Mal was a little more circumspect, but she was incredibly complimentary, too. Of course, they hadn't had their gifts ignored.

"Did you like your gift?" Donovan said when Julia finally looked at him.

She jolted. "Yes, thank you. The staff and I enjoyed it very much."

She'd shared it with her staff? The thousand-dollar bottle he'd handpicked from his stash to give to her personally had been passed around the kitchen? But even as the thought flashed through his mind, Donovan could appreciate the magnanimity of her gesture. What better way to show people how much you appreciated them than by sharing your good fortune, which was exactly what he'd done with her. He'd just hoped she might return the favor by sharing the bottle with him. "I'm glad to hear it."

Julia nodded, a light flush rising on her cheeks. "Well, if you'll excuse me, I need to get back to the kitchen."

"Of course," Donovan said before Owen could. He watched her walk away, the sway in her step that made him forget all about the skinny blondes of his past. Tatiana who?

"I didn't know we were sending wine to our staff now."

"We're not." This was a personal gift from him.

But he didn't tell his sister that. And he wasn't even sure what had brought on the generosity. He needed to concentrate on getting the restaurant up to par so that when he managed to get his father's agreement to sell, they could list the property immediately. He needed to focus on work. They all did.

Donovan glanced at his brother, who was smiling at the bartender across the room. "Owen." His voice was sharper than he'd intended, but first Julia and then the bartender? Was there anyone safe from Owen's charms? "Don't you have to work tonight?"

Owen should be on-site at Elephants, making sure everything was running smoothly, not sitting in a restaurant. He didn't appear upset by Donovan's tone. "I'm heading over after dinner. The staff can handle things without me."

Donovan was sure they could, since the assistant manager at Elephants was incredibly competent. She could probably handle the Apocalypse without batting an eye. Still, that didn't excuse Owen from his work. If he wanted to get paid, he needed to put in the hours. "You're expected to be there—"

"I haven't had a day off in two weeks and I'm working tonight. Okay?" Owen patted his lips and then rose. "If it makes you happy, I'll go now."

But Donovan noticed that Owen stopped by the

bar, charmed the woman working behind it, and chatted with the hostess on his way out. Donovan wouldn't have minded any of that. Owen's people skills were his greatest attribute. But when Donovan saw Julia duck back out of the kitchen and head straight toward his brother, saw them hug and kiss each other once more, his hands fisted.

No. His brother was welcome to spread his charm across the city. He could date a different woman every night. He could bring them into his bar and comp them drinks and food all night. But he could not date Julia. Hell, no. Donovan had just gotten her to sign a contract. He wasn't about to have Owen risk that for a quickie.

But he kept his aggravation hidden under a polite smile. This was nothing to get into now. Especially since he'd be sure that it wouldn't amount to anything.

Donovan and Mal chatted about work for a while, and when their server came by to ask if they'd like anything else, he ordered dessert and coffee. Just getting the full meal experience provided by the restaurant. And if he got another look at Julia, that would be okay, too.

Mal declined. "I'm exhausted," she told him. "If I have coffee this late, I'll be up all night." She did look tired.

"We can go, then." He started to lift a hand to call for the check and cancel the dessert.

"No, no." Mal waved a hand. "You stay." She stood and came over to give him a kiss on the cheek. "Enjoy the dessert. I'll see you tomorrow."

He considered leaving anyway. He didn't need the dessert, but he really should try to get a handle on the customer service provided by La Petite Bouchée.

Instead of remaining at the table, he caught the server's attention and said he'd like his coffee and dessert at the bar. The server nodded and walked him over, making certain he had everything he needed before disappearing. Donovan was impressed. Julia had trained her staff well and the food was excellent, which would make his job much easier.

The bar stool he was on was rickety and the cushioning was almost nonexistent, but the bar was clean and the woman behind it was friendly. She answered all of Donovan's questions knowledgeably, keeping an eye on the other customers and segueing between all of them easily.

While he sipped his coffee, Donovan studied the beer-and-wine list. Satisfactory, but with the number of craft breweries and boutique wineries that permeated the West Coast, Donovan knew it could be better.

The pair of men beside him were waiting for their

table and chatting about their day. He eavesdropped, only half listening while he mentally planned the changes. New interior, new seats and bar stools, new menu. Then one of them said something that caught his ear.

"If this place didn't look so terrible, I would totally consider having our wedding reception here."

"Excuse me." He turned on his friendly business smile. He was no Owen when it came to people skills, but he was entirely capable of holding his own. "I'm Donovan Ford. My family just bought this restaurant." He shook their hands and proceeded to elicit their feelings on the restaurant.

They had a lot to say.

"So why do you come?" he asked after they'd filled him in on their many observances. Apparently, they came often. At least once a week.

"The food," the dark-haired man said.

"As good as anything we had in Paris last year," said the blond. "The chef is too good for this place. No offense."

"None taken."

The blond smiled. "I didn't think she'd stay this long."

"Have you been coming awhile?" Donovan was interested to hear this. Loyal, regular customers were the lifeblood of the industry. If these men were regulars, he wanted to know why.

"Oh, yeah, at least three years. We started coming because we were friends with Alain, the original owner. But when Julia took over cooking from her mom, we started coming for the food."

"Her mom?" Donovan tapped a finger against the side of his coffee mug. What did her mother have to do with the restaurant?

"Suzanne was the chef here before she got sick. When she couldn't work any longer, Julia came back to Vancouver to help. I think she only intended to stay until her mom got better..." His voice trailed off.

Donovan studied them, noting the sad tilt to their eyes. "But she didn't."

"No." The brunette shook his head. "She died. We thought Julia might leave then. Go back to Paris."

Donovan ignored the clamp of his own heart. His father had survived. According to the doctor, as long as he continued to take care of himself, Gus Ford would live a long life. "But she didn't leave."

"No, she settled in." The dark-haired man smiled. "I think it's sort of a tribute to her mother."

Donovan could understand the desire. And felt as though maybe he knew Julia a little better than he had before.

He chatted with the men until they finished

their drinks and moved to their waiting table. Then he waited for Julia.

JULIA REMAINED IN the kitchen until the last plate was served and she was sure there were no further orders coming in before she made her way back into the dining room. She knew Donovan was still there. Had been informed by the staff the moment he'd left the table and taken up a stool at the bar instead of leaving.

The room was only a quarter full, which wasn't terrible considering it had been only half-full this evening to begin with. She saw Donovan across the room, still sitting at the bar. He had a menu in his hand and was frowning. Even with twenty tables and about twenty-five feet between them, she could feel his magnetism. But that magnetism, that draw of attraction, wasn't why she walked over. She was simply being polite, making nice with the new owner.

Still, when he noticed her, putting down the menu and focusing all his attention on her, Julia felt the pull all the way to her toes.

"Donovan." She slid onto the stool beside him. "I didn't expect you'd still be here." A subtle hint that he shouldn't be.

He smiled, either ignoring or missing the gentle rebuke. "I thought we could talk."

"Oh?" The bartender, Stef, arrived to place a

glass of water in front of her. Julia stilled the sudden fluttering in her chest with a sip of it and smiled at the woman who was working her way toward a law degree. "Thanks."

"The menu's dated," Donovan said.

Julia stiffened. She knew the menu was dated. It hadn't changed in thirty years. But her attempts to modernize it had fallen on deaf ears. First with Alain, who hadn't wanted to change anything, and then with Jean-Paul, who'd refused to spend money.

She reminded herself that she should be grateful Donovan saw the need, too—she wouldn't have to convince him—but something about his tone put her on the defensive. As if he thought she was the one responsible for it.

"I happen to agree. I hope this means you're open to changing it."

He nodded, his eyes already scanning the room. At least the space was decent. It needed a bit of polishing, but nothing major. Julia had convinced Alain to repaint the walls so they were a crisp white, and the photos on the walls were full of charm. A mix of pictures from Alain's childhood in Bordeaux and some from her mother's personal collection of travels through France. Besides the one of Julia playing in the fountain, there was also one she'd taken during her first year living in Paris. In her opinion, they created a friendly, welcoming atmosphere. A personalization that let diners know the meal wasn't just about eating but was an experience.

The floor could use a good sanding and restaining to return it to its former golden glory and the light fixtures should be swapped out for something more current, but other than that, the restaurant looked nice. It was classic, like the food they served.

"And the space needs a major update."

Apparently, Donovan Ford felt otherwise.

Julia felt the stiffness travel up her spine, across her shoulders and settle in her jaw. "Don't you think that's a bit of an overreaction?"

His eyes met hers and held. She felt that spark of attraction again and doused it with a quick toss of common sense, like flour on a grease fire. Always best to tamp those things out before they had a chance to catch.

"I'd say the renovations are a necessity. The seats aren't comfortable." He shifted as though to prove his point. "And the decor is at least twenty years out of style."

Out of style? Well, only if you thought looking like the inside of a snowflake was style.

"It's old-world," she countered, recalling the lovely bistros and family-owned restaurants she'd favored during her years in Europe. She didn't want La Petite Bouchée to be quite as authentically homespun as that—it didn't suit the food she wanted to serve—but the aesthetic of appearing like something that had lasted hundreds of years and would last hundreds more appealed to her. Classic was what she aspired to. Glossy white bar tops and Lucite seats were tomorrow's Harvest Gold appliances and velvet wallpaper.

"It's old-fashioned." Donovan lifted one dark eyebrow, a quirk Julia always wished she'd been able to master. Mostly because she hated it being directed at her and wished she could do the same in return as a way to negate the skill. "Who is the target market?"

She scowled. "Are we talking about numbers, then?"

"If you want."

She didn't want. She'd looked at the numbers often enough to know they weren't going to support her argument. The fact was La Petite Bouchée was lucky to break even on any given night, but Julia didn't think that was because of the decor.

"I know it could use some freshening up," she admitted, "but the decor is part of the charm." And she wanted him to stop talking about any potential changes. One thing at a time. It was enough that she'd signed the contract today and agreed to the marketing blitz. She didn't want to hear how he planned to rip the heart and soul out of the place, as well.

"It's not charming." Now she did feel insulted. "But it could be. It will be when we're finished."

Julia peeked up at him. "I'm not going to let you make this a carbon copy of every other place you own."

To his credit, Donovan didn't get his back up or look put out by her comment at all. "You don't like the wine bars?"

His calm tone helped her find her own cool. "I do like them. For bars. But that's not what La Petite Bouchée is about. We're an iconic and classic fine-dining establishment. The decor should reflect that." And since she was the one who'd hopefully be buying it from him in the future, Julia felt she should have some say in the matter.

Donovan watched her, and Julia felt a warm flush crawl over her skin. "I'll take that into consideration." And before she could get her back up about how he should do more than consider her opinion, he said, "The service was good and your food was excellent."

"Not dated?" She couldn't help sniping.

He grinned and accepted the verbal tap. "Not dated. But nothing about the decor showcases just how good it is." Julia opened her mouth to object. Her food was classic. The decor needed to follow suit. But he had more to say. "Which is why it needs updating."

Julia sipped her water instead of arguing. He was right. She knew that. She just wanted to protect the traditional charm that would make La Petite Bouchée stand out. But she should hear him out before deciding that he was wrong. "Okay. Like what?"

He smiled and it slipped through her like warm chocolate sauce. "That is a question for my designer. Why don't we table this discussion until she's had a chance to look the space over and come up with some options."

Julia frowned. In her experience—okay, from what she saw on TV—designers rarely kept anything the same. They wanted to make a bold statement, something bright and flashy that held no reminders of what the space had looked like before. A designer would eradicate all the good years La Petite Bouchée had experienced. The happy memories that used to fill the space before time and customers began to slip away.

She wanted to bring that back, to revive the space, not revolutionize it. "Part of the restaurant's heritage is in keeping things the same. If you change it too much, it'll just be like any other restaurant." It was a good point and one Julia was prepared to make over and over until he got it. "People will have no reason to come here."

Donovan glanced around the room, which had emptied out completely while they talked. "Is anyone coming here now?"

She bristled at that. "They come. Just not often enough."

"Exactly."

CHAPTER FOUR

JULIA WOKE UP after only a few hours of sleep, and instead of rolling over and drifting back off, she found herself staring at the ceiling and thinking. Alone with her thoughts didn't always feel like a good place to be. Not when her head was filled with worries about the restaurant. Or worse, like this morning, memories of her mother.

Julia had always planned to come back to Vancouver after she got all her European living out of her system, her various training at both Michelin-starred and nonrated establishments. She'd thought she'd have years left to live in the same city as her mother. And instead, she'd received a phone call one hot August afternoon just before her twenty-eighth birthday. Only, instead of hearing her mom's cheerful voice on their weekly phone call, it had been Alain telling her that she needed to come home because her mother wasn't well.

It had scared her. Badly. And when she'd gotten hold of her mother—while sitting at the Orly airport in Paris, waiting for her flight to Vancouver to board—she'd heard the truth in her mother's voice.

That she'd been sick for some time. That she hadn't wanted to tell Julia because she'd believed she was going to get better and hadn't wanted to worry her. And that the doctor's prognosis had been dire during her last checkup and he'd recommended that Julia return to Vancouver. Now.

But her sudden return had given Julia something besides the fear that she was about to lose her mother. It gave her the chance to get to know her mother through the eyes of an adult instead of a teenager. The opportunity to share their love of food and each other. Most important, the time to say goodbye.

Which was still hard to accept some days. When the ache in her heart refused to be eased, Julia went to the restaurant. The one place that felt truly instilled with her mother's essence. Her joy of cooking and spirit of life. And in those moments, she truly saw what La Petite Bouchée had once been and could be again.

So she pulled on her favorite jeans, the comfy ones that had been broken in just right and didn't require her to wear five-inch heels, a simple silk T-shirt and a cashmere cardigan that she'd gotten 80 percent off years ago and still wore on a regular basis.

Her mom had been the same way with her clothing, choosing quality over quantity. Julia's closet wasn't bursting at the seams with the latest styles and trends, and she didn't have a different outfit for every occasion. What she did have were classic pieces that fit any situation. A little black dress that could be dressed up with sleek heels and pearls for a night of formal dining or paired with colorful flats and a printed scarf for a casual drink on a sunny patio. A beautifully cut blazer that she could wear with a skirt and kitten heels for a business meeting or skinny pants and leopard-print ballet flats for drinks after work.

And it meant that she didn't need to update her wardrobe every season or even every year. She simply added a few inexpensive accessories to keep her look fresh and in tune with what was in the fashion magazines.

She made coffee, deciding to forgo the stop at one of the many artisan coffeehouses that dotted the Vancouver landscape. She was a woman who needed to save her pennies, not for another pair of shoes, but to purchase her restaurant. Though her pennies weren't ever going to amount to the asking price, the more she could contribute to the pot, the larger the stake she'd hold.

She also felt it increased her bargaining power. She wasn't going into meetings with nothing to her plan but her name and a dream. She had her own hard-earned cash to put down, too. It helped not only to prove her own seriousness and determination in taking on the project, but also invited the same from her backers. She exhaled. Of course, that was assuming the Fords put the place back on the market.

But she had no reason to think they wouldn't. Donovan had seemed serious about wanting to sell and he'd never been afraid to share his true feelings. He certainly hadn't spared hers when he'd talked about the current decor.

She probably shouldn't enjoy his company as much as she did. He was a distraction and one she couldn't afford. But when he wasn't insulting her restaurant's looks, he was charming and interesting. He'd traveled a fair bit—not as much as she had, but then, he hadn't lived overseas for six years, either.

Her heart didn't feel quite as heavy when she slipped into the back door of the restaurant. She expected to be greeted by cool silence, the kind that floated over her and soothed her irritations. The kind she could bask in for a couple of hours or longer since La Petite Bouchée was closed on Mondays. Instead, she heard voices coming from the dining room.

Someone was here? Her heart thumped once and then calmed. There was no need to worry. Although she hadn't expected company, the restaurant was a busy place and she wasn't the only person with keys. Sasha had a set, as did her floor manager, and the Fords would have a set. And whoever was inside certainly wasn't making any attempt to be quiet. She thought she recognized the low timbre of Donovan's voice.

Julia pushed open the swinging doors and found Donovan in gorgeous black wool pants, a blue dress shirt and a charcoal sweater, standing with a trio of strangers. The trio were nodding and draping bolts of fabric over everything that stood still. The designers.

She felt a small niggle of apprehension. Donovan hadn't mentioned anything about the designers coming in this morning. And he'd been here after closing last night. Of course, he didn't have to tell her everything.

He must have heard the doors because he looked up when she walked into the dining room and smiled. Julia felt a low thrum run through her. "Julia. Come in. Meet the design team."

The team of three, two men and one woman, all looked the same. Three variations on tall and skinny, with sable hair and blue eyes, clad in black with one single focal point, or as they would probably phrase it, "a pop of color." One of the men had a striped purple tie, the other wore sapphire-colored cuff links with matching shoes, and the woman, who seemed to be in charge of the trio, had a gorgeous scarf in red, pink and orange, as if the sunset had been swirled onto the fabric before being draped around her neck.

They each greeted Julia politely if a bit indifferently. She wasn't sure if that was because they didn't like anyone who might have an opinion on their style selections joining them or they were simply going for that mannequin effect. There wasn't a wrinkle or a hair out of place on any of them. By comparison, she and Donovan both looked as though they'd just rolled out of bed after some hot and sweaty sex.

Julia felt her cheeks heat and pushed the thought away. Donovan and her bed were two things that didn't mix outside her fantasy life.

"Are we picking colors?" she asked when she reached the group.

"No. We're merely getting a feel for the space." The woman started talking while the two men began gathering up the bolts. Her words were full of terms like "flow" and "maximizing table space." Whether the new bar should be in dove gray or champagne and questions on whether the accents should be silver or gold. It sounded beautiful but cold and a clear imitation of the Fords' other bars.

Julia listened, gathering information and context. When the designers finished extolling their grandiose plans and gathering their materials, they left. Julia waited until the door clicked shut behind them before she looked at Donovan. "I thought we agreed that I would be a part of the design discussions."

Donovan pulled out a chair that had been draped with a burnt orange—no, just no—and sat down. Julia sat down, too. "It was unplanned. The designer called this morning with a free block of time, and I took her up on it so we could get things moving."

"Why didn't you call me?"

"You said last night that you were looking forward to sleeping in today." He reached out to touch the back of her hand. "Nothing has been decided yet. It was only an initial meeting to get a scope of time and cost. I didn't think you needed or wanted to be involved in those aspects."

"Well, I do." She wanted to have a say in everything. "The space has to reflect the menu and service. Those are my domains."

Donovan nodded. "How do you picture the space?"

She looked around, picturing her favorite spaces in her mind and superimposing them on the room around her. "Pretty much the same. Just fresher. Maybe some new chairs and stools for the bar, a softer color on the walls." The white was a bit bland with no other design to highlight, but it was a lot better than burnt orange. "Some updated light fixtures." She glanced up at the chandelier, which was the one piece she wouldn't change. It was huge and gorgeous, all crystal and platinum swoops of sparkle. "Maybe a ceiling medallion to highlight the chandelier."

"And what about the floors? The bar? The poor use of space?" He squeezed her hand and heat shot through her. "Julia. We have to make changes." His dark eyes seemed to tilt down at the corners. "We can't leave it as it is and expect anything else to change."

"We could. With the marketing campaign, we'll gain new business." All they really needed was for people to remember they were there, to walk through the door and taste the food for themselves.

"But they won't come back." He let go of her hand and sat back. "They'll take one look at this place and decide it's not cool or hip or whatever."

"This isn't about being cool or hip or whatever." La Petite Bouchée was classic and would stand the test of time.

Donovan ran a hand through his hair. "Actually, it is. We need the social scene to give it the stamp of approval. Once we've got that—"

"But we're not a bar," Julia interrupted. She understood where he was coming from. The part of the industry that relied on the young and pretty to fill their tables and their coffers. But a restaurant was different. And she felt as if everything was changing so fast. As if her life was once again in upheaval. "We need the foodies."

"Julia, the foodies *are* the social scene. And right now, you and your food are being wasted."

She sat up straighter, stinging from the implication that her food, her staff wouldn't be good enough on their own. "I think my food speaks for itself."

He reached out and caught her hand when she started to stand. "The decor, the layout, even the menu is working against you right now. I want to bring everything in line to work together."

His hand was large and strong but held her fingers loosely enough that she could break free if she wanted to. She should want to. His eyes drilled into hers, searching. "Why are you so afraid of change?"

"I'm not afraid." But her pulse pounded in her ears and made her vision shimmer for a second. "I just don't think we need to change for the sake of change."

It felt as if her whole life had been nothing but change for the past two years. A sick mother, taking over the restaurant, dealing with Alain's death and then the nightmare that had been Jean-Paul's reign. And now the Fords also wanted to do things their way.

Was it so wrong to want a little stability? A little time-out so she could get her legs under her and figure out what to do next?

She studied his hand as it curled over hers. They looked good together. Strong and supportive. "I just don't want to see this place turned into a replica of every other restaurant out there. I don't want us to lose what makes us different, special."

The parts that reminded Julia of her mother and the traditions she'd built during her ten-year tenure as executive chef in the kitchen.

Suzanne Laurent had been part of the heyday of La Petite Bouchée as a junior kitchen slave, and she'd always believed that with hard work and a concerted effort it could be a top-tier restaurant again. Given a little more time and money, maybe she'd have been able to get it there. Now it was up to Julia.

"And you think that's what I want?" His voice was low and serious. Sexy.

Julia looked up from their hands. It wasn't a connection she could pursue anyway. Even if they did look like something sculpted by Michelangelo. She tugged free and put her hands in her lap. "I don't know what you want, Donovan. You say you want to sell the restaurant and know that I'm an interested buyer. Yet you don't include me on the decisions that will affect the future of the restaurant. Wouldn't it make more sense to get my opinion?"

There was a pause, a long, silent pause. She could hear the rumble of voices outside, tourists braving the February weather to visit the popular market next door, and the whoosh of cars and wind. He nodded slowly. "Of course. You're right." He stood. "Come and look."

He led her to another table to a trio of poster-board mock-ups. "These are just some ideas based on my suggestions and work the designer has done for us in the past." His arm brushed hers as he pointed, and his scent filled her head. That spicy, clean scent that made her think of the windowsill herb garden she'd had in Paris.

Julia prepared herself for shiny white and lots of cold, oversize mirrors. A restaurant version of Elephants. Instead, she saw something more beautiful than she'd imagined.

Louis XVI oval-back chairs in dark wood and a silky ivory moiré. The golden parquet floor replaced with light gray wood. The walls were no longer slabs of plain white decorated only with scattered pictures, but had strips of white wood installed as panels, and the walls themselves were a foggy gray with mirrors and other objets d'art. The bar was longer, stretching to fill up that awkward corner that was too small for a table and too big for a plant.

It looked like her restaurant, only better. So much better.

She inhaled, sucking in wonder, excitement and eau de Donovan. God, he smelled good. She shoved that discomforting realization out of her head. No matter what she might personally think of Donovan Ford, he was off-limits.

How could she grow her own name, increase her cachet in a city full of world-class chefs if she allowed herself to be waylaid by the first amazing-smelling man to cross her path?

Julia concentrated on the mock-ups in front of her, on the impersonal wall displays, and her gaze skittered up to the photos that were hung there now. The walls of La Petite Bouchée were currently covered in personal photographs taken by current and former staff that displayed a French life in stunning black-and-white imagery. They were part of the restaurant's tradition.

"I want to keep the photos on the walls," she told Donovan, turning her face from the pictures to look up at him. He leaned over her, one hand planted on the table as he, too, reviewed the papers on the table.

He glanced down, a lock of hair falling over his forehead. "Why?"

Julia swallowed, told herself she should really break this eye lock or at least shift in her chair so their bodies weren't so close to touching. "They're part of the restaurant's history. Of all the people who worked here." At his furrowed brow, she explained. "They're *our* pictures. Alain's photos of his childhood home, a picture I took of the Tuileries Garden my first winter in Paris, one that my mom took of me the first time she took me to France, one that Sasha took when she went to the French Alps last year."

He glanced behind him at the closest wall and the photos displayed there. "I didn't know."

"And now you do."

He straightened up. "Show me." He started toward the wall she'd been staring at only a minute earlier. "Which ones are yours?"

Julia stood, too, slowly, trying not to drag her feet and wanting to all the same. There was no reason to think this was anything more than polite interest, and it provided her an excellent opportunity to sway him to her side. The photos weren't just displayed at La Petite Bouchée; they were part of the restaurant. "This one."

She pointed to the garden photo she'd taken when she'd first moved to Paris. She could still remember the day she'd taken it. A bad day when she'd been feeling lonely and lost, still working hard to be fluent in the language, and had just been thrown out of her first kitchen among extremely loud and spittle-laden cursing.

She knew it was a rite of passage, one that all

young chefs experienced in this particular kitchen, but it was still difficult, and she'd promised herself that when she ran her own kitchen, she'd never do the same to anyone else.

"It's beautiful." Donovan stepped closer, really looking at the picture then back at her. And even though she hadn't told him about the day she took it, she felt exposed, as if she'd just bared a piece of herself to him without realizing it. "Where's the one your mom took? I'd like to see it."

She felt her heart hiccup. She shouldn't. She really shouldn't. She pointed it out anyway. "It's one of my favorites."

He was quiet as he studied the picture. "You can see the love." And Julia felt her heart hiccup again. "The way you're looking at her. You love her."

"I do." She swallowed the sudden lump in her throat. "It was hard when she died."

He only nodded and opened his arm, offering support if she wanted to take it. She did; she so did. But she was afraid to move.

"I was living in Paris when she got sick," she told him. "But I haven't gone back." Hadn't been able to. Not yet. "We had six months together." To say those goodbyes that so many people never got the chance to say.

Julia knew she should consider herself lucky, but sometimes she was infuriated. She'd had only one parent. Onc lone family member. And that person had been stolen away. While other people had piles of family—aunts and uncles, parents and stepparents, brothers and sisters, and all sorts of second cousins and cousins once removed that they needed a spreadsheet to keep track of all of them. It wasn't fair.

"And I don't know why I'm unloading all of this on you."

"I want to hear. Tell me about her."

Julia clasped her hands together and looked at the picture of herself in the fountain as a little girl. Donovan was right; there was love in every aspect of the photo. The splash of the water. The way the sun shimmered on the water. The gleam in her eye. She knew her mother would have been looking at her with the same gleam. She drew in a deep shuddering breath and started talking.

She had Sasha to talk to, but she was conscientious about not dwelling on her loss, not bringing every conversation back to her mother. And she had the staff at work, but Julia had been careful not to exploit those relationships. She needed to seem in charge, and crying all over the dishwasher's shoulder about the way her mother used to make beef stock wasn't likely to inspire the kind of respect an executive chef needed.

She didn't know why she felt comfortable talking to Donovan except that he'd asked to see the picture and had pointed out something that no one else had ever seen. Not even Julia, and she'd been looking at the photo from the time she was old enough to remember.

"She sounds special."

Julia smiled. "She was."

"I wish I'd had the chance to meet her."

Julia's throat clogged and she could only nod. Donovan took a step toward her and she met him partway, taking solace in his gentle hug. When she felt that the urge to cry had passed, she looked up. "Well, now that I've blabbed all my family secrets, you have to do the same. Tell me about your family."

Donovan left his arm around her. She was glad. "My dad had a heart attack three months ago."

Julia's mouth fell open. "What? I hadn't heard."

"No, we kept it private. A family matter. He didn't want people to know, didn't want them to come bearing casseroles and other pity gifts."

"So why are you telling me?" He simply looked down at her and she knew without him answering. He felt comfortable talking with her, too. "I'd like to meet him."

"Oh, you will. We won't be able to keep him cooped up permanently. My mother's already threatened to lock him in his room if he doesn't follow the doctor's orders."

Julia laughed, and it felt good. Knowing that other people's parents recovered even if hers hadn't.

"Donovan?" She lifted a hand to touch his cheek but stopped. What was she doing? Yes, they'd shared a moment, but that was it. She started to pull it back.

He caught her wrist and pressed a light kiss to her palm. "Thank you for telling me about your mother."

She should look away, should step away. She didn't.

It was a mistake. Suddenly, he was surrounding her. All dark and tall and staring down at her as if there was nowhere else he wanted to be.

Julia sucked in a breath. A quick one because she didn't have time for more. And then his lips were on hers and her fingers were tangling themselves in his soft, dark hair, her body pressed into his tidy suit and she was just in the moment.

And not savoring it, either. *Savoring* was too wimpy a description for what they were doing, and Julia should know. She did plenty of savoring in her daily life. Taking a quick taste of sauce before adjusting spices, swirling and sipping wines to see what paired best with her dishes. If her staff were going to pitch pairings to the clientele, she needed to be sure they worked. Nibbling an appetizer from a competitor to ensure she tasted every component both alone and together. But this? This was no savoring.

Donovan's mouth was pressed against hers, firm and demanding. Julia sank into it, allowing herself to revel in the moment even as she knew this wasn't the way to help her career.

The way his hand slid up her back then back down before pulling her into him. The light bristle of stubble that scraped across her skin as he dragged his mouth across hers. The scent of strong basil. An herb she loved and always kept a fresh pot of on her windowsill.

She wanted more.

Donovan's body rocked into hers, the press of his thigh between her legs. She felt her body relaxing. All those tight balls of tension that she carried around most days unwinding and slipping away, leaving behind pockets of heat.

His hand pressed her lower back, nudging her more tightly to him. Her muscles loosened, threatening to let go. If they'd been in a different space and different situation, she might have done it. Just let go. Might have peeled off her cashmere sweater and silk top. Might have shucked her jeans to the side and divested herself of her pretty bra-and-panties set and found a comfy spot—preferably one that was king-size and sturdy enough to handle some vigorous bouncing—to take this where it needed to go.

Because this didn't have to be forever. What was one night? One afternoon? Her body melted against his, the press of hard pecs and firm abs against her softer physique. She liked her body, appreciated the difference between women and men. Hard planes to soft roundness. The contrast heightening the sensation.

His hand slid down to cup her ass, then up to finger the hem of her T-shirt. She slipped her hands under the collar of his coat and slid it down. It got caught on his shoulders, so she switched tactics, slipping her hands along his collarbone to unknot his tie and undo the first few buttons of his fancy dress shirt that probably cost as much as her sweater. Only she'd bet he'd paid full price and had a closet full of them. Not that it mattered. All that mattered was getting her fingers inside it so she could touch his bare skin.

She felt a sprinkling of hair on his chest, the sharp crispness of curls, and appreciated that he hadn't waxed them away. She wasn't into a pelt of hair the way Sasha was, but that was probably due to seeing one too many on the beaches of Europe. A hair sweater coupled with a banana hammock was enough to make a person lose their appetite for the rest of the day. But she didn't think baby-soft smoothness was much better.

Donovan's chest was just right. She undid a couple more buttons just to be sure and was rewarded when his fingers sneaked beneath her shirt to dance across her back. A trail of shivers followed his touch. And she felt a little shudder work its way through her body.

Maybe they could use a chair. They were getting rid of them anyway. And she was pretty agile. But then Donovan flicked his tongue against hers and moved his hand around to caress her stomach, and all thoughts about chairs and beds and using whatever apparatus was available flew out of her head on a wave of enjoyment.

She knew she should back away, gain her head and the thread of why she shouldn't be kissing Donovan Ford in the middle of the restaurant.

She didn't. Not until a knock on the door interrupted them.

"What the hell?" Donovan mumbled the questions against her lips, his hands still all over her. "Are you expecting someone?"

"No." Her staff never came in on their day off. She wouldn't allow it, knowing they needed a break to decompress.

"Me neither." He started kissing her again. She started to seriously wonder if the chairs could hold them. Or there was always a tablecloth laid across the floor. Or up against the wall. Donovan looked as if he was strong enough to support her in that position.

The second knock was louder, more insistent.

Donovan groaned and rested his forehead against hers for a moment. "Don't move," he said and started buttoning his shirt over that gorgeous chest.

Julia drew in a breath and straightened her T-shirt and sweater, smoothed her hair, hoping it didn't look as though some hot man had just had his fingers buried in it.

Donovan grinned at her over his shoulder as he headed toward the door. "That looks like moving."

Well, sure, easy for him to joke. He wouldn't be the one standing there mussed and half-undressed. "I didn't see you staying still."

"Someone has to answer the door." He turned to look through the glass windows on either side of it. Julia couldn't make out any faces, but apparently Donovan could because he swore.

"Who is it?" she asked, her fingers toying with the edge of her sweater.

"My family." And Julia felt alarm and nerves rise up her throat as his entire family—Owen and Mal, and an older woman and man who, judging from appearances, could only be his parents—walked inside. Oh, God. Would they be able to tell she'd just been contemplating how to do Donovan in the restaurant?

Julia wasn't sure if she should run or hide. She hesitated and then it was too late. Owen grinned and headed her way. Spotted. Left with no option but to stay and stand her ground or look like a nutcase, she chose the former.

"Jules." Owen's tone was warm and welcoming. "I didn't expect to see you here today." He greeted her with a brief hug.

Julia felt some of her nervous energy ease. She already knew Owen fairly well. On the nights that Donovan didn't show up at the restaurant for dinner, Owen did. He had already offered some good suggestions on how she might smooth out some of the flaws in their front-end service. Julia got the feeling that Owen's suggestions sometimes fell on deaf ears with his family, which she didn't understand. He had a natural gift with customers and an ability to home in on the root cause of an issue and resolve it quickly without hurt feelings. Quite honestly, she wished she could hire him to be her restaurant manager, but she knew he was already working full-time at Elephants.

"Is my brother cracking the whip?" he asked as he released her from his tight hug. "Making you work extra hours?"

"No. I just happened to be in the area." Julia swallowed her nerves and forced a smile. Mal waved hello as she slid out of her coat, showing off a gorgeous black suit that displayed her long legs and sleek figure. She and Mal had been in touch through email about a planned media blitz once the renovations were under way and Julia had the free time to give to it, and though they hadn't spent time together in person, Julia liked her decisiveness and confidence.

There was no reason to be nervous. The Ford siblings were lovely people; there was no reason to think their parents would be any different.

"Julia." Donovan's voice spread through her like butter melting in a hot pan with a bubble and froth. "I'd like to introduce you to my parents, Evelyn and Gus Ford."

Julia smiled at the couple. Evelyn was her height and slender with a bright smile and the same expressive eyes as Mal. She wore a beautiful wool coat in heather gray that Julia recognized as expensive and vintage. Gus was an older version of his sons. Both the older Fords wore friendly and interested expressions.

"Mom. Dad. This is Chef Julia Laurent."

She was pleased that he'd used her title. Not everyone would have. But her nerves remained fluttering just below the surface. Julia inhaled slowly and reminded herself that although her lips were still tingling, there was no visible indication that she and Donovan had been engaging in some decidedly nonwork behavior in the dining room mere minutes earlier. She was simply the executive chef in to check on her kitchen and make sure everything was ready for tomorrow's service. No

making out in the dining room to be found here
at all. Nope, not at all. Nothing to see here.

"Mr. and Mrs. Ford." Julia held out her hand.
"It's a pleasure."

Mrs. Ford stepped forward, taking Julia's hand
in hers. "Forgive us for intruding. And please
call me Evelyn." She hugged her, surrounding
Julia with warmth and a familiar feeling. That of
being loved by her own mother. "I hope I'm not
being too forward, but we've been so excited to
meet you."

They had? Julia stood still, caught by surprise
and the rush of memory brought on by the hug. It
reminded her of summer nights in Paris, of holding her mother's hand as they tried out a new café
by the Seine, of walking into the family kitchen
where her mother was testing out a new recipe
she wanted to put on the restaurant's menu, and
of those last days when her mother, laid up in a
hospital bed and unable to handle much of her
own basic needs, still insisted on dabbing the insides of her wrists and pulse points behind her
ears with her signature scent.

She hugged Evelyn back, reveling in the thoughts
of her own mother, appreciating the easy affection
the Fords offered. Evelyn's hold was soft and soothing and just for a moment Julia felt as if it was her
own mom hugging her. Only it wasn't and would
never be again.

She swallowed the tears that prickled in the back of her throat. Yes, her mother was gone and she desperately missed that connection, but that didn't mean she was going to cry all over a virtual stranger.

Still, when she moved to step back, Evelyn held on for one extra moment and then released her with a squeeze. "Welcome."

And Julia felt the prickle return. Just a flash before it was replaced by a slow warmth that seeped through her and smoothed some of her jagged emotions.

"Thank you." Julia wanted to say more but her throat was tight and mouthing platitudes was all she could manage. She settled for smiling, hoping what she felt inside showed on her face.

"Step aside. Step aside." Gus, whose dark hair was the same shade as all three of his children's and showed only a touch of lightening at the temples, moved to stand in front of her. He was tall with broad shoulders. His handshake was strong, no sign of the heart attack Donovan mentioned he'd suffered. His color was good, too. In fact, had she not known, Julia would never have guessed he'd suffered such a major health crisis a few months earlier.

Of course, Julia knew better than most how deceiving looks could be. Her mother hadn't looked sick at all, not until her illness left her with only months instead of years. And even then, on her good days, Suzanne had looked like the same woman Julia had always known. A bit too thin and with a tendency to move gingerly, but not like a woman who would be dead within the year.

"Mr. Ford." She pumped her hand up and down. "A pleasure."

"Gus," he corrected. "We don't stand on ceremony in this family. And you're one of us now."

"One of us. One of us," Owen chanted until Donovan pinned him with a glare. "One of us," he whispered.

Julia bit the inside of her cheek and tried not to laugh. But it felt good to be referenced as part of the family. Even if Gus had only meant she was part of the business family, it was something, and more than many business owners were inclined to give.

"So tell us something about yourself, Julia." Gus released her hand but remained close. "I understand you have some family history with the restaurant."

Julia explained that her mother had worked in the kitchen of La Petite Bouchée for more than thirty years, starting as a sous chef and working her way up to the executive position. She didn't say why she'd taken over for her mother or that she'd passed away, and she was grateful that Gus didn't ask.

"Your mother might have been working here the night Evie and I got engaged. How long has it been? Thirty-one years?" He looked to his wife for confirmation.

"How old is your son?" Evelyn asked.

"Thirty-one?" Gus guessed, darting a glance at Donovan.

"Right age, wrong son," Donovan said, coming over to stand beside his father and far too close to Julia for her comfort.

She eased over a step, but Gus and the rest of the family simply moved with her. All except Mal, who was looking over the mock-ups Donovan had left on the table.

"That's one of the reasons we wanted to buy this particular space," Gus said. "There's history here and not just for us."

Julia was surprised. That sounded like someone who planned to keep the business, but she shoved the thought away. Donovan had been clear that his intention was to sell and he'd given her no reason to distrust him. "I'm pleased to hear it." And she meant it. "I very much want to see her restored to her former glory."

"Then we have something in common," Gus said.

Donovan cleared his throat. "Dad, why don't

you sit down and I'll show you some of the ideas Julia and I were discussing."

Discussing before he'd laid a lip-lock on her that still had her insides in disarray.

Gus frowned at his son. "I don't need to sit down. I'm perfectly fine standing."

"Dad." Donovan frowned back, leaving no question as to whether or not they were related. They looked like a before-and-after for anti-aging cream.

"I'm not an invalid and I'll sit when I'm ready. It's bad enough with your mother hanging over me, worrying about my diet and my blood pressure. I don't need it from you, too."

Julia watched Donovan's lips tighten, but he did as his father asked and backed off. "Fine. Then why don't you *stand* and I can show you some of the ideas Julia and I were discussing before your arrival."

Gus's mouth twitched. "Well, now you're just being a smart-ass."

Donovan nodded. "And we both know that's Owen's role in the family."

"Hey," Owen said, "how did I get dragged into this?"

And then Evelyn stepped in, assuring Owen that he was only a smart-ass some of the time, that Donovan was perfectly capable of being a smart-ass in his own right—as he'd just shown—but that he was also correct in noting that Gus should take a seat if he wanted to stay longer.

Gus grumbled at his wife, but took a seat at one of the tables. "I would have sat down when I needed to."

"No, you wouldn't have," Evelyn said and planted a kiss on his cheek. "Now, let's see some of these ideas."

Julia stood by quietly, curious to see how Donovan interacted with his family. She'd always been drawn to large, noisy families. So different from her own singular upbringing. Also, it gave her free rein to eyeball Donovan without appearing to do so. Yes, he definitely looked strong enough to support her against a wall.

And then she reminded herself that those were not the thoughts she was supposed to be having. She was supposed to be grateful that they'd been interrupted. She was supposed to remember that she had a career that needed all her attention.

Instead, when she looked at Donovan, her insides lit up, flared as though they'd been touched with a match. And she not only found the idea of kissing him delicious rather than deplorable, but she also wondered if she might find a good excuse to do so again. Which was really, really bad.

Julia was so focused on her own thoughts, she didn't immediately notice when Donovan's attention turned toward her. Not until he cleared his throat and she looked up to find a knowing smirk on his face.

Great. Just great.

"This is wonderful," Gus said, giving Julia a reason to break the eye contact without looking as if she was backing down. "I think you've got a great start here." He reached out and laid a hand on his wife's arm. It was an easy gesture and clearly one that happened often based on the way Evelyn leaned toward him.

"I agree." Evelyn included all of them in her comment. "I can't wait to see the finished product."

Julia let Donovan take the reins in describing the time line, how long they'd need to close the restaurant to complete the renovations and some of the plans Mal was already putting in place for the reopening. She adored the overlap of voices and ideas as others chimed in, the web of support that was clearly the family's normal way of communicating, and felt a pinch of sorrow that it was something she'd never experience with her mother.

But it was too late for regrets. She felt a prickle behind her eyelids and swallowed. "Can you stay for lunch?" Any excuse to get out of the room, away from the togetherness she'd never have again, and gather herself.

Evelyn looked at her husband. "How are you feeling?"

"I already told you, I'm fine." Gus's hand fisted until Evelyn gave it a calming stroke. "And we'd be honored to stay."

Julia had always enjoyed the social aspect of cooking. Food was such an integral part of the human experience. More than just fuel or survival, but a bond between people. A way of nurturing and cherishing, and an indication of trust. Eating someone else's cooking meant allowing them unguarded access to your person, and was something Julia thought about with each dish she prepared. It did something to her soul, helped fill the space that was left when her mother died.

She pushed through the swinging doors of the kitchen, glad that it was an off day and she didn't have to worry about the staff rolling in at an inopportune moment. Not that she planned for anything inopportune to happen. No, she was just here to cook. Not have sex against a wall.

She stepped into the walk-in, perusing the silent and gleaming shelves and plucking quart jars and other food items that she'd bring together to make a fantastic meal. Gus would probably be on a special diet. Low-fat and heavy on the veggies due to his heart attack. But cooking for health-conscious, heart-smart Vancouver residents for the past couple of years had given her an excellent place to start.

Chicken breasts, marinated and roasted, and green beans with a lemon-mustard sauce. A light hand with oil and other fats. Because, in this particular instance, butter didn't make everything better. She'd make some other dishes, too, ones that were mainstays on the menu.

Julia set to work, twisting her hair into a tight, work-safe bun, slipping on an apron, heating up pans, chopping ingredients and whisking spices and herbs with oil for the marinade. She figured she'd be finished in about thirty minutes, give or take.

The sound of the kitchen door swinging open interrupted the rhythm she had going. She didn't mind. Until she saw who it was.

"What can I do for you, Donovan?" And why did he have to look so good? Or maybe it was the heat from the stove that was making her cheeks flame. Ignoring the fact that the stove and pans were nowhere close to temperature yet.

"You don't have to cook for us, you know."

She did know. "I want to."

"Julia." Donovan crossed the kitchen and stopped beside her. Close. Maybe a little too close. Or maybe she just liked it a little too much.

"Careful. The stove is hot." Like her face.

But he didn't move away. Neither did she. "About before."

Julia swallowed. "I don't think we need to discuss that." Didn't need to think or dream about it, either.

"And what if I want to?"

Her breath caught in her throat. She wished she had a glass of water. Surrounded by taps and fridges and all means of food prep and not a drop to drink. She swallowed again. "This is going to take a half hour. I need to start cooking."

She could hear the sizzle of the pan, knew exactly how any ingredient placed into it would react.

Donovan exhaled. "Ignoring it won't make it go away."

"It might. Have we tried?"

He stepped even closer. "It won't."

Julia could feel the tear of indecision inside her. He was probably right, but she didn't want him to be. "I can't, Donovan."

"Can't what?" His breath tickled her ear. She didn't respond, just gripped the handle of her spoon more tightly and stared at the pan on the stove in front of her.

She couldn't do this. Not with him. She had a career that needed her attention, a reputation she was trying to build. And her hard work and position weren't things she would throw away over a handsome face.

"You okay?" he finally asked.

Julia blinked, still staring down. "Fine." But she didn't look at him. Couldn't.

She sensed when he took a half step back, but somehow that didn't give her any relief. "Look, I didn't mean to cross a line here. I'm attracted to you. I thought you felt the same."

She did. She totally did. Which was why she couldn't look at him now. Afraid that if she did, he'd see the invitation in her eyes. To do it again. Kiss her again. Take her right here against the wall of the kitchen, even with his family outside.

"If I misinterpreted that, I apologize."

He hadn't. Not even a little. She looked up and knew it was a mistake even before she saw the flare of heat in his eyes. Her brain stuttered, causing her mouth to open and shut. So attractive. "I need to start cooking," she told him.

But he merely smiled and brushed away a lock of hair that had slipped out of her bun and across her eye. She shivered and his smile widened.

Yeah, this wasn't over. Not by a long shot.

CHAPTER FIVE

Donovan was still thinking about Julia when he parked in front of his parents' house later that night. The feel of her skin under his hands, the responsive tilt of her body, the knowledge of how close he'd been to getting down on his knees and worshipping at the altar of her body. He thought about when he'd pulled back to look at her and she'd been standing there, staring back at him with those eyes that made him picture wicked, naked fantasies. When her body had wavered toward his and he'd read her invitation as clearly as if she'd delivered it to him on a platter.

And then his family had barged in and wrecked the moment. As if they'd planned to cock-block him. Which might have been funny, if it hadn't actually happened.

He walked up the steps to the house he'd grown up in and pushed open the door. Hell. He wanted to be walking into Julia's house, picking up where they'd left off and learning how her body felt underneath his. Or on top of his. Really, he was willing to try both ways. He found his mother in the kitchen tossing a salad. "Hello."

"Hello, dear." Evelyn lifted her cheek for a kiss. "Are you staying for dinner?"

"Of course." He stole a carrot from the bowl and popped it into his mouth. He tried to have dinner with them at least once a week. "I even brought wine." He stowed it in the fridge. "Do you need anything?"

"I've got it under control." She waved him away. "Go visit your father before he comes in here and starts whining about having to eat salad with his meal instead of potatoes."

Donovan grinned. "Where is the old man?"

"In the den." Evelyn turned to check on something in the stove. "And don't give him a beer, even if he begs. Doctor's orders." Though kind and caring in every way, Evelyn Ford could be ruthless when it came to those she loved. And she loved her family fiercely.

Donovan decided against pouring one for himself—that would just be cruel—and went to find his father. He discovered him just where his mother had said, lounging in his den, trying to hide a beer behind his seat. He straightened when he saw it wasn't his wife.

"Dad." Donovan plucked the bottle out of his father's hand. "You know Mom is going to think I gave this to you."

"A good son would give it back."

Donovan took a sip and then handed it over. "I saw and know nothing."

Gus grinned. "It's only one. But your mother. You know she worries." They all did. But his dad looked better every time Donovan saw him. Perhaps not as robust and energetic as he'd been pre-heart attack, but the gray pallor to his skin was gone and the gleam of ideas was back in his eyes. "I like your new chef."

"What? No hello, how are you, good to see you?"

"I did see you only a few hours ago."

Donovan had to admit that his father had a point.

Gus lounged back on his favorite padded leather chair with a tall back that he refused to replace. Just getting it re-covered when the leather had been torn—a youthful incident involving Donovan, Owen and a Scout knife that they never saw again—had been a battle. "She's a hell of a cook." He patted his stomach in appreciation of the food Julia had served this afternoon.

Julia was a hell of a lot of things. Chef, woman, kisser. But Donovan wasn't about to share that with his father. "She is. That's why she runs the kitchen."

"Pretty, too."

Donovan pointedly ignored that comment. Prior

to his health scare, Gus had seemed content to let Donovan and his siblings run their personal lives as they saw fit. If they wanted to be serial monogamists, play the field or ignore dating altogether, it didn't bother Gus.

But since then, his concerns appeared to have shifted. Donovan didn't know if it was the fear of missing out on their future families, weddings and grandkids or if he just had too much time on his hands, but Gus was becoming a busybody.

"Julia is very attractive," Donovan agreed, knowing that glossing over the comment or changing the subject entirely would only make his father think he was onto something. "Should be useful for the marketing push Mal's got planned."

He settled on the chair beside his father's. It wasn't quite as tall or as padded, but it was just as comfortable.

But if he thought his polite acknowledgment of Gus's words would be enough to satisfy any interest his father had, he should have known better. His father would never be so easily dissuaded from his cause. "Good job, good cook, good looks. Sounds perfect."

"Mom will be thrilled to hear it."

"Be thrilled to hear what?" Evelyn Ford entered the den that was supposed to be Gus's domain but was co-opted for family use the majority of the time. She noted the bottle of beer in her husband's hand and removed it from his grip without comment.

"Dad's in love with my new chef." But Donovan's attempt to twist the subject and make light of his father's sudden interest in his personal life could only be deemed a failure.

"*Your* new chef?" Gus grinned at his wife as he tugged her hand so she perched on the armrest of his chair. "Did you hear that, love?"

"I heard." His mother shot Donovan a what-can-you-do look. They both knew Gus had laser-beam focus when he set his mind on something. Sharp, direct and difficult to hide from. She patted her husband's cheek. "Don't tease your son."

"Or pick on one of your other kids," Donovan suggested. "Shouldn't I get some brownie points for being the one who's actually here?"

He was the one who'd stepped up to lead the company when it became clear that Gus wouldn't be returning to the office anytime soon. Yes, he knew Mal and even Owen had taken on more responsibilities and larger roles, too, but the majority rested on his shoulders. He should, therefore, be excused from any paternal harassment, well intended or otherwise.

Gus didn't get the memo. "My heart attack put some things into perspective for me. I want to make sure my family is happy."

"I'm happy," Donovan said, and for the most

part it was true. "Of course, I'd be happier if you'd consider my idea about putting the restaurant back on the market."

He hadn't mentioned it to his father lately. But if his father was well enough to make a surprise visit to La Petite Bouchée and hassle him about his personal life and his pretty chef, then he was clearly feeling better and could listen to what Donovan had on his mind.

Donovan had crunched the numbers and knew exactly how much they needed to get to turn a profit, even with the planned renovations. While he'd originally considered trying to make a quick flip, he saw now that seeing the renovations and grand reopening through made better business sense.

"I know you have a personal attachment to the restaurant." The nostalgia in his father's voice when he'd talked about it over lunch had made that clear. But this wasn't about personal attachments. "Branching out into the gastropub market is a better fit with what we already do and it has higher profit potential."

Gus nodded. "It's not always about profit, though."

"No, it isn't…" Donovan paused, considering his next words. "I think we should sell."

"Really." But that was the only outward reaction from his father. Donovan shouldn't have been surprised. It wasn't as if he hadn't told his father this before. Gus steepled his hands in front of him. "Why?"

Now, *that* was a surprise. Every other time Donovan had mentioned his thoughts on the matter, his father had remained unshakable in his stance that a restaurant was their ideal growth market.

Gus smiled. "I know you've got a plan."

"I do." Donovan felt the fizz of excitement. The hope that maybe this time his father could be convinced.

"So tell me."

Donovan's mind whirred. He wanted to share everything, all the details big and small, because he knew he could make the transition not only smooth but successful. But as with most plans, he decided it was best to start with the first step. "If we list the property—"

"No." His father interrupted before he could even get going. "You've told me that before. Plus the financing, the marketing, every aspect of the business side. I want you to tell me why it's important to you." He looked at Donovan, his watchful gaze taking everything in. "I can tell this isn't just business."

Donovan felt the fizz die out. "It's not." But he wasn't sure he wanted to tell his father the rest of his reasons.

They sat in silence for a moment, engaged in a

quiet contemplation. Donovan didn't want to hurt his father's feelings, but it didn't feel right to sit on his thoughts any longer, either. And his dad had said he just wanted them to be happy.

"Did you mean that? About wanting us to be happy."

"I did."

"Even if it means doing things differently than you would?" Up until the heart attack, Gus had had the last word on all company decisions, which was why they owned La Petite Bouchée in the first place.

"Yes."

Donovan drew in a bracing breath. "I need to make my own name." Make up for his failed initial attempt to crack the market on his own.

His mother blinked at him, but his father merely pressed his fingertips to his lips. "I see."

"I don't know if you do, Dad. You're recognized in the industry." Gus Ford had been a success right out of the gate. He'd been a young man with a little money and a big work ethic, who'd studied the Vancouver market and decided that an upscale lounge where people could have excellent drinks and high-quality appetizers was missing. He'd been right. Elephants had been a hit from the moment they'd opened the doors, and nothing had changed in the following years.

His mother sat forward. "So are you, Donovan."

"Not really." Yes, he was successful as part of the brand his father had developed. But when he'd tried to follow in his footsteps, fresh out of university with a degree in business management and a trust fund to support his dream, his restaurant had failed.

Donovan knew it was nothing he'd done wrong. He'd had a good location, a great kitchen, a solid business plan that he'd executed cleanly. Sometimes, businesses failed. Even when he looked back on it years later, with an eye for something he might have overlooked, he'd found nothing. It had just been one of those unfortunate things. And yet, that didn't make it any easier to accept.

"Donovan," his mother began.

"No." Gus quelled her words with a hand on her arm. "I want to hear."

"I just want something that's my initiative. That I can look at and know I created it and made it a success. Like you did with Elephants." And since Donovan had invested the majority of his trust fund in his failed restaurant, he needed to look to the family company to back the dream. This time it would thrive. He had more experience, more success and he knew now that the money was in liquor sales. Lower cost, higher profit. And he was ready to put all his learning to use.

"Are you thinking of leaving the company?"

"No." Donovan's response was swift. He had no intention of removing himself from the day-to-day running of the family company. "I'd just like to be able to have my own section under it." A way to prove to himself and everyone else that he was more than his one failed attempt.

His mother was silent, but his father made a humming sound in the back of his throat. "I didn't know you felt so strongly about this."

"I do." They'd never really discussed his restaurant going under. Though it had been a difficult time for Donovan, he'd tried to grow from it. He'd applied and been accepted to Cornell, where he'd received a master's of management in hospitality. He'd learned from his years working under his father's guidance. He still had no guarantees, but if anyone was ready to succeed with a new opening, Donovan felt it was him.

"I love knowing that I'm part of the tradition you started," he tried to explain, "but I want to start something new, too. My own tradition." He looked from one parent to the other. To his relief, they both nodded. As if what he said wasn't completely far-fetched.

"And you think we need to sell La Petite Bouchée to do that," his father said.

The relief expanded. "Yes." Since he no longer had the necessary funds to expand on his own, this plan would have to go through the company accounts. "We need the capital if we want to pursue my preferred investments." And he had an eye on a location a few blocks away from Elephants that was ideally suited to the project. "But aside from the cash flow, I need the ability to focus my energy on the project, and I can't do that as well as oversee the restaurant and our other holdings."

"Okay."

Okay? Okay they understood? Okay they'd heard enough? Or okay they were willing to sell the restaurant as soon as they received an acceptable offer?

"Let's hear the details of this plan."

And while Donovan talked, his father listened, asking a few questions, but mainly just absorbing the information. When Donovan was finished, Gus nodded.

"I don't see why not." He leveled a gaze at Donovan. "But I don't want to sell the restaurant."

Donovan frowned. Wasn't that the whole point of his spiel? That he needed the time and the funding if they were serious about expanding into the gastropub market?

"I'll take over La Petite Bouchée when I come back to work."

That would solve half the problem. "What about the funding to buy another locale?"

Gus opened his arms. "Money isn't a problem, Donovan. Send me the business plan for a look and we'll start taking next steps."

CHAPTER SIX

DONOVAN SAT IN his office looking at the finalized marketing materials his sister had pulled together. It was a nice clean campaign. Effective in its simplicity and reliant on his chef, who was now—he checked his watch—fifteen minutes late.

But he wasn't too annoyed. He knew how hard Julia had been working, seeing as he was at the restaurant most nights for dinner. Partly to see what they were doing, looking for ways they might make improvements with the renovations, but mostly just to see her. To watch her chat with their few regulars, to see the way she handled her staff and to watch the way she smiled at him when she saw him sitting at the bar.

She often came out after closing to sit with him, ask about the renovation plans and state her own opinions on the matter. He loved watching her face in those moments. The way her eyes focused on him, her lips pouting in his direction.

Donovan hadn't kissed her again. Not yet. But he sensed it was only a matter of time. The more he saw her, the more he wanted her, and since she wasn't ignoring him, asking him to leave or otherwise expressing disinterest, he figured she felt the same. Whether or not she would act on it was another matter. But that hadn't stopped Donovan from ending his casual relationship with Tatiana or from avoiding entanglements with any other women. The only woman he was interested in was Julia Laurent.

He tried calling her cell phone again, but it kicked him through to her voice mail without ringing. Unfortunately, he was unable to leave a message because, as the computerized voice had informed him, her inbox was full.

Instead, he cooled his heels with a glass of cold water and by familiarizing himself with all of Mal's initiatives. They were meeting to discuss the marketing plan, which would be moving forward in the next couple of weeks.

Normally, Mal would have led the meeting, but she'd been invited to join a coalition of other eating establishments in the city to discuss a charitable project that would both raise awareness of the hungry in the region and encourage residents to eat out in one of the participating locations.

They thought the opportunity would dovetail perfectly with their hopes of elevating La Petite Bouchée back to the position it had once held. Gus had wanted to attend the meeting, too, but Donovan and Mal had convinced him to let them handle it. Still, it was becoming clear that it wouldn't be much longer before Gus was back in the office working his twelve-hour days and taking the restaurant off Donovan's hands.

He hadn't yet told Julia about the change in plans regarding ownership of the restaurant. Not because he was trying to hide anything, but because he wanted a new contract in place to offer her. She'd made certain concessions in her current contract based on the assumption that they'd be putting the property up for sale and she'd have rights of first purchase. But if that wasn't happening, Donovan felt it was only fair they offer her other perks and bonuses.

He dealt with other business while he waited for Julia. An email from his real-estate agent to set up a showing for the space near Elephants that they thought might be viable for the gastropub. Another from his father with questions and suggestions on the business plan Donovan had sent him last week. A third from Mal, who was hoping to wrap up her meeting in time to catch the tail end of this one. Plus, the myriad questions and details that were part of running a successful business.

Donovan answered some, forwarded others and placed a few in his to-be-handled-later file, as they required information that he didn't know off the top of his head. Then he turned his attention to the amendments his father had made to the business plan.

Some of them were things he had already considered and decided against. Like the choice to pursue quick growth versus slow. While normally cautious, Donovan worried that any delay in getting the idea to market could be the difference between success and failure. It was only a matter of time before the Vancouver market was flooded with these kinds of upscale establishments that combined a casual atmosphere with high-quality food and drink. A place where you could pop in after a yoga class and not look out of place.

He envisioned a place that his current clientele would flock to on those nights and afternoons when they didn't want to dress up. Somewhere they could be a bit more relaxed and still enjoy the high-end service that the Ford Group was already known for.

"Mr. Ford?" Bailey, his pretty, young receptionist, knocked at the door, interrupting his thoughts. "Ms. Laurent is here to see you. I've placed her in the meeting room."

About time. He thanked Bailey and gathered up his materials before heading to the boardroom. He wasn't pleased that Julia was late, but he was still glad to see her. The small pricklings of irritation ebbed away completely when he saw her smiling at him. "You're late," he said anyway.

She frowned. Was it wrong that he looked at it a moment longer than might be deemed professional? "We said eleven thirty," she told him. "I'm actually ten minutes early."

"We said eleven." He spread the papers out on the desk—Mal's media plan and other events that his sister felt would raise the profiles of both Julia and the restaurant. "But you're here now. Let's not waste any more time."

"Donovan." Julia ignored the paper he slid in front of her, her eyes pinning him. "I don't want you to think I'm not professional. If we had agreed on eleven, I would have been here at eleven." She reached out and put a hand on his arm. Her fingers were warm through his sleeve. And suddenly Donovan was thinking about the bedroom instead of the boardroom.

He could feel the tips of her fingers pressing into his skin. No prick of lengthy nails, though. He glanced down. No sign of polish, either, which made sense as she worked in a kitchen. And yet her hands were intensely feminine.

"I think we can chalk it up to miscommunication." He didn't move his arm when it would have been logical to step away. Though he knew she wouldn't have been to the restaurant yet, she still smelled like lemon and white wine. The aroma of his new favorite dish. Her coq au vin blanc. Delicious.

Their eyes met, locked. *Ignoring this would make it go away*, his ass. It wasn't going away. Not now, not before and definitely not in the future. He pushed the folder containing an outline of Mal's ideas toward Julia without looking at it. No, he was still looking at her.

At the light color that rose to her cheeks, the way she licked the corner of her mouth and the way she didn't look away from him, either. "I wasn't late."

If she looked at him this way, she could be late anytime she wanted. "Fine. I was early." She smiled and he wondered if he should just forget propriety and kiss her now.

Instead, he nudged the folder until it bumped her hand. "Take a look at Mal's plan and then we'll discuss." Because the next time he kissed Julia, it wouldn't be with an office full of employees just outside the door. It would be somewhere private, where they could explore this attraction without fear of being interrupted.

But she didn't look at the folder. "Donovan. We…I need to keep this professional."

"We're professional." Wasn't he in a suit? Hadn't he just decided that kissing her in the boardroom was inappropriate?

Julia shook her head. Her hair was down. He usually saw it pulled back in a low knot as required by food-safety standards. He liked it this way, wanted to slip his fingers through those soft strands. "We're not." She lowered her gaze. "We both know that."

Donovan started to reach out to take her hand but stopped himself. Trying to convince her things were perfectly professional between them meant not holding her hand, even if she let him. "Then let's talk about it." He took a seat two away from her, creating a barrier of air between them. "What do you want?"

She lifted her eyes from her lap. "This isn't about what I want, Donovan."

"I think it is." He maintained his casual pose in the seat. "Clearly, you have some concerns. Tell me what they are so we can figure out how to solve them."

"You think it'll be that easy?" Her eyes dropped again.

"Not if you're going to play the mysterious woman, no." She shot him a look full of fire and conflict. He shrugged it off. "So tell me."

"I just…" She paused. "We can't act on whatever this is." She waved a hand between the two of them. He waited for her to elaborate. She didn't disappoint. "I have to think about my future, my career."

"And dating isn't part of that future?"

She scowled. "It is. It will be," she amended. "But not with you."

That stung. "Is there something wrong with

me?" Donovan tried to keep his tone light, but even he heard the whip of hurt behind his words.

"No." She exhaled. "But I need to focus on my career right now. I'm still new in this market. I need to make a name for myself."

"And that's what we're here to talk about." But he didn't nudge her back to the plan in front of her. He stared at her, watching her tongue dart out to lick her lips, noting the lock of hair that curled across the curve of her cheek. "Julia."

"I have to focus on my career, and part of that is my reputation. How things look to other people." She lowered her hands to the chair arms, squeezed. "If we get involved, people will talk."

What? "Who?"

"It doesn't matter who." Her eyes rested on his. "It's what they'll say." He saw her deep intake of breath. "If we get involved, they'll think I'm sleeping with you to keep my job."

Her words caught him off guard. "Do you really think that will happen? You were the executive chef long before we bought the restaurant. It's not un-heard of to keep the staff after a purchase."

"No." She leveled a gaze at him. "But it won't matter. It's juicier to make up salacious details about our sex life."

"We have a sex life?"

But she didn't smile at his joke. "I'm serious, Donovan."

"I know. Sorry," he apologized. "But do you honestly think people will still say that after they've tasted your food? Personally, I think it speaks for itself."

"Thank you for saying that." The tension around her eyes eased, but for only a moment. "Unfortunately, it won't be enough. People will say the food is good but not that good. They won't be able to untangle my professional skills from the ones they'll think I'm showing you behind closed doors."

He considered it, then shook his head. "No, you're wrong. Maybe in the past that might have been true, but times have changed and your food is good enough."

"Donovan." Her voice was soft. He wanted to reach out and tuck the loose hair behind her ear. "We should get to work."

"We should." But he didn't move. Her words were eating at him. "Are you really willing to let everything go because you're afraid?"

"I'm not afraid." But her eyes skittered away from his.

"It's okay to feel that way." He rolled his chair next to hers so the arms bumped. She blinked but didn't say anything, not when he swiveled her seat so she faced him. Not when he leaned forward. And not when his lips were less than an inch from hers. "But don't let that define you."

"Donovan."

He leaned forward and then they were interrupted by a knock at the boardroom door.

"Oh, good." Mal pushed her way inside, nodding at both of them. "You're still here. What did I miss?"

Seriously? Again? He was going to get his entire family bells that they had to wear around their necks like cats so he could hear them coming and make necessary plans to prevent them from barging in when he was just about to connect with Julia.

Julia rolled away from him and lifted a hand to move that lock of hair away from her cheek. He wasn't certain, but he thought he saw a shudder run through her.

Donovan looked at his sister. "Nothing," he said. Absolutely nothing thanks to his sister's heinous timing.

"Great." Mal sat down in a chair across the table. "Then let's get started." She motioned to the closed folder still in front of Julia. "Take a look through that, Julia, and then we'll talk details." Mal shrugged out of her coat, draping it across a chair beside her and pulling a laptop out of her leather briefcase.

"Of course." Julia flipped open the folder and started to read the contents.

Donovan studied her. Until he realized he was

gawking and that would surely be noticed by his sister. He turned to Mal, who was thankfully still tapping away on her laptop. "How did your meeting go?"

"Good." She didn't raise her eyes. "I think it'll be great for business."

Donovan suddenly realized she might spill the beans about the restaurant and decision to keep it in the family. Hell. He darted a glance at Julia, but she didn't look up, apparently not sensing his sudden panic. "Good. We'll discuss details later."

Julia did look up then, but to Donovan's relief her question wasn't about the meeting he'd just mentioned. She pointed at the paper in front of her. "You want me to do *Wake Up, Vancouver*?"

Wake Up, Vancouver was the most popular morning news program in the city. An appearance there would be sure to boost both their profile and their reservations.

"We both think you'll be perfect," Donovan said. He and Mal had discussed how they should take advantage of Julia's sultry French looks. "We thought maybe the first week we're open." So the people who saw the show could call and make reservations right away.

Julia blinked and looked back at the paper. "And we're participating in Bounty of Whistler next month?" Bounty of Whistler was a spring food festival created as a counterpoint to that town's wildly successful winter event, Cornucopia. This was its first year. "The restaurant won't even be open yet."

La Petite Bouchée was closing next week and would remain closed for three weeks while the renovations they'd agreed upon were made. The food festival, happening the first week of March, fell right in the middle of that.

"Yes, it's perfect timing." Mal stopped typing. "It'll be a test run of sorts. You can serve some of your new menu items and I'll get us some good media coverage, so when we do open, there's already interest built. I was thinking of just a booth, but we have the opportunity to take over a restaurant for the night. One of the other participants backed out."

"Take over a restaurant." Donovan saw the spark of interest in Julia's eyes. "A tasting menu paired with wines."

"Exactly." The same spark lit Mal's eyes. Donovan was glad to see it. For too long, his sister had seemed quiet, too inwardly focused for his liking. He knew it was her personal life, whatever was happening between her and Travis, but he didn't like seeing her so unhappy. Mal had always been fiery, the kind who gave as good as she got, but most days, that Mal seemed to be in hiding. "Donovan will be with you at the festival, so all you'll have to worry about is cooking and introducing each course. Everything else will be handled by him."

Donovan blinked. This was news to him. When Mal had mentioned the idea earlier this week, she had been clear that she was the one who knew media and public relations, so she was the one who should be there. And Donovan could hardly say that his crush overrode her business sense. So why was she handing him the reins now? But when he looked at her, she merely gave a quick head shake. A sibling gesture that meant they would talk about it later.

Julia flicked a glance at him and then back to Mal. "It sounds great."

"Good." Mal made a few notes on her laptop and then pushed it to the side. "I realize this is probably a lot to take in all at once. Why don't you take the folder home and look it over this week. We can meet to discuss any questions or concerns you have after that."

When Julia looked at him, Donovan inclined his head in agreement. "Or you can call. You have my number, and I'm always around to answer."

She nodded. Donovan considered adding that she could just call him if she felt like it, but bit back the words. That was a conversation for another time, one where his sister wasn't listening in on every word.

"Unless there's anything you can think of now?"

"No." Julia looked at the folder. "No, you've given me plenty to think about, though."

When he returned to his office after walking Julia to the elevator, Mal was waiting for him. With Owen.

He swallowed the sigh that threatened to push through his closed lips. He loved his siblings; he really did. But sometimes a man just wanted to be alone with his thoughts and his raging libido. Sometimes a man didn't get that choice, though.

"What's up?" He sat behind his desk, jiggling his mouse to wake up the computer and subtly—okay, maybe not so subtly—letting the pair know that this needed to be short and sweet. Where had Owen come from, anyway? He hadn't been in the office earlier and he certainly hadn't arrived while Donovan had been escorting Julia out because he would have spotted him in the hallway. "Why are you here?"

Owen blinked, his head pulling back fractionally. "I wanted to hear about the meeting."

"Oh." Donovan frowned. He wasn't sure how he felt about that. Over the past month, rather than showing signs of disinterest in the family business as he always had, Owen was taking on a larger role and asking for more responsibility. Donovan still wasn't sure if he appreciated that his younger brother was showing some initiative or was annoyed that he was sticking his nose into things that had been running perfectly well without him. Probably a bit of both. "Why's that?" Owen's responsibilities lay with Elephants—that was it. He had no current role in La Petite Bouchée and, given the fact that Gus would be the one to take over from Donovan, no role in its future, either.

"Because I want to help."

Donovan didn't doubt his brother's sincerity, just his ability to follow through. "I appreciate the offer, but Mal and I have got this covered." *Now, run along, little brother, and let the grownups talk.*

Owen must have sensed his thoughts because his face tightened. "You know I want to be more involved."

"And you are," Donovan pointed out. "You've been handling Elephants for a while now."

"And?"

Donovan frowned. Did Owen want a parade? A gold trophy for doing the same things that he and Mal, before she'd left to start her own bistro in Aruba, had been doing for years? "And what?"

"Never mind." Owen shook his head. His usual easygoing demeanor replaced with something sharp and a little sour. "You know, Donovan, you've been on my ass for years about how I don't take enough responsibility with the company. But now, when I'm trying, you shut me out." He pushed himself out of the chair. "I'll talk to you later, Mal." Then left without a backward glance.

Donovan watched him go, feeling a twist of uncertainty in his belly, and then turned to his sister. Mal scowled. At him. "What?"

"Don't you think you're being a little hard on him?"

Donovan ran a hand through his hair and shoved the uncertainty aside. He *was* hard on Owen. He knew that, but he had to be. The business needed him to be. It was all well and good for Owen to claim an interest in the family holdings now, to offer his help and quite probably to act on it. But his history indicated it would be a passing fancy and Donovan wasn't interested in training his younger brother only to have it be a waste of time. "He's had plenty of opportunity to get involved before."

"I know." Mal heaved out a sigh and crossed her legs. She'd removed her suit jacket. Her shirt was bright red and matched the soles of her shoes. "But maybe he's finally ready. Don't you think we should give him the chance?"

"Probably." Donovan told himself that this was a special situation and poor timing on Owen's part. "But Dad's not ready to come back and the restaurant is a far bigger project than we usually have in spring. Maybe once the renovations are done and the campaign is over." Once their dad was back, maybe Donovan could start to bring Owen in a little more. A bit of extra work here and there, see if it was something Owen could stick with or if he'd start to blow them off. Something that wouldn't destroy their bottom line or productivity.

"I think you need to give him a chance."

"I will, Mal." He really would. But not now. Not with La Petite Bouchée and Julia. "But this isn't the right occasion." He leaned back in his chair, finished with that topic. "Now, you want to tell me why I'm going to the food festival and not you?" Not that he wasn't looking forward to it, but it wasn't like Mal to pass her load on to anyone else without good reason. He wanted to hear it.

But instead of the quick rejoinder he'd expected, Mal looked worried, a frown on her lips and a furrow to her brow. She'd been looking pinched in general lately, but when he'd asked, she'd brushed off his concerns with a brisk wave and a terse reminder that she was fine.

"Mal?" The tickle of concern about his sister turned to a full death rattle. "What's going on?"

She looked away, to the side of the room. "I have a thing."

"A thing?" It wasn't like Mal to conceal her thoughts. "What thing?"

Her leg started to jiggle. "Just a thing."

Donovan didn't say anything, sensing that any

pushing on his part would cause her to close up and start in on how she was just fine and he didn't need to worry. But Mal hadn't been herself lately. Actually, she hadn't been herself in a while. She came in early, stayed late and generally ran her department with skill and confidence, but the smile she used to share so easily was gone and her satisfaction with life seemed diminished. And he was pretty sure this *thing* had something to do with it.

"I'm going to see Travis." She still didn't look at him.

Donovan kept his expression neutral. "I wasn't sure you were still together." He hadn't asked anything specific about his little sister's love life after the first time, when she'd bitten off his head and reminded him to stay out of her personal business. But the sapphire ring hadn't reappeared and she never mentioned Travis's name. "So, you're going to Aruba?"

"Yes." She didn't offer any more information on the matter and Donovan didn't ask for details. He'd been fortunate enough to end all his relationships amicably and with no lingering feelings, but that didn't mean he couldn't recognize what his sister was going through would be hard. She and Travis had been together more than five years. They'd met in university and he'd been a fixture at their family gatherings ever since.

"Is there anything I can do?"

Finally, she turned her gaze toward him. "Yes—go to the food-and-wine festival." Mal tapped her finger on the seat. "Unless you think we should send Owen. He does love that kind of thing."

"No." Donovan cut that thought short before it could take root. "Terrible idea." His gut churned at the thought of Julia relying on his brother instead of him.

"Donovan." Mal sounded disappointed, as if he was the one doing something wrong. "Owen wants to be more involved."

"I know, but this is the wrong situation." It wasn't just the restaurant and Julia on the line; it was Donovan's reputation, as well. And while Owen had certainly been showing initiative and growth, Donovan wasn't ready to put his personal reputation in his brother's hands. "I'll go."

CHAPTER SEVEN

JULIA STOOD IN the kitchen of La Petite Bouchée stirring the sauce in the pan in front of her. A variation on hollandaise, one of the master sauces in French cooking, and incredibly tasty. Even in her currently tense state, she knew that she had a winner. Too bad she had no one to share it with.

She'd sent the staff off an hour ago, with instructions to enjoy their time off since the restaurant was now officially closed for renovations. The construction team would be in first thing tomorrow morning to start tearing down and then building up. Julia and Sasha had already rescued the pictures from the wall, stowing them in Julia's office until they could be put back up.

Part of her was excited to see what the space would look like, but another part of her was still worried. Worried that the changes would ruin the classic style she wanted to keep, worried that the space would no longer remind her of her mother. She sighed. But Donovan had been right when he'd said things needed to change. She knew that.

And she was trying to embrace it, or, at least, not run screaming from it.

Julia pushed the distracting thoughts out of her mind. She'd stayed behind not to mourn the coming changes but to work on her menu for the Whistler food festival. In a week and a half, she and some of her staff would be on their way to what was already being touted as a foodie must-see. And Donovan.

She swallowed. Despite their near kiss in his boardroom a few days earlier, he hadn't made another move. He'd continued to show up for dinner most nights and stayed after closing to recap the night with her, but there had been no lean-in and no brush of lips across her skin. She wasn't sure how she felt about any of it.

She liked him and liked spending time with him. But this was as far as she could go. At least for now. She stirred the sauce again, trying to drown out her conflicting thoughts. That she was already spending lots of time with Donovan and that getting involved wouldn't change anything. That she should stop wasting the free time she had by flirting with him and instead should concentrate on building a better business plan and ensuring her investors were all on the same page.

She should be focusing on her new menu. The one she was responsible for creating and perfecting. The reason she was standing over the stove now. Julia had no intention of doing anything too drastic. Instead, she envisioned a menu of updated classic French cuisine. Small changes that wouldn't scare away traditionalists but would encourage those looking for something different to try.

But late at night, lying in the emptiness of her bed, she didn't think about the menu or about the new look La Petite Bouchée would have. She thought about Donovan Ford.

She stirred the sauce faster, keeping it from congealing into clumps while it reduced. Julia might have been able to let it all go, to move on and think only about the restaurant, if she'd been able to wipe that kiss from her memory. That heart-stopping, leg-weakening kiss that she also thought about when she was alone in her empty bed.

Sasha thought she should just sleep with him and get it out of her system. Which Julia wasn't going to think about because it did little to help her already-tender stomach or case of rollicking nerves.

She wished her mom were here. Suzanne would have a strong opinion on the matter. Not just on the food—which protein was best suited, whether or not the sauce needed more pepper, if she should serve a traditional accompaniment like asparagus or something less common like a green papaya salad—but on any potential relationship with Donovan, as well.

As a woman in the industry at a time when they were badly outnumbered, Suzanne had managed to navigate the dangerous waters with style and panache. Julia wished she'd asked her more about that. It had never seemed necessary. As the industry shifted and more and more women turned to cooking as a profession, as well as running and owning their own restaurants, Julia had assumed the path would be relatively straightforward. And it would have been had Donovan Ford not appeared to put a wrinkle in things.

But her mother wasn't around to ask and never would be again. It was up to Julia to choose her own path.

She wished she'd let Sasha stay when she'd offered. Instead, she'd shooed her best friend out, not wanting Sasha to cancel her plans just so Julia wouldn't be lonely. And she wasn't lonely. Even if the deserted state of her kitchen indicated otherwise, she was just alone.

It was just that some nights it felt like the same thing.

Julia shook her head, dislodging the thoughts and the moroseness that came with them. She didn't need to fix her entire life tonight. She tasted the sauce, then drizzled some on the piece of salmon and chicken she'd cooked to test it with. It worked for both, though the salmon tasted better when she added a few more drops of lemon.

Satisfied, she cleaned her dishes. Tomorrow, she could try again. Maybe Donovan would finally show up for dinner and she could ask his opinion.

She tossed her chef jacket into the linens hamper and switched her comfy pants and sneakers for jeans and red flats and headed outside. When her phone rang, she considered ignoring it. She didn't feel like talking, but she didn't feel like going home to stare up at her bedroom ceiling, either.

"Hello?"

"Don't tell me you're still at the restaurant." Sasha's voice was a bit fuzzy, partially drowned out by the noise of the bar she was at.

"Just leaving," Julia admitted. She made sure the door was locked behind her and then started the trek toward the bus stop and home.

"Excellent—then I don't have to come over there and pry you away from the stove. Come out."

"Sasha." Julia started to decline, then paused. Hadn't she just been thinking that there was nothing for her at home but another lonely night of staring at the ceiling? And what was the point of that? Clearly, it wasn't getting her anywhere. And maybe a night out would get her mind off her current situation. "Where are you?"

"Elephants."

Julia jerked. And maybe a night out would just highlight her conflicted life. Yeah, suddenly studying the ceiling sounded excellent. "You know, I'm pretty tired."

"Your man's not here."

"I never should have told you about that kiss."

"Should have, could have, would have." Sasha laughed and the sound lifted Julia's mood. "Come out."

Julia sighed. She was tired and it had been a long, draining night. Even closing the restaurant down temporarily felt like saying goodbye.

"Don't make me come to your apartment and drag you out." Julia knew she would, too. Sasha had done it before. Right after Suzanne's funeral, when it had taken all the energy Julia had just to get out of bed and get herself to the kitchen.

Those had been dark days, full of pain and regret, and Sasha had pulled her through. Showing up at her apartment, forcing Julia to get into the shower, styling her hair and doing her makeup, even choosing her clothes and then making her come out for the night because it would be good for her. And Julia had to admit that Sasha had been right.

Those nights out had done a lot to improve her mental state and help her deal with her grief. Not that this was the same thing at all. She wasn't grieving Donovan or what might have been. There was hardly anything to grieve, even if her body did sometimes ache for his touch.

"Fine. I'll see you in ten."

It took less time than that since she got lucky, spotting a cab just after hanging up and making every green light on the drive there. Julia's heart thumped as she paid the driver and climbed out the back door.

The bar was full. Julia could see the mass of bodies through the window, and when she opened the door, she was met with a wave of sound and heat. She tugged at the sleeve of her wraparound sweater, glad that she'd been wearing something going-out appropriate, as she wound her way through the crowd and into the heart of the bar.

She squinted but finally spotted Sasha and some other people sitting in a booth by the back corner. She wound her way through the tables, her years of working in the industry allowing her to avoid potential spills and bumps easily.

Sasha greeted her with a big hug and a kiss on the cheek as though it had been years instead of hours since they'd last seen each other. Her green eyes were bright with excitement as she wagged them toward the end of the table and then whispered in Julia's ear, "What do you think of the blond? I want to take him home tonight."

The blond was tall and thin, built like a marathoner, and had a wispy growth of hair on his upper lip, but he smiled politely when he saw their attention on him. "He looks nice," Julia agreed. He also looked unemployed and as if he'd barely left high school, but Julia didn't worry about that.

Sasha didn't get involved. Not for long, anyway. She flitted from man to man like a bee drunk on nectar, never allowing anyone to get deeply attached. Julia thought it seemed lonely, but Sasha appeared to like it. And on those nights when Julia was alone in her bed with nothing but the sheets for comfort, she wondered if Sasha might have it right.

Surely, one hot and sweaty night with a hot and sweaty man would absolve her of these uncomfortable fantasies starring Donovan Ford.

"He's got a friend." Sasha pointed to an equally thin, equally wispy-looking brunette. Julia hid her shudder.

"Not interested." And wouldn't have been even if she'd never met Donovan Ford.

Sasha shook her head. "I'm telling you. One night of hot sex. It'll do you a world of good." She tugged Julia down beside her. "More important, how's the tasting menu coming along?" Julia had been fretting over the choices for the special dinner they'd be hosting at Bounty of Whistler for the past week. "Are you happy with it?"

"I think so." Julia was pretty sure she'd gotten the right balance this time. But she'd have to try it a couple more times in larger batches to ensure the flavors translated properly. She didn't even want to consider things going wrong the night of the special dinner. "Want to come over to my place tomorrow and taste for me?"

"Sure." Sasha leaned closer. "Alternatively, you could make better use of your time off and invite Donovan over for personal tasting." She wiggled her eyebrows.

"If you say 'and you don't mean a food tasting,' I'm leaving," Julia said.

Sasha laughed. "I wasn't going to. But I would have if I'd thought of it." She slung an arm around Julia's shoulders. "Since you brought it up, I feel it's my duty to point out that since *you've* thought of it, it must be on your mind at least some of the time."

"No," Julia lied, which wasn't a total lie because it was on her mind *all* the time. "I wouldn't even consider it." Because it was a bad idea. A bad, bad idea. Being alone in the restaurant had been enough to have them kissing. How far would she go in her apartment, where there was no one and nothing to remind her that she needed to think of her future and the restaurant's? "Besides, we don't have that kind of relationship."

"And why is that? I thought you liked the kiss."

Julia knew she should have kept the incident to herself, chalked it up to an impulsive error and pretended that it had never happened. That would have been the professional thing to do. Of course, she'd blabbed the minute she'd seen Sasha. "It didn't mean anything and nothing will come of it. That's why."

Sasha rolled her eyes and leaned closer to be heard over the noisy crowd. "Maybe that's your problem. You're all tense because you haven't gotten any."

"That's not why I'm tense." Julia had many reasons to be tense, but getting some wasn't part of it.

Sasha patted her on the shoulder. "So stubborn, so unable to see what's right in front of you. I'm telling you. Just one night to blow off steam and you'd feel all better."

"No. I wouldn't. I'd just be tenser." But Julia's lips tingled and a low heat crept up from her belly. If only she could indulge in the spark that sizzled whenever Donovan was in the vicinity. Allow those hands to do more than cup her face or stroke her cheek.

"Not if he did it right, and he looks like the kind of man who would know how. It wouldn't have to be serious. Just a really hot fling. No harm in that."

Julia understood that was true in Sasha's world and she would be lying if she said she'd never engaged in a short fling or one-night stand herself. But… "I'm not interested in a hot fling. With anyone." She ignored Sasha's raised eyebrow. "I have other things to think about, Sash. With all the renovations and menu changes, I don't have time."

Sasha laughed. "Oh, please. There should always be time for good sex. And if not, you should make some. It would probably go a long way toward easing your stress."

"And maybe I'll just get a massage."

"You know, it isn't healthy to ignore your personal needs."

Julia shook her head. "I'm not ignoring anything." She had a perfectly good vibrator that lived in her nightstand drawer. Not that she'd had much time to use him lately. Which only served to prove her point. If she couldn't even clear out a block of time when she was alone and in bed, then actually connecting with a real live human seemed out of the question.

Sasha patted her shoulder again. "You keep telling yourself that."

Julia straightened and tried not to look as though she was thinking about a naked Donovan. "I will."

"Good." Sasha smiled and dropped the subject, but Julia's brain didn't.

The wispy blond and his friend decided they wanted to move on to another nightclub, but when Julia said she wasn't interested, Sasha decided to stay, too.

"Go," Julia encouraged her. "I should probably head home anyway."

Sasha sent her a withering look. "This is the first time you've come out in two weeks. You're not going home at eleven thirty." She waved the boys off. "Besides, I'm thinking he might be a little too thin. I don't want to break him or get bruised by his protruding hip bones."

Julia laughed.

"It's a legitimate concern."

"Ladies." Julia glanced up to see Owen towering over them, a water bottle in his hands. "I didn't know you were coming tonight. You should have called."

She smiled and lifted her cheek for Owen to kiss. "We didn't know you were working." And even as she said it, her eyes darted around the room, searching to see if the other Ford brother might be nearby.

Sasha wasn't so subtle. She kissed Owen on the lips and asked, "Where's your handsome brother?"

Owen put a hand to his chest, a pained expression on his face. "I'm crushed. Am I not enough man for you?"

Sasha laughed while Julia stepped on her foot under the table. Seriously, what was she doing?

"Oh, you're plenty of man." Sasha laid a hand on Owen's chest. "I'm flattered you'd sit with us."

They flirted away while Julia sipped her water

and tried not to feel jealous that she didn't have a Ford to flirt with. Not that she would. Because she so wouldn't.

Owen turned, including her in the conversation, and soon Julia forgot all about Donovan. Except when Owen tilted his head a certain way, or when she noticed the way his hands looked laid flat against the table or saw the way his dark hair seemed to absorb rather than reflect the light. Just like Donovan's. So really, barely at all.

Owen turned all his attention to her when Sasha excused herself to go to the bathroom. "I hear you and my brother are taking a trip."

Julia nodded and pretended her abdomen hadn't twisted. The trip was for work only, and no matter what kind of ideas Sasha might try to put in her head, there was no reason to think anything other than that would happen during the weekend. "Just a few days."

He picked at the label on his water bottle, shredding off a small strip of paper. "Are you looking forward to it?"

This time she couldn't ignore the twist, but she did her best not to show it and kept her tone light. "Bounty of Whistler should be a great event." Julia was excited to be part of the festival's inaugural season. Plus, she hoped to be far too busy, cooking and glad-handing and serving, to think about sexy times on the mountainside with Donovan. "Are you coming?" That would be great—to have at least one other person who might act as a buffer between her and Donovan, because Julia knew she couldn't count on Sasha to do it.

"No." Owen lounged back against the booth. "When Mal had to cancel, I'd hoped I might, but…" He shrugged. "Apparently, I need to prove that I'm serious about the family business." The corners of Owen's mouth turned down. "It seems I spend too much time playing and not enough working."

Julia didn't know what to say to that, so she reached out and offered his hand a sympathetic pat. She had sensed there was some distance between the brothers. There were many evenings they both came to the restaurant to eat, but never together. But she didn't know how deep it went. Whether it was just a difference of opinion on lifestyle or something more serious.

"I think you're doing a great job," she told Owen. "Look at this place. It's a Tuesday night and it's packed." She didn't even have to exaggerate. Though plenty of businesses would be half-empty or closed entirely on what was traditionally a slow night, Elephants showed no sign of anything other than success.

The bang of pans from the open kitchen and the clink of bottles from the bar told her that they weren't slowing down, either. Owen smiled, but his fingers still worked that water-bottle label until it was a pile of torn strips lying on the table. "Yes, well. That's expected. I need to go beyond that." He put his hand on top of hers. "But thanks for being so nice."

"I'm not just being nice, Owen. It's true." She put her free hand on top of his, sensing he needed kindness as much as reassurance. "This is amazing. Maybe you could help at La Petite Bouchée once we reopen. We could certainly use this kind of business."

Owen smiled, but there was bitterness in it. "Maybe." And he didn't sound as if he thought it would be a possibility.

She squeezed his fingers. Sometimes actions meant more than talk and a simple touch could be more soothing than a lecture's worth of words.

And that was how they were sitting when Donovan found them.

Julia's heart thumped when she heard his voice flowing around her, cloaking her entire body. "Julia." His eyes didn't leave her. "And Owen."

"Ah, yes. The ever-working brother." Owen smiled, but Julia heard the tension in his voice. She folded her hands in her lap. "I didn't expect to see you here tonight. I hope you're not checking up on me."

"No. I just stopped in for a drink after work." He glanced around the room. "Busy night."

"It is." Owen might appear relaxed, but beneath his jovial chatter, Julia had noticed the sharp eye he kept on the crowd around them. The servers were well trained, gliding between tables and caring for patrons with a friendly demeanor. There was no reason for Owen to be hovering over anyone, cracking the whip.

Donovan turned, his eyes meeting hers, and Julia felt the glimmer of attraction flutter through her. She tamped down on the sensation and wondered exactly how long Sasha was going to take in the bathroom.

"Owen, will you give us a minute." Donovan spoke to his brother while his eyes remained on her, and it was clearly a statement, not a question.

"I'm fine where I am," Owen said.

"Then I'll join you."

Julia hadn't expected Donovan to nudge into the minuscule space beside her. Not when there was practically an arena's worth of space beside his brother. But nudge he did, the bump of his thigh against hers sending another glimmer of heat through her.

She tried not to notice. "You know, Owen and I were just discussing the possibility of him joining us in Whistler."

"Were you?" Donovan stretched an arm along the back of the booth, his hand hovering just above her shoulder. If she shrugged, she was pretty sure his fingers would tickle her.

"Yes. He mentioned he'd like to attend. I think that seems reasonable, don't you?"

"No." His eyes caught hers and didn't move. Julia felt her lungs swell, but she couldn't really breathe. Just stare back. What was it about this man that clouded her thoughts? "Owen—" Donovan's voice shifted but his gaze didn't "—could you give us that minute?"

"Julia?" She turned to find Owen watching her with a concerned tilt to his brow. He even reached out to touch her arm and she realized he was worried about her. He wanted to protect her from his big bad brother, which was sweet though unnecessary.

She could manage Donovan, and it was clear their fraternal relationship was strained. She didn't know why, but she sensed encouraging Owen to stay would only exacerbate whatever the issue was. She wouldn't do that. She might not have siblings of her own, but she held family relationships in high respect. She held all family in high respect, maybe because she no longer had any of her own.

She smiled at Owen. "I'll be fine."

"Are you sure?" She nodded, sure she'd done the right thing when the tightness around Owen's mouth relaxed. "Okay. I'll be at the bar. Let me know if you need anything."

She waited until he'd moved out of eavesdropping range before she looked at Donovan. "You want to tell me what that was all about?"

"Not really." He didn't slide closer to her, but he did relax, his long body sinking into the cushioned padding of the booth.

Julia slid away from him. Not because she didn't trust herself to be near him, but because it was a big booth, large enough to seat five comfortably, and the two of them snuggling up in one tiny section seemed silly. And just a little too intimate for her own comfort.

Donovan tilted his head and looked at her. "Why are you asking about Owen joining us in Whistler?"

"It came up in conversation." But she was having trouble thinking when he watched her with that intense gaze and he sat so close. She could see the outline of his thigh muscles under his pants. He had the kind of body a woman could grab, grip hard and hold on to for the ride. And out of her chef coat, away from La Petite Bouchée, it was harder to remember that her focus needed to be on work. She forced herself to turn her head and glance around the room in a show of disinterest while her temperature returned to normal. Or it might have had Donovan not still been staring at her when she turned back.

"So you just happened to be holding hands with him when I came in?"

"We weren't holding hands." She'd been supporting Owen—that was all. "Why does it matter?"

Donovan shrugged and after a long moment of staring seemed to let it go. "I missed you."

Heat spiked beneath her skin along with irritation. "You saw me last night."

"It was too long."

Julia knew she shouldn't like it when he talked that way, when he hinted at more. But she did like it. A lot. "You'll survive."

"I might not." He leaned toward her. But he didn't kiss her. And she wasn't sure if she was happy or sad about that.

So she changed the subject. "You know, we need a general manager at La Petite Bouchée when we reopen. Someone to manage the floor." Because her previous one had quit when she'd announced they were closing for three weeks to renovate and she wasn't particularly sad to see the back of him. He'd been officious and quick to palm off duties that he felt were beneath him. Julia guessed he didn't realize that in a restaurant, there was no job beneath you.

Heck, she'd been known on more than one occasion to jump into the dish pit and scrub if that would get the line moving again.

"Do we?" He watched her, all dark eyes and cool smile.

Julia tried not to think about how appealing it was. She had a job to focus on. And even if she wasn't trying to build a career and a name for herself, getting involved with her boss was a bad idea. People might think she'd gotten ahead based on her skills in the bedroom, not in the kitchen. Or that was what she told herself when her hormones tried to get the best of her. "Yes. I think Owen would be perfect." She flicked a look around the wine bar, which she knew would be busy right up until last call. "I like how he handles Elephants."

"He doesn't handle Elephants." Donovan's smile wasn't quite so cool now. "That would be the assistant manager, Jeannie."

Julia frowned. That wasn't right. She'd met Jeannie once and she seemed capable and polite, but Owen was definitely the one in charge. The one captaining this ship. "Owen's pretty involved," she insisted. In fact, he was heavily involved, taking care of concerns from both patrons and staff, all without losing his easy demeanor.

Of course, she didn't know what went on behind closed doors, but that was the beauty of her idea. The general manager needed people skills. She took care of the back end of ordering and inventory control.

"I'd like to at least ask him if he's interested."

Donovan's lips tightened. "And if I recommend that we don't?"

"Why would you do that? Because you're not keeping the restaurant and Owen works for the family?" It was the only thing she could think of. She could even understand his reticence. But there was no reason Owen couldn't manage La Petite Bouchée until then.

Donovan's lips tightened again. "No. That's not it." He looked as if he was about to say more, but a throng of customers bumped their table, sending the liquid in their glasses sloshing, and by the time they'd reached out to right them and sop up any spillage with their napkins, the moment was gone.

"Then why?"

"Listen." He paused, wadded up the wet napkins in his hand and put them in one of the empty glasses. "Owen's job is here. At Elephants."

"I know. But I think we should at least offer him the choice. Even if he says no, I'm sure he'd appreciate hearing about it." Owen had clearly indicated to her that he was ready for a bigger challenge. What bigger challenge than helping set up and overseeing the grand reopening?

"I know he would. That's not my concern."

"Then what is your concern?" Julia didn't realize she'd leaned closer until she felt the heat from Donovan's body wash over hers. She swallowed.

"Owen is…excitable. He jumps in with both feet and he's ready and willing to do whatever it takes."

"Uh, those sound like good things," Julia pointed out. She didn't point out that Donovan's thigh had shifted and was now pressing against hers.

"They are. Until the next new, exciting thing comes along." Donovan blew out a breath. "Then he'd be off chasing that butterfly. I can't guarantee that he'd be reliable. He might get invited on a safari or a cruise to Alaska and just like that—" Donovan snapped his fingers "—Owen would be gone."

"Are you sure we're talking about the same Owen? Tall? Dark hair? Lives at Elephants?"

"You don't really know him."

"No." She drew the word out. But everything she'd seen of Owen said he wasn't the type to leave her, or anyone, high and dry. Maybe he'd been that guy in the past, but people could change. "Or maybe you don't know him anymore."

Donovan shrugged. "I probably don't. But I know the way he was, and past behavior is a good indicator of future behavior." He closed his eyes for a moment. "Owen is my brother, and even though he can drive me insane, I do love the guy. But—" he opened his eyes and looked at her "—I don't know if I can trust him."

Julia saw the guilt wash over his face. A flash

of emotion and then it was gone, replaced by his usual calm bearing. She reached out to him. She didn't think about it, wonder how it might be perceived or whether it was a bad idea. She just thought he needed support and she was willing to give it. Her hand landed on his, curled through his fingers. "That's a pretty serious statement."

Donovan's fingers curled around hers. "It is. But I have to be honest with you. Owen and I have never seen eye to eye. Not even when we were little."

"That's a lot of years to overcome."

"Yep." He didn't explain and Julia didn't ask him to.

"I guess it's part of being brothers." She couldn't fully understand, being an only child, but she thought she could imagine what it might be like. "But don't let that relationship drift away. He's your only brother."

Julia would have loved to have a sibling. She couldn't remember not wanting one, always begging her mother for a little sister because boys were gross. But Suzanne would only laugh and say not right now.

She thought about it again now. Wondering if dealing with her mother's death might have been easier if she hadn't been alone. "Not everyone is lucky enough to have one."

"You can have him."

"Donovan."

His quick smile faded. "I know. I just… It's hard. I don't like thinking of you looking at our relationship and judging me lacking."

"I'm not judging you. I like Owen. And I like you." His fingers tangled with hers. She felt her heart give a long, slow thump. A beat that filled her entire body. "It seems to me that you should like each other."

"I knew you liked me."

"Okay, that was so not the point." Not the point at all.

"Oh, I think it was." And when he bent his head toward her again, it took every ounce of will-power she had to turn the other cheek.

CHAPTER EIGHT

JULIA'S INSIDES WERE all knotted up, had been that way since she'd nearly kissed Donovan at Elephants last week. Which really would have been a mistake. Owen had been there, and Sasha, who would never have let her hear the end of it.

Although Sasha wasn't letting her hear the end of it anyway.

"Why don't you just admit you're attracted to him?" Sasha asked from the driver's seat. It was Saturday morning and they were on their way to Bounty of Whistler for the weekend. They had a private dinner scheduled tonight, where festival-goers had to purchase special tickets to participate. Julia had been pleased that the event had sold out. Tomorrow, they'd be in one of the booths in the convention center, serving up food to the masses.

"What does that have to do with anything?" Julia's eyes tracked to Donovan's car, grateful that she'd declined both his invitation to ride with him and for her and Sasha to stay at his family cabin. Much safer to stay in a hotel.

Sasha looked at her as if she was crazy. "Because you want to do him, and maybe if you did, you wouldn't look so tense."

"Eyes on the road," she told Sasha. "And I'm not tense." But even as she said it, Julia felt her shoulders rise up.

Sasha turned her attention back to the road, but she didn't let the subject drop. "So this pinched look around your mouth is the latest fashion?"

Julia forced her mouth to relax. "I'm not tense." Or no more tense than any other head chef who was trying to find a way to buy her restaurant from the current owners. It was hard, Julia noted, liking the people she worked for and yet wanting them to fail.

Although that wasn't exactly true. She didn't want them or the restaurant to fail—she just wanted them to sell to her. Which wouldn't happen unless the space failed.

A bit of a problem, really, since that would also reflect poorly on her. It had been easy to explain to potential investors that the reason La Petite Bouchée wasn't already a huge success was because it needed refreshing. Not quite a face-lift but some Botox. A touch-up on decor that brightened and lifted, an updated menu and a proper launch to let the foodie community know that La Petite Bouchée was back and better than ever.

Which was exactly what the Fords had planned. And she didn't see it failing.

"You know what gets rid of tension?"

"Don't start."

"Too late." Sasha gave a merry laugh. "And it's well past time that you got some. Don't make me bring up your dry streak."

"A streak I'm on by choice."

Sasha sent her a pitying glance. "Oh, honey. No one goes on a streak this long by choice."

"It hasn't been that long." Julia glanced at Donovan's car again. It had been only, what? Four months? Six?

"Just over a year," Sasha announced. "With that guy you picked up after we got drunk in Seattle."

Had it really been that long? A year? Julia opened her mouth to argue, until she realized Sasha was right. Good God. Twelve months? "I don't know why you're keeping track of my sex life."

"Someone has to look out for you." Sasha nodded as if it was her duty as a best friend. "Which means it's high time to get back on that horse, if you will. And Donovan Ford appears to be quite the stallion."

"Sasha," Julia hissed, even though there was no one around to hear them. "Stop."

"I think you should do him tonight."

Julia didn't answer. Instead, she looked out the

window at the gorgeous view provided by the Sea to Sky Highway that ran from Vancouver up to Whistler. The road was carved into the mountain while the ocean brushed up on the opposite side of the road. Beautiful and deadly.

"Seriously, Julia, it's perfect. You're out of town at a beautiful resort. What better time to make your move?"

"I'm not making a move. I told you that. I don't have time for dating."

"Who said anything about dating him? Just ride him like the good little cowgirl I know you want to be."

Julia tried not to laugh. "I am not a cowgirl and I don't plan to ride anything." But she couldn't deny the vivid image that popped into her head. Straddling Donovan, her hands on his chest, his on her hips as she rocked back and forth on top of him. She shifted in her seat. "Can we talk about something else?" Anything else.

"No. Not until you agree I'm right."

Julia refused to do so, but she couldn't get Sasha's words out of her mind, either. Not even after they'd arrived, checked into the hotel and then headed to the restaurant where they were taking over the kitchen for a private dinner tonight. Those local restaurants that weren't participating themselves rented out their spaces to chefs and owners who were.

It would be only for tonight. A taste. Just enough so that she could stop wondering and get back to focusing on what mattered—her career and finding a way to buy La Petite Bouchée for herself.

But thinking about Donovan, under her, on top of her, beside her, made her feel overly warm, as if her chef coat was too tight. She left the top buttons open while she prepped in the borrowed kitchen.

Julia had brought along half her team. Since they were doing only one service tonight, they didn't need everyone, but she did need her best. Tonight was a showcase. Most ticket holders would be from Vancouver, and a good meal was one they would talk about with their friends, creating buzz so when La Petite Bouchée had the grand reopening, there would already be demand.

Which was exactly what she should be focused on.

Julia kept busy in the kitchen, checking and tasting and doing it again until she was certain she hadn't overlooked anything. Her shoulders felt tight and she rolled them back and forth before she called for plating.

She'd peeked out a few minutes ago and seen Donovan working the crowd, making sure everyone had wine and chatting up the fixed menu they were serving tonight. Julia would go out with each course to talk about the food and spend a little time with people she hoped would become future regulars. Since Whistler was only two hours away from Vancouver, it was a regular destination for many city dwellers. More than a few were at the festival and had bought tickets to their dinner tonight.

Her heart skipped a beat as she checked every plate for consistency and beauty before allowing the servers to carry them out. Tonight was a big deal. A chance to make or break her reputation since most people here hadn't been to La Petite Bouchée during her tenure—or if she were honest, probably at all, since the restaurant had fallen off the foodie landscape more than a decade ago.

Julia followed a short distance behind the servers, a smile on her face, as though she hadn't just spent hours slaving over every detail, throwing something out when it didn't work and starting again.

"Ladies and gentlemen." Donovan's low voice carried through the room, drawing every eye. Even hers. Julia clasped her hands in front of her and hoped they wouldn't shake. It wasn't that she was nervous. It just felt as if this was a marquee moment in her career, a turning point. She felt her nerves run higher when Donovan moved to stand beside her, turning a smile in her direction. "I'd like to introduce the amazing chef at

La Petite Bouchée, Julia Laurent." There was a polite round of applause.

Why did her knees feel as if they wouldn't hold her up? She'd worked the front of the house plenty of times. She loved to talk about her food. She was good at this. She felt the steady press of Donovan's hand on her lower back and her nerves eased.

"Good evening." She leaned back just slightly, making sure not to lose that comforting connection as she launched into her spiel about the first course. She probably shouldn't take so much solace, so much confidence, from the simple feel of his hand on her waist. But she did. He curved his hand over her hip and gave it a reassuring squeeze before she returned to the kitchen.

He did. And during courses three and four, as well. Julia's entire body was tingling when she returned to the dining room for the final time that night, accepting accolades, good wishes and questions about when La Petite Bouchée would reopen.

"You're a hit," Donovan murmured in her ear, which did nothing to stop the tingling or the flash of Sasha's words through her head. *Who said anything about dating, cowgirl?*

Julia did her best to ignore it. "*We're* a hit." She might be the one who'd created the menu and perfected the dishes, but he'd been the one to set up the event and warm up the crowd.

A slow smile spread across his face. One that sent a shiver all the way to her toes. "Shall I pop some champagne to properly celebrate?"

"No, thank you. I need to oversee cleanup and..." And then she would return to the room she was sharing with Sasha and go to sleep so she was rested for her demos at the booth tomorrow. Fun, fun, fun.

"I can wait," Donovan said, and Julia wasn't sure if he was talking about tonight or something further in the future.

"Go," she told him, putting a hand on his arm to nudge him along. Big mistake. Even that minimal contact through layers of fabric created a burst of attraction. "We'll have that champagne when we reopen." When there were other people around and they weren't staying in a romantic mountain-resort village.

But Donovan didn't move. "You sure?" His gaze warmed her, as if she needed any help after having just spent the past eight hours in the kitchen.

She gave him a firm nod and hoped he couldn't see her indecision.

He might not have, since he left after congratulating the staff on a job well done, but Sasha homed in on it like a hummingbird to sugar water.

"Oh, you are not coming back to the hotel with me."

"Of course I am." Julia concentrated on cleaning her knives, making sure there was no sign of the ingredients they'd diced, minced and chopped earlier this evening.

"Did you see the way he was looking at you?" Julia glanced up to find Sasha fanning herself. "I thought I'd accidentally left some burners on."

"You're imagining things." But Julia had noticed, too. She refused to fan herself, knowing it would only encourage Sasha.

"No, I'm not. Ask anyone—we all saw it." But when she opened her mouth to call for confirmation, Julia stopped her with a hand.

"Don't."

Sasha's eyebrows shot up. "Aha. Then you admit I'm right."

"Even a stopped clock," Julia countered, and slid her blades into her knife roll. "He invited me for champagne."

"And you declined?" When Julia nodded, Sasha released a long-suffering sigh. "Fine. I guess I'll have to take one for the team and go in your stead. Hair up or down?"

"You're not going." Julia knew Sasha was only teasing and yet she felt irritated, edgy, thinking of Sasha—or any woman—drinking champagne with Donovan.

"Then you are."

Julia didn't answer right away. She should have.

Sasha leaped on the opening like a starving person at an all-you-can-eat buffet. "Excellent. It's decided. You'll go have champagne with the hottie and I'll pretend not to notice when you don't come back to the hotel tonight."

"Sasha." Julia glanced around the kitchen. There was nothing left to do. Her stomach tumbled. She wasn't actually considering it, was she? No, it was crazy.

"Go. Drink champagne. Have fun."

"But—"

"But nothing." Sasha shook her head. "Think of it as getting him out of your system."

She had a point. Maybe if Julia slept with Donovan, she could stop thinking about him.

"But this can't go anywhere after tonight."

"So what?" Sasha wiped down the last counter and shot her a cheeky grin. "Have one hot night and then never think about it again. Well, except when you tell me the details. Every single dirty one."

Julia knew the moment the decision was made. And it wasn't there standing in the kitchen with her best friend grinning at her like a loon. No, she and Donovan had been moving toward this moment from the second she'd spotted him sitting in her dining room that first night, looking as sinful as the dark-chocolate torte on her menu. It was time to stop pretending.

DONOVAN WAS LOUNGING on the couch of his family's Whistler home, wondering if he should open the champagne on his own. It was an expensive bottle and he had reason to celebrate the event tonight. There was no doubt that when La Petite Bouchée reopened, their reservation list would be full. He knew it not only in his mind—his number-crunching, risk-evaluating, budget-balancing mind—but in his gut. And despite the fact that he'd never wanted to return to the restaurant business after his initial debacle, he wouldn't deny that this felt good. Amazing, in fact. That he'd proved that his first restaurant hadn't been the rule.

There was no reason to let the Veuve go to waste. Yet, he remained on the couch, unable to drum up any interest in opening it. He flicked on the TV and wondered what the rest of his staff were doing. Partying in one of the village's many bars? The weekend would be hopping, with everyone in town for the festival. Maybe they'd cordoned off a back room in a restaurant, clinking glasses as they talked about the dinner service this evening. And was Julia with them?

If he were honest, that was what he really wanted to know. Sure, he'd be pleased to hear the staff had gone out to celebrate a night well done, but it wasn't the reason for his interest. No, that was the pretty dark-haired chef with the dark eyes who had refused his offer of Veuve. Seriously. Who did that?

So when his phone rang, he grabbed for it. Even if it was something work related, it was better than torturing himself by thinking about drinking Veuve with Julia, sipping it from her lips, licking it out of the hollow of her throat, lapping it from her navel.

He was surprised to see her name on the call display, but he muted the throb of interest that followed. Probably a question about tomorrow, a concern regarding setup or food prep, or to double-check timing. Nothing worthy of a throb. "Hey. What's up?"

"Donovan…" She paused. He could hear her breathing, not soft and smooth, but rough and jagged. There was a small hum as she cleared her throat. "I was wondering… Is the invitation for champagne still open?"

He blinked, that throb of interest becoming a steady drumbeat. "Absolutely. Where should I meet you?" He wouldn't give her the opportunity to change her mind. "I can be there in ten minutes." Which was exactly how long it would take him to grab his keys and navigate his car the short distance from the cabin to the village center.

He'd changed out of his suit, but his jeans and T-shirt were fine for the casual village atmosphere. Even in the fanciest hotels.

"Actually…" There was a brief pause and another hum of throat-clearing. "I thought I might come to your place."

Donovan wondered if it was possible for his head to pop off. Not that he was assuming anything. Maybe she just wanted to sit somewhere quiet, away from the foodies who would be out full force tonight. Maybe she didn't want to run into her staff. He inhaled slowly, willing his head and other parts of his anatomy to return to the at-ease position. "You're more than welcome to come here."

"Okay." Her word was an exhalation.

"I'll pick you up at your hotel in ten." He had his keys in hand before he even hung up, and made it there in seven.

She must have been waiting for him because she came through the large sliding glass doors as soon as he pulled up under the porte cochere. He was thrilled when she tossed an overnight bag into the backseat. He waited until he'd pulled the car out of the hotel's roundabout driveway and onto the road before he mentioned it. "Can I ask what you're bringing?"

Maybe it was food? Or she'd brought her own bottle of champagne? Or any other number of things that some women seemed to cart along with them everywhere they went.

His mother had a purse that was large enough

to contain half a department store's worth of items, and she'd been known to retrieve a pair of socks, chopsticks or a small sewing kit from its depths. If Julia was just looking to share a platonic drink, he should know before he made her uncomfortable by kissing her the second they got through the door.

She was quiet. Donovan stayed silent, too.

Finally, she exhaled. "Maybe this isn't such a good idea."

"I disagree. It's a great idea." He felt it necessary to jump in before she talked herself out of this, because if she asked him to turn the car around, he would. "I just wondered."

"If I have to explain it to you, then it's probably a terrible idea."

Donovan smiled. He had his answer. He stepped on the accelerator. "Forget I asked."

They pulled up to the cabin a mere three minutes later. The roads were empty and there were no streetlights between the village and the family property.

The cabin was actually more like a full-service lodge, built to host the entire family, including future spouses and kids. But except for when Owen used it to throw a party for all his hangers-on, there were rarely more than two people up at a time.

Donovan had left the main lights on when he bolted out the front door, more intent on getting to

Julia than on energy saving. They glowed through the large floor-to-ceiling windows. From inside, it felt like being in the middle of the forest at a rustic retreat. Albeit one with steam showers, a glass-front fridge and its own path to the ski hills.

He pulled into the garage and hopped out of the car to help her out of her side. She allowed him to carry her bag, which he took as a good sign, and they stepped inside.

He'd been prepared to drop the bag and turn her to face him, to look into those dark eyes and lean forward to take possession of her mouth. He hadn't been prepared for her to do the same.

But he wasn't complaining. Wouldn't have even if his lips hadn't been occupied.

Which they were. He wasn't sure what to do first—pull her beautiful, luscious body against his or drag her up the stairs to his bedroom. Instead, he just stood there for a second, lips pressed to hers, filled with gratitude at his good fortune.

She pulled away first and for a second he feared that she was going to change her mind, reiterate that maybe this wasn't a good idea and she was having second thoughts. And though it might kill him, he'd drive her back to her hotel without complaint. And try to satisfy his needs with a long cold shower.

"Donovan?" But the smile on her face, with the sexy little curve to her lips that made him want to lick the edges and see if they tasted as sweet as a strawberry, didn't look as if she was having second thoughts at all.

He hauled her against his body and kissed the side of her neck. "Yes?"

"Where's the bedroom?"

He didn't waste any time carrying her up the stairs. He ignored the art on the walls that she'd probably enjoy, the gourmet kitchen with its gleaming appliances and the bathroom with its jetted tub and eight showerhead walk-in. Though he was certainly amenable to having her give them a thorough once-over later. Perhaps he'd go in with her to show her how everything worked.

Lust clouded his vision as he crossed into his room. Not the master because that was his parents' room and the other rooms were more full suites, anyway, with their own king-size beds, designer chairs and lavish bathrooms. He could picture Julia under the spill of water in his shower, her body naked and rosy from being touched and teased.

He barely got them both to the bed, wanting only to drop to his knees and worship her right then and there.

He didn't know where to start first. Kiss her again, run his fingers through her hair, slowly remove each article of clothing from her body? But when he lowered his body against hers and she snuggled against him, all heat and lush curves, the idea of moving away even just long enough to remove the material between them flew out the window.

Julia ran her hands down his chest and then slipped her fingers beneath his shirt. Donovan pressed closer, kissing her neck, appreciating her sharp intake of breath and the way she leaned into him, the cushion of her breasts pushing against him.

And then what was already turning out to be a pretty perfect way to end the evening got a little more perfect.

She stepped back and shrugged out of her soft sweater, grabbed the hem of her black T-shirt and pulled it over her head, exposing her breasts in their pretty black bra. Her skin looked smooth and creamy against the dark material and his mouth watered.

He wanted her. All of her. Now. But he clenched his hands and forced himself to watch, to appreciate the show as she placed one hand on the waistband of her jeans and flicked open the button.

Oh, hell. He hoped she was wearing matching black panties. A little covering of lace and silk that teased and tormented more than it protected. He held his breath as her hand moved lower, only the sound of the zipper breaking the silence. And then she slid her jeans over her hips and Donovan exhaled.

A teeny, tiny scrap of black that pointed him in the direction he wanted to go. And he realized he'd had enough of watching and it was time to participate.

He shucked off his clothes in a hurry, hungry to touch as well as look, and tossed them toward the chair in the corner of the room. He wasn't sure if any of the garments actually made it to the chair. Didn't care, either.

Julia's skin felt cool to the touch, like slipping into a snowmelt lake at the height of summer. Refreshing and invigorating. Donovan wanted to dive in and stay there forever. Or as long as she'd let him.

He put his hands on her hips, turning them so that her back was to the bed. Then slowly, he walked her toward it. Kissing her, tasting her and wishing he'd thought to bring the bottle of champagne with them. He hadn't given up on the fantasy of dribbling it on her, letting the liquid catch and pool in her secret depths and then slowly lapping every drop of it up.

Maybe later. Along with that shower-and-bath fantasy.

Her arm reached up to stroke his, her hand curling around his biceps when his tongue tangled with hers, and then curving around the back of his neck to tug him down to her. Closer to her.

Wherever she wanted to take him, Donovan was willing to go.

He reached down and flipped back the down comforter. It was high-quality, as was everything in the house. But Donovan didn't care about any of that. All he cared about was Julia spread out on the bed, her pale body lit up against the silvery-gray sheets.

He lowered himself to her. Their lips remained fused. Long, hot kisses, his hands tightening over her hips, feeling the difference of the scratch of lace and the softness of her skin.

Julia stretched up to meet him, looping both arms around his neck and opening her legs to cradle his body. He wasted no time in showing her his appreciation. He felt her smile when he pressed his hard ridge against her.

Donovan wasn't the kind of man who went straight for sex. He enjoyed the foreplay just as much, bringing his partner to orgasm with his fingers and tongue, watching the glaze fall over her eyes, the flush that rose up her chest, turning her nipples a dark, rosy shade as they tightened and budded. He drew pleasure from hearing a woman's soft cry of release, feeling her thighs clamp around his head as her legs began to shake.

But he didn't think he could wait with Julia. She was too much. Too soft, too lush, too sexy. He was like a horny teenager looking through a girlie magazine for the first time, ready to pop off at the slightest touch. And he was ready to pop. More than ready, if the strain of his underwear was any indication.

Hell, she wasn't even naked yet.

Donovan raised his head just enough to break their lip-lock and ran a hand along her side. Her knee curled up, curving around him, and he felt his control slip another notch. "Julia?"

"Hmm?" She opened her eyes to look at him, a small satisfied smile on her lips, and ran her hands through his hair. He had to grit his teeth and breathe through his nose for a second.

"This isn't how I envisioned this." There hadn't been time to light candles, to set up a playlist on his iPod or give her a long, slow massage.

He lowered his forehead to hers, the heat throbbing through his body threatening to take over. He wanted to just act, to peel her out of her bra, fling those panties off and take her body until they were both drenched in sweat.

She hooked her leg over his back, pulling him back down so their bodies were once more plastered together, the only thing separating them a few measly scraps of fabric. "Funny, because this is exactly what I had in mind." She slid a hand down his spine and back up, gently running her nails along each knob.

Donovan shuddered and felt the involuntary

jerk of his body as it rocked into hers. He really wasn't going to be able to hold back. Not with her wrapping herself around him, licking his earlobe. He sucked in a wheezing breath. "I just…"

What? What did he just? Hell, he couldn't think. And she certainly didn't seem interested in anything he had to say. At least not right now. He slipped a hand under her back and flicked open the hook of her bra, growled when it sprang free, releasing her breasts.

Donovan rose up only long enough to strip it down her arms and off her body before dipping his head again. He cupped one breast in each hand, pushing them together so he could taste both nipples with one long lick. From side to side and back again.

Julia moved restlessly beneath him, her hands falling from his body to clutch the sheets. Donovan licked again, stopped over the right to suck the nub into his mouth, letting his tongue lie flat against it, then spinning it around in a quick swirl.

Her back arched, bowed against him as she gasped and buried her fingers in his hair, tugging and pulling but making sure he didn't go anywhere. Donovan had no problem with that. He did the same to her other breast. First, pressing his tongue down, warming the area, and then, with a quick twist, swirling his tongue around.

She responded with the same aching gasp and a renewed rubbing of her body against his. It was heaven being surrounded by softness and curves instead of the hard, sharp lines of his last few relationships, and Donovan wondered why he hadn't noticed it then. Maybe because he hadn't known what he was missing.

Urgency was beginning to rear up with each rub of her chest along his. The peaks of her nipples brushed against his pecs, letting him know how much he excited her.

Donovan lifted his head enough to admire the view. A flush crept up her body, turning her chest rosy. He laid his palm on her belly then slowly ran up the center, stopping in the middle of her chest. She didn't feel cool anymore. Her breathing was rapid and she watched him with hooded eyes.

The thin thread of control he'd managed to grab started to slip, done away by her bold excitement. Flew away completely when she placed her hand on his crotch and stroked. Once, twice. Stars burst along the edges of his vision as his body jerked, strained toward hers, feeling her lush heat surround him, warm him from the outside in.

He wanted to be in. In bed. In a relationship. In Julia.

With great disappointment, he pulled back. It was hard to drag his gaze away, to look somewhere other than those pearling nipples and soft, white skin, but he could look his fill later. In the shower. In the tub. In his bed. He'd show her delectable body all the care in the world once his mind wasn't burning with desire and threatening to blow up.

Donovan didn't think Julia was bothered. Not when he hooked his thumb in her underwear and tugged them down her legs and she only reached forward to do the same for him. His body jerked again and he gritted his teeth to keep from shredding her underwear in one strong yank.

He had a stack of condoms in his nightstand drawer, not that he generally brought girlfriends to the family cabin, but he was responsible and prepared just in case. Because excusing himself to make a quick run to the village drugstore would surely kill any mood.

He pulled one out now, hands shaking as he fought to get it free of the foil packet. It probably would have helped if he'd watched what he was doing, but that would mean taking his eyes off Julia.

Oh, Julia. He felt the heat boil up inside him

as he watched her. The teasing way she curled onto her side, balancing her head on one hand, letting her arm slide along her body while she watched him.

He managed to roll on the condom, his body demanding that he hurry up, then turned her onto her back and took one of her ankles in each of his hands. He pressed a kiss to the inside of one. He'd have liked to lick his way to her knee, along her thigh and directly into her heat, but just the thought was enough to make his body ache for release.

Instead, he ran a hand along the smooth firmness, the hours a day she spent on her feet showing in the sleek muscles, and cupped her core. She sighed and wriggled against him, drawing his fingers inside.

Donovan saw no point in waiting, in continuing to play. She was ready, he was well past ready and it would be better for them both if they gave in to the fiery need now and took their time later.

He positioned himself at her entrance and nudged inside. Her body stretched around his, adjusting as he glided in with one long stroke. He held still for a moment by squeezing his eyes shut and mentally counting to ten, and then he looked down at her, saw the line of her exposed neck, head tilted back and couldn't wait any longer.

She moaned as he drove into her, and Donovan might have said he was lost, except he was exactly where he wanted to be.

CHAPTER NINE

OH, YES.

Julia couldn't catch her breath. Couldn't get enough. Couldn't say or do anything except moan in pleasure.

Oh, yes. Oh, yes.

Thank goodness she'd admitted what she wanted and told Donovan. She gasped when he pressed a thumb to the aching bud between her legs. Lightly, so there was only pleasure and the continued climb toward release. Then kissed him again and again. Wanting to be closer, to feel more, their bodies locked together.

Tension was beginning to coil in her muscles, encouraging her to draw him deeper, roll her entire body into his. Her lungs hitched with each new sensation. The feel of his muscles under her hands, each one bunching and shifting in a harmony of movement. The smell of his skin, masculine and strong. The rustle of the sheets as he pushed them to the side and rocked his hips against hers.

She pulled her mouth from his and tilted her

head back, fighting to pull in a breath, fighting to pull him closer. His thumb paused and then dipped down, circling in a firm steady twirl. Her nails dug into him, her knees rose up and the tight, winding tension in her body twisted to its peak.

Julia had had sex before. Maybe not lately, but definitely her fair share over the years. She knew what she liked and she wasn't afraid to guide a man in the right direction. To show him with her mouth and her body and her words what she liked, what made the heat blaze through her limbs and left her sated and limp.

It had never been quite like this. The ability to read a lover's body as though she'd been given a list of directions and had handed over her own in return. She ran her hands over his ass and thighs and back up again, loving the feel of the strong muscles tightening and releasing. And then he did that thing with his thumb again at the same time he bucked into her.

If she'd been able to speak, she'd have told him to keep doing that, not to change a thing, right there. Luckily, she didn't need to. Donovan stroked and circled and Julia broke.

Simply let go of everything and allowed the rippling, throbbing sensations to carry her away on a sea of sighs.

Donovan kept moving, increasing his pace until

the sound of their bodies meeting filled the room. Then he paused, gave one hoarse shout and collapsed on top of her. Julia was too full of her own pleasure to care that his body was crushing hers, that she couldn't draw a complete breath or move.

Instead, she ran her hands up from his ass, traced his spine to his shoulders and his neck. She brushed her fingers along his hairline and along the curve of his ears. A low moan of approval rumbled through him and she felt it in her chest, as well.

Julia smiled, appreciative of both his skill and her own, and hooked her arms around him, not ready to break the moment. Not yet.

His face lay in the curve of her neck. She could feel his breath slow and grow steady. Each pulse of air was a small shudder across her skin. A reminder that they remained linked and neither of them seemed interested in breaking that.

Even when his weight became noticeable, pressing her into the mattress and pinning her legs in place, Julia wasn't interested in moving. She skimmed a hand over his arm. She felt whole here. Complete.

The thought surprised her. She'd never been the type of person who needed a partner to feel satisfied or happy. She'd always been content with her own company, with her work. But maybe she was changing. Or maybe it was just the hormones talking. Really, a person might agree to anything when caught in the sex haze.

Donovan murmured against her neck when her hand trailed back down his arm and then swept across his body. "I think your nails left marks in my ass."

Julia would have lifted her head to check, but that would have taken too much effort and would likely have dislodged him. She smoothed her other hand over his hair. "Poor baby. Do you need me to kiss it better?"

He raised his head just enough to look at her. "If you're offering, I'm accepting." Then he kissed her and she forgot about the marks until he finally rolled off the bed and walked to the bathroom.

Julia didn't bother to move. Not even to drag the covers over her rapidly cooling body. But she did note the marks on his ass. And when he crawled back into bed and lay on his stomach beside her, she stopped him from pulling up the covers. "Not yet."

"Julia." It was half groan, half barely contained anticipation. "I'm not sixteen anymore."

"And thank God for that." She sat up, her hair falling across her shoulder to tickle her chest. "No sixteen-year-old has moves like that."

He twisted his head to glance at her, his eyes glinting with mischief. "You like my moves, then?"

She patted his cheek. "Don't get cocky."

"Too late."

She stifled a laugh and crawled on top of him, paying particular attention to the red marks she'd left in her excitement. Soothing them with light brushes of her fingers and then a lighter brush of her lips.

The skin on his buttocks was smooth and pale and soft. He groaned under her ministrations. She kept doing what she was doing since he so clearly liked it. First, a stroke then a kiss and repeat.

Steadily, she began to make her way up his back. Stopping to investigate any freckles, shadows and anything else that caught her attention. It was some time before she got to his upper back, where she pressed her hands into his shoulders and bent over to kiss the nape of his neck.

Her only indication that he had something planned was his quiet exhalation before he flipped over, keeping her on top of him, steadying her hips with his hands while he adjusted their positions.

Julia glanced down at the bulge now fully on display. "I thought you weren't sixteen anymore?"

"I said I wasn't sixteen. I didn't say I was dead."

She laughed, but the sound drifted away on a contented sigh when he rubbed his thumbs across her stomach and slid his hands up. His fingers knew just how to move, just where to touch. He palmed her breasts, the heat from his hands causing them to tighten. She swallowed, fitted her hands over his and let her neck fall back.

They rocked into each other, slowly, gently. More like people who were used to each other's rhythms and needs than new lovers. He watched her, his eyes scanning up and down her body, along her face, noting everything. But she felt powerful instead of shy. Confident in the knowledge that she was the one who caused the heat in his gaze, the curve on his lips, the hardness even now nudging the warmth between her thighs.

And when she'd teased long enough, when it grew obvious they needed to move to the next step, she reached into the nightstand drawer, snagged one of the foil packets and opened it with her teeth. She saw the bob of Donovan's throat, felt his hands curl into her hips and smiled as she moved down his legs so she could put the condom on.

Then she rose above him, all female power and attitude, and slid her body around his. This time she set the pace. Slow and easy. Different from their first time but just as good, just as fulfilling. And when Donovan's hands cupped her breasts, rolling her nipples between his forefinger and thumb, she felt the ripple of release flow through her. Her body pulsed around his until he came, too. A quiet, soft release that was no less powerful for its delicacy.

"Julia." His voice was soft, too, more breath

than words. And she knew exactly what he meant without him saying anything else. She bent over him and kissed him, openmouthed and openhearted. Leaving everything she had, everything she was, between them. Because there was no point in hiding for herself or from herself anymore.

DONOVAN WOKE HER up twice more in the night, under the shade of dark where he loved her silently, softly. Their bodies wrapped around each other so there was no indication of beginning or end, just skin on skin. And once more in the pearly-gray dawn, with the hum of day beginning around them as they stared into each other's eyes. She reached up to hold his cheek in her hand, stroking the bristle of his beard growth, and felt her heart squeeze when he turned his face to kiss her palm. So small, so minimalist, and yet she felt as though it spoke to their connection.

When she finally woke up and stayed awake, the morning was no longer the soft light of dawn. But even the sight of the gloomy overcast day couldn't dampen her spirits. Not when she saw the circles under her eyes in the mirror. And not when she realized that although she'd been far-thinking and organized enough to bring along a change of clothes and toiletries, she hadn't seen it through to the final and necessary step of taking the bag upstairs with her.

She slipped on last night's shirt, which was just long enough to provide full-body coverage, and padded downstairs to find Donovan tapping away on his laptop at the breakfast counter in the kitchen. She hadn't gotten a good look at the space last night, but she drank it in now.

The thick granite slab the color of honey, the white cabinets and large windows that looked out onto a patio. It was a place to create and test. She suspected the huge stainless-steel fridge would be stocked and wished she'd brought her knives with her.

"You're up." Donovan rose and greeted her with a kiss. "Coffee?"

"Please." She tucked a lock of hair behind her ear and adjusted her shirt, which had ridden up thanks to his enthusiastic hug. He patted her hip and then moved around the kitchen island to the coffee machine on the other side. It had plenty of shiny knobs and emitted a soft hiss when Donovan turned one of them.

Julia shivered, partly from the memory of the way his hands had touched her last night. And partly because she was dressed in only a T-shirt. She found her overnight bag inside the coat closet and returned to the kitchen with it.

Donovan turned from the coffeepot, his eyes

flicking to the bag in her hand. "Leaving already? Do you need a to-go cup?" His eyes flicked farther down to her bare legs. "And maybe some pants?"

"Very funny. Just the coffee."

He grinned at his little joke. "Cream? Sugar?"

"Straight up." The way she'd gotten used to drinking it in Europe. Her French and Italian friends had insisted that everything she added to the coffee was muting the flavor, hiding it, and had eventually broken her of her habit of adding shots of vanilla, sweetener or dairy.

Donovan pulled down a mug, filled it up and handed it to her. She inhaled deeply and then sipped, letting the hot liquid coat her tongue before swallowing. The flavor was rich and bold, the coffee of the same fine quality as everything else connected to the Fords.

And she was standing around in a T-shirt with no panties. She shifted, one hand clutching the bag, the other her coffee. Donovan looked as if he'd already showered, so there was no need for her to linger with her ass hanging out.

"I'm glad you're here." He came around the island, plucked the cup out of her hand, set it on the counter and hauled her up against him. His jeans were rough against her skin, but his hands were gentle. "Really glad."

Julia felt the heat from his body sink into her,

and knew that she would never regret this. Not one minute of it. She smiled up at him. "Is it all right if I shower before I go?"

"I'd be offended if you didn't." He barely paused before adding, "Is it all right if I join you?" She blinked, and when she didn't answer right away, Donovan said, "Now you're supposed to say that you'd be offended if I didn't."

She shouldn't. She should clarify that while their time together had been wonderful, it was for only one night. Just a way to get him out of her system so she could focus on her career. Instead, she took his hand and tugged. "Come on."

It was still the same night. Sort of. Right?

By the time they made it up the stairs, Julia had stopped thinking. Her shirt got left behind, as did Donovan's, and his jeans made it to only the landing.

The bathroom had a luxury shower with multiple heads and spray that could be adjusted so there wasn't a single part of the body unattended. It certainly improved the showering experience. No one had to stand on the cold side and get only the bounce of spray off the other's body. Not that Julia would have noticed cold water when Donovan's hands and lips were everywhere.

She gripped his shoulders when he sank to his knees, and leaned against the wall for support while he showed her just how talented his tongue was. Her eyes closed while the water beat down on her and Donovan's tongue swirled around and around. Her head dropped against the tile, but he kept up his relentless teasing until her skin grew taut and her body strained toward him and she released, crying his name as she came.

He stayed on his knees and pressed a soft kiss between her thighs, which caused an avalanche of shivers. And then placed his tongue flat against her, staying perfectly still while her body hummed in pleasure.

"Donovan?" She lifted her head. Her neck felt wobbly, and it took some effort to hold her head up when all she wanted to do was lie back and let the sensations take over. He watched her with dark eyes that saw her at her most vulnerable, and then licked, long and slow. She shivered again.

"I feel like I didn't really show you what I was capable of last night."

Julia blinked at him. "Six times wasn't enough?"

"Counting them, were you?" He stood, a smug look on his face, and braced his arms on the wall around her. He blocked most of the spray, but heat rolled off his body. "I didn't want you to think I wasn't generous."

She placed her hands on his shoulders and slid them over and down his back. "No worry about that." And then they took turns washing each other until they were wrinkled and relaxed and very, very clean.

Julia was toweling her hair dry when Donovan returned with her cup of coffee. She put the towel down and took the cup, draining half of it in one swallow.

Donovan grinned. He had only a towel wrapped around his waist. It dipped when he moved behind her and wrapped his arms around her. "That was amazing."

She loved the feel of his lips brushing across the back of her neck. He could have been discussing the most mundane and banal details, but with his lips on her, it felt like sex. As if she hadn't gotten more than her fair share in the past twelve hours.

"Can I see you tonight?" He rocked back and forth, holding her against him.

Julia felt her body stiffen. "About that."

She felt the squeeze of tension roll through him. "Do not even think of telling me this was just a one-night stand."

"How about a one-morning stand?" But Donovan didn't smile and Julia couldn't blame him. She didn't feel like smiling, either.

"No." His gaze met hers in the mirror. "I wouldn't be okay with that, either."

Julia shivered, slipping deeper into his embrace. "I just—"

"Just what?"

She didn't know. "I feel like the restaurant and you... They're tangled together."

She felt the softening of his muscles as some of his tension eased. "Are you using me for my connections? Because I would be fine with that." He pressed his lips to the side of her neck. "For now."

"No, I just—" She stopped again. She just what? "I feel like we're crossing a line here."

"I think we crossed that line last night."

He was right. And yet... "I think it would be better if we kept things professional for now."

Donovan didn't say anything for a moment. She could feel every breath he took, brushing against her jawline, pressing against her back. "Is that what you think?"

"Yes." But even to her own ears, the assertion sounded weak. "At least until—"

He cut her off by spinning her in his arms, his lips hot on hers. "I don't want to lose this." He kissed her again. "Or you."

She'd be lying if she said it wasn't heady, being shown with actions and words that he wanted her. And she'd be lying if she said she didn't feel the same about him. But she wanted the restaurant, too.

"Let's find a way that we can both have what we want." He ran his tongue along the edge of her earlobe. "For example, I really want to open that champagne we didn't drink last night and sip it from your body."

Her knees wobbled. Good thing her hands were clutching his shoulders for support.

"And then I want to feed you a nice meal that you didn't have to cook."

Julia's heart knocked against her chest. People rarely cooked for her. A drawback of the job. Most people were too intimidated to offer up their own creations to a trained chef. But the fact was, most chefs loved having someone else do the cooking for a change.

"Which I think is entirely professional." He murmured the words against the back of her neck this time.

"Do you?" The question came out on a puff of air, which was all she could manage with his mouth teasing across her skin.

"Yes, and I don't hear you disagreeing. But feel free."

She might if she could ever catch her breath.

"Or we could just see how things go." He dipped a finger into the front of her towel and tugged at the knot.

They could. And the idea had appeal. A lot of appeal. She made up her mind. Donovan was a great guy and she liked him. Yes, he was her boss for now, but he'd made it clear that he had no long-term plans for La Petite Bouchée. She wasn't so wrapped up in her career to think guys like him came around every day. "All right. But we're just seeing how things go and we can't flaunt it. Especially at the restaurant." Kitchen staff were notoriously incestuous, sleeping with each other, breaking up, sleeping with someone else and then getting back together. Lather, rinse, repeat. "I don't have time for anything serious."

"That, or you're embarrassed to be seen with me," he teased.

As if. But he didn't need the ego stroke. She spun in his arms to face him, reached up to cup his face. He hadn't shaved yet and the stubble scraped her palms. "Completely embarrassed."

He snorted. "Well, I am pretty embarrassing. And I've been known to streak on occasion." He whipped off his towel, then hers.

Julia laughed as he picked her up and started for the bed. "Consider me warned."

As he lowered her to the bed, and blanketed her with his body, he said, "I hope you're not too embarrassed because I would like to take you out on a real date."

She nodded and wrapped her arms around his warm body. "Later."

"I didn't mean this second." His fingers trailed the inside of her thigh.

"I know." She squirmed, encouraging him to reach for the good bits. "I meant later, when I'm not trying to work out financing to buy La Petite Bouchée and—" She sucked in a long breath as his fingers slid home. "Why are we talking about this now?"

"I have no idea."

CHAPTER TEN

DONOVAN FELT GUILTY for not telling Julia that his plans for the restaurant had changed. Well, no, that wasn't entirely true. At least not the part about his plans.

He still had no intention of being involved in the day-to-day running as soon as he could unload those duties. But the restaurant wasn't likely to be sold anytime soon, either.

It just hadn't been the right time with his fingers between her legs and his mouth on her breast. Much the way that now, standing in the greenroom of the TV studio with Julia about to go on air, also wasn't the right time.

And neither had any of the preceding days and nights while he and Julia spent their days at the restaurant overseeing the renovations and their nights in his bed overseeing each other's bodies.

He told himself that he didn't want to distract her. And he didn't want to start that conversation until he had a new contract with an additional bonus structure for her to sign. Legally, he wasn't obligated to do anything, but it felt like the right thing to do in order to keep her as La Petite Bouchée's executive chef.

The restaurant would be reopening in one week and Donovan was more than ready. The interior looked amazing, Julia's food was better than ever and Mal's marketing plan was in full swing. Donovan watched it in action now, on set at a local TV station's breakfast show where Julia would be doing a brief demo for the audience.

Mal stood with him in the greenroom, the pair of them watching one of the overhead TVs as the hosts talked about the segment coming up, which was Julia's demo. Mal had been looking more and more run-down of late, her usual snappy attitude dulled. Donovan had hoped her visit with Travis in Aruba during the Whistler food festival would resolve whatever problems they were having, but it had clearly caused more strain than relief.

It was obvious something had happened. He'd broached the subject once, asked if she wanted to talk and let her know he was there to listen, but she'd brushed his concerns aside, told him she didn't want to talk about it and changed the subject. So he'd let it go, but his little sister's evident unhappiness bothered him.

Still, there was nothing he could do about it this second and he had a job to do. He turned his attention back to Julia and felt some of the weight on his shoulders lighten, the way it always did when he saw her. She was a woman who'd been through a lot and she'd survived it all. He had to trust that Mal would, too.

Julia was wearing a brand-new chef's jacket, one with the updated logo over the breast. Just a simple swirl of logos and her name in block print over top. She smiled at the camera as it panned to her and the station cut to commercial.

He turned and found Mal watching him, her gaze taking in everything. She'd been like that even as a baby. Five years older and wiser, Donovan could recall the day his mom and dad had brought his new baby sister home. He'd been excited, but that had soon turned to disillusionment when the new baby couldn't play soldiers or swim or do much of anything except cry and hog all of the attention.

But she'd always had those big, watchful eyes. Staring at him from her crib, her high chair, her playpen in the corner of the family room. And, even once she learned to talk, keeping his secrets quiet.

Donovan shifted under that gaze now. "What?"

"I'm confused." Mal glanced at the TV screen above them, but they were still on a commercial. There were at least thirty seconds before the morning show returned and Julia's segment started.

"About?"

"I thought you didn't want to be as involved in the restaurant." There was a gleam in her eyes that he recognized. Mal already knew his answer and was taking this opportunity to amuse herself. Since he would have done the same, Donovan couldn't hold it against her. "And yet here you are at an interview at—" she made a show of checking her watch "—six in the morning."

Since Julia had been at his place and he'd woken up with her, Donovan hadn't seen the point in staying home. He wouldn't have been able to go back to sleep—he was someone who was up once he woke up—and he was curious to see how things went. Well, mostly he was curious to see how Julia did.

"Is that a problem?"

"Of course not." Mal's dark hair swung around her face. She looked tired, but then, she always looked tired these days. Something Donovan was smart enough not to mention. "I just find it odd. Exactly how uninvolved do you plan to be?"

"As uninvolved as I want to be." Which wasn't very much these days.

"So you're together." It wasn't a question.

Donovan didn't answer. He pinned his sister with his own gaze. He knew it was nothing compared to Mal's, but it had served him well in a boardroom or two. She didn't flinch, merely folded her arms over her chest and raised an eyebrow.

Donovan mirrored her movements, which drew a small smile.

"Look, I think she's great and whatever you do in your personal life is up to you." Mal's arms dropped to her sides as she took a step toward him. "But have you thought about what happens next?"

There was a flicker on the TV above them as the commercial break ended and the show returned. Donovan used the remote to turn up the sound.

The female host's voice echoed through the space, the speakers giving it a tinny quality. "I'm excited about this next segment. As many of you know, I love to eat." She ran a hand over her pregnant belly.

"Donovan." Mal's voice rose above the TV show. He turned to look at his sister. "Is it serious?"

He didn't know how to respond. He should say no. He and Julia had started sleeping together only a week and a half ago. They hadn't talked about a future. They hadn't even been out in public as a couple. And yet, he couldn't bring himself to claim that what was happening between him and Julia was casual. Because it wasn't.

"Have you told her that we're keeping the restaurant?"

"Not yet." Mal was the only one who knew

that he'd virtually promised to sell the restaurant to Julia back when he'd thought he was going to have to be responsible for it.

Mal's eyebrows shot up. "Really?"

"Yes, really." He knew he needed to. But he still hadn't called the lawyer to draw up the new contract. And there had been so much going on—the food festival, the TV spot today and the restaurant's relaunch in a week. He didn't think burdening Julia with that information was a good idea. They needed her. He needed her. And he'd have to walk the tightrope of her wants and needs carefully.

Mal frowned. "Oh." The one word was ripe with meaning.

Donovan swallowed his irritation. He wasn't annoyed with his sister, but with himself for not dealing with the situation yet. "I know, Mal. I'll take care of it. I promise."

"It's not that. Or it *is* that, but not in the way you think." She plucked the remote out of his hands and lowered the volume on the TV. "You care for her."

Donovan nodded. He did. More quickly than he'd expected. Already he missed her on nights when she didn't stay with him.

"Does she feel the same?"

"I think so." He bloody well hoped so. Because

the idea of Julia slipping out of his life wasn't one he wanted to contemplate.

"Then you have to tell her."

"I know."

"I'm serious, Donovan. These kinds of things… Personal relationships and—" Her voice broke, but she got it back a moment later. "Personal relationships and business. They don't always mix. You have to draw a clear line between them."

Though her expression was primarily neutral, simply a marketing and media-relations director giving the acting CEO some advice, Mal's eyes told a different story. One that said mixing business and pleasure was a dangerous game that could have no winner.

"This isn't the same situation." Donovan didn't specifically refer to his sister and Travis and whatever had happened between them. But he didn't have to. They both knew what he was talking about. "I'm keeping the business separate, and when the time comes to tell her, I plan to offer fair compensation. It's a business decision. I'm sure she'll understand."

But Mal didn't look relieved. If anything, her eyes narrowed. "It's never that easy, Donovan. You think it will be, but it isn't."

He sensed she wasn't talking about his relationship but her own. "Mal…" He let her name trail off. He'd made it clear that he was there if she wanted to talk; she wouldn't appreciate hearing it again.

"I'm just telling you to give it some careful consideration." She pressed her lips together, indicating that she was done talking about it. "But I trust that you'll make the right decision. For all of us."

Donovan nodded. He would. He had no doubt of that. But Mal was right—he couldn't keep ignoring the situation with Julia. He'd need to talk to her about it, pitch his idea and future plans for the restaurant. Surely she'd be able to see that staying at La Petite Bouchée was good for her career, too. No, it wasn't ownership, but it was the next best thing. Because Donovan already knew that Gus had little intention of getting involved with the kitchen. He was just happy to eat the food.

But not right now. Not when the restaurant's grand reopening was days away and they all had a lot on their plate. Later, when things were more settled, when his father had selected his return date and Donovan had the contract in hand for her to sign. He'd bring it up then.

LA PETITE BOUCHÉE glittered on opening night. The chandeliers overhead, the shiny new floors and gleaming bar, the glassware, the metallic threads in the ivory fabric on the chairs. And the people.

Everywhere Donovan turned, there were flashes of icy diamonds, cool sapphires and warm rubies. The social scene coming to see and be seen.

He'd be lying if he said he didn't feel incredibly proud. All his hard work, all Julia's hard work—really, everyone's hard work—had paid off.

Although the room looked very little the way he'd initially imagined, before Julia had given her suggestions, he could see now that it was perfect. He'd known his design team would do a fantastic job—they always did—but this was a step above.

There were no high-gloss bars or Lucite chairs. No shiny metal stools or color-free walls. But the round-back chairs that reminded him of Paris were out in full force and the prints on the pale blue walls were all black-and-white. The bar was dark, burnished wood and the mirror he wanted covered the wall behind it, highlighting the gleaming glass and rows of bottles. The chandeliers dripped crystals and spilled warm, golden light.

It might not be the modern style he'd imagined, but it was warm and rich. A mix of old and new that surpassed both. He was proud of what he'd accomplished, what his team had accomplished in only two months.

His family hadn't yet arrived. Mal was dealing with some things at the office and had texted to say she'd be about ten minutes late, and Owen was coming with his parents, which meant they'd be about fifteen minutes late since Owen rarely showed up to anything on time.

Donovan refused to let that annoy him tonight. If Owen wanted more responsibility as he kept claiming, he could start by showing up on schedule. Donovan glanced down at his heavy watch. Which meant he had about six minutes. But his brother's lack of punctuality was really of no concern other than Donovan knew it would stress out their father.

They'd all been working hard to keep Gus's stress level as low as possible while he recovered from his heart attack. Occasionally, this meant being sneaky. But it was worth it if it meant that Gus's health continued to improve.

Tonight would be the first time his father had laid eyes on the restaurant since the renovations. There had been times it had been tough to keep Gus away, but they'd managed with a combination of fibs and bribery. And now he'd see the finished product, see what his dream had become under Donovan's guidance.

Donovan hoped he liked it.

As Donovan worked his way around the room, chatting to those he knew personally, nodding to those he didn't, he couldn't help thinking of Julia. She'd been in the kitchen since the early hours. Checking and double-checking everything. Tonight was a big deal for her, too. Her performance for a new and opinionated crowd.

Donovan had no doubt that she would wow them completely. He wanted to go back to the kitchen and see her, even just to wish her good luck, but like so many other times tonight, he stopped himself before he even started.

She had a lot to do, and as much as he'd love to touch her, to look over all they'd created together, he knew that would be selfish. His only role tonight was to chat to the patrons, make sure everyone felt welcome and be there as backup for the extremely competent staff should something go wrong. Julia's role was harder and more detailed.

Not only did she need to ensure that every single plate that left the kitchen was good enough to be served to the harshest critic, she'd be expected to make multiple appearances in the dining room to greet each guest personally. There were reporters here, contacts Mal had lined up to cover the event. But when he'd reminded Julia of that in bed this morning and wondered if she might take some promotional photos, she'd explained those would have to be taken before service, because once the orders started coming in, the food had to be her number one priority.

Then she'd kissed him and he'd forgotten about the coffee he'd just made, and by the time he'd remembered, the autotimer had shut off and he'd had to make a second pot. Really, not such a trial when he considered how the time had been spent.

"Donovan." He spun when he heard his name, a welcoming smile already in place. The smile warmed when he saw his mother. She kissed him on the cheek and hugged him. "You look wonderful. The place looks wonderful."

He saw his father coming up behind her, just a little slower than before, but Donovan doubted anyone but those who knew him well would notice. He looked almost back to his old rugged, active self. The doctors had assured them that everything looked good and Gus should continue to lead a long and healthy life, but it was hard not to worry. Even Owen, the least likely Ford to twist himself into a knot of what-ifs, stuck close to Gus as they traversed the restaurant.

But in typical Owen-style, he charmed the room as he went, nodding and smiling to the various people he passed. As Donovan watched, his little brother paused at a table hosting a trio of particularly attractive women. No doubt he was checking out their impressive cleavage. Same old Owen.

But rather than hang around, Own moved on quickly and didn't appear to get or give a phone number before doing so. Donovan was surprised. Maybe Owen had changed a little. Donovan just wasn't sure how much and if it was enough to trust him with more than managing Elephants.

He brushed the thought away. Tonight wasn't about Elephants or any location except La Petite Bouchée, and Donovan wasn't concerned with what changes his brother may or may not have made.

"Dad." Donovan reached out to give him a handshake and backslap, the standard male-Ford greeting. Gus's color was good and there was no pinch of pain around his mouth.

"Donovan." His father's voice boomed through the room. "Look at this place. Great. Just great. You've done a fine job." All of this was said at full volume, just in case anyone in the vicinity wasn't listening. "Show us the place."

Donovan led them to the bar, where he'd pre-ordered drinks. He handed them around with a pleased flourish. White wine for his mother, beer for Owen and a single finger of scotch for his father. Owen declined the beer and requested a glass of water, like the one Donovan carried. Okay, maybe Owen had changed more than a little, but considering how he'd been before, he still had a long way to go.

"Where's Mallory?" his mother wanted to know as she sipped.

"Just running a little late. She'll be here soon."

His father was studying the bar itself, a smile on his craggy face. "Good craftsmanship." He slapped a hand on the black walnut, sealed and polished to a high gloss. "They don't make things like this any longer." He eyed his son. "I thought you'd make it all cold and sharp. Glass or something. This is much better."

Donovan kept his former plans to himself. "Actually, the bar was Julia's idea. She wanted to mix new and old." And she'd resoundingly shot down the glossy white bar he'd originally picked out.

Gus looked around as though expecting her to appear out of thin air. "Where is she? I want to say hello in person. Let's go to the kitchen." He started to push himself off of the bar stool, no longer a rickety cushion-free experience, but one with full back and seats that shaped around a person's body, encouraging them to stay, have another drink and enjoy the evening.

"Later, Dad." Donovan laid a firm hand on his father's shoulder. "She's busy." He gestured around the full room. A full room of people waiting to eat.

Owen frowned. "It'll only take a second. I don't think Julia will mind."

"Julia has promised to come out and say hello when she has a moment." Donovan shot his brother a pointed look. He didn't appreciate Owen jumping in and acting as if he had authority here. Owen wasn't the one who'd overseen renovations, menu planning or media events.

After his parents had admired everything about

the renovated restaurant, they sat at their reserved table. Mal joined them a few minutes later, still not looking herself. But she smiled on cue and made polite conversation.

"Amazing. Just amazing." Gus looked around again. "Nicer than I remember." He reached out to clasp his wife's hand. "You've done a good job, son."

Donovan felt a swell of pride at his father's accolades. Gus had always been quick to recognize his children's accomplishments, but that didn't diminish hearing them now. He had done an amazing job, and was pleased his father said so.

"I have to say, it was kind of nice not to see it happen gradually." They'd encouraged Gus to take it easy, instead gear up for his return to the office slowly, which did not include dragging himself to the work site to check on the renovations. He'd probably have tried to pick up a hammer and swing it along with the construction crew. These weren't facetious concerns. Gus had done it before. "It has a lot of impact this way."

Donovan smiled. "I'm glad you like it." Particularly since all of it would soon be under Gus's command.

There was no sign of Julia until dessert, when she brought out the dishes herself. Donovan's heart jumped when he saw her. Her cheeks were flushed, probably from standing in the kitchen all night, but she was smiling and looked to be buzzing on energy. She should be buzzing—the night had been an unmitigated success.

He'd personally seen two different food critics leave with smiles on their faces and had no doubt their reviews would be raves. Julia was a hit. No, *they* were a hit. And they deserved it.

"Chef." He didn't hide his grin. "Congratulations."

It felt as if Owen had one-upped him, jumping out of his seat to plant a kiss on her cheek. "Amazing, Jules. Just amazing." But Donovan reminded himself that he was the one she went to bed with at night. And that it was good that she got along with his family. Even those members he himself didn't always get along with.

The family all cooed over her, telling her how much they'd enjoyed the food, asking her to describe the dessert, complimenting the service and being polite and engaged food connoisseurs in general. Donovan merely watched Julia. The way she bloomed under their attention, the way she answered in her friendly and cheerful manner.

He wanted to touch her, to kiss her and let everyone know she was with him. But they'd agreed to keep things casual, and even though he knew that wasn't true, he didn't think forcing her to admit it in front of an entire restaurant of people was the way to go.

So he kept his seat, pleased when Julia looked directly at him and her smile changed, warmed her eyes and made them glow with a look that was for him alone.

She stayed another minute and then excused herself to visit other tables. Donovan watched her move through the crowd, his eyes tracking the way she stopped to say hello, shake hands and offer a kiss if it was someone she knew well enough. Even under her bulky chef's coat she looked great. Or maybe that was because he knew every inch of the lush curves that lay beneath it.

JULIA KNEW THE night had been an utter success. No one would disagree. Not if they had eyes and taste buds.

The plates had been cleaned, no scraps left behind. The dining room had been full and there hadn't been any major hiccups in service. There were always little things that could go better. A server had tried to verbally call the order instead of printing a ticket when they had a last-minute change; the bar had run out of the wine they'd suggested as a pairing for her signature dish; and one of the commis chefs had misfired an order and been unable to get back on pace. He'd struggled until Sasha had jumped in and taken over.

Julia would have to watch him closely, see if he could handle the pace she expected to be the norm. Tonight might not be out of the ordinary for a weekend, and if the cook couldn't keep up, he'd have to go.

But even the possibility of letting someone go wasn't enough to dim her good cheer. She oversaw the kitchen cleanup with a smile that she couldn't contain. No matter that she'd been up for close to twenty hours and on her feet for the past sixteen of them. It had been worth it. Worth every worry, panic, fight to have everything turn out exactly as it had.

"Chef?"

Julia turned to find her head server standing in the pass between the kitchen and the dining room. She bestowed a smile on him, too. He'd been fantastic tonight, keeping everything running smoothly and ensuring all tables were well cared for. "Great job tonight, Jase."

He smiled. "Mr. Ford is waiting at the bar. He'd like to see you when you're done."

"Which one?"

"Donovan."

A wash of pleasure increased her already-high spirits. She nodded. "Thanks." She'd been hoping Donovan might stick around so they could celebrate their success together. Because it was their success. Another trickle of pleasure flowed through her. Them. A pair. Who'd have thought?

The closing routine was finished twenty minutes later and Julia shooed everyone out with her thanks and congratulations. Stef was the last to leave, making sure there was nothing else she could do before she finally headed out the door.

Julia had no doubt the entire staff was headed somewhere together. There was too much adrenaline, too much excitement to call it a night so early. No doubt there would be much hooking up, too. She hoped her own night would follow suit.

She flipped the lock on the front door and then returned to the bar, where Donovan sat, nursing a soda water. "We did it."

His eyes followed her as she moved closer to him. Heat pooled in between her thighs. "You did it."

"No." She threaded her fingers through his hair just above each temple. "This was definitely a team effort."

Donovan looked at her but didn't lean forward for the kiss she'd been anticipating. His brow creased. "Are we a team?"

Julia tilted her head and looked at him. She'd pulled out her hair tie before leaving the kitchen and her hair spilled over her shoulder and down her arm. "I think so."

"Good." He patted the stool beside him at the bar. "Let me get you a drink."

Julia wavered and eyed the bar. The light was out behind the wall of bottles and there was no one to serve from it anyway. "We're closed." And she really wanted to go home.

"Our license allows us to serve until midnight." He got up, his arm brushing hers as he moved. She felt a small jolt rock through her, felt it grow when he pulled down a bottle, twirled the neck over his fingers. "Water? Soda? Something with a little bite?" He spun the bottle over the back of his wrist and caught it neatly.

"Exactly how many times did you watch *Cocktail*?" The movie had always been one of her favorites.

"No more than ten. And it was for business, so a tax write-off." He flipped the bottle behind his back, letting it spin end over end before catching it at hip height. Julia just stared at him. "What?" His lips curved into what could only be deemed a smirk. "You think I just walked into my job based on nepotism?"

"Um...yes."

He laughed. "I won't say that didn't help, but no. I worked at Elephants as soon as I was legally permitted to do so. First as a busser, then a bartender. I did that all through university, and after I went back East for my master's, I worked at the wine bar every summer."

"Did you really? Spinning wine bottles before serving them?"

"You know we serve more than wine, and the ladies used to go crazy for my moves."

"I'm sure."

He raised an eyebrow at her. "Test me. Order something crazy and I'll make it."

She crossed her arms on the bar and leaned closer. "What if I don't want something crazy?"

"Then that will make it much easier to impress you."

"And why are you trying to impress me?"

"Maybe *impress* isn't the right word. Soften, win over." He put the bottle down and leaned forward to kiss her. "You tell me which one you like best and that's the one we'll go with."

"You don't need to do any of that." She felt her breath catch. His lips hovered just over hers, so close she could feel their warmth.

"You sure?" he murmured.

Julia didn't feel like talking anymore. She nodded.

"Then why was my brother allowed to kiss you in public while I had to keep my distance?"

If he'd told her that he'd decided to give her the restaurant free and clear, she couldn't have been more surprised. She slumped against the back of the bar stool. But when she studied his face, she saw he wasn't kidding. Oh, sure, he was smiling and there was a slight lift to his eyebrow, but his eyes were serious. He really wanted to know.

In some little way, it thrilled her. That he cared enough to ask. That he cared enough to notice.

"Donovan." She reached out to cup his cheek. "Are you jealous?"

"Yes." He pushed the bottle farther to the side and levered himself half onto the bar so they were within kissing distance again. "I know you said you wanted to keep things casual, but I'm not crazy about the idea of my brother macking on you in public."

"I'd hardly call a peck on the cheek *macking*." She peered up at him. The main overhead lights were off, only the sconces behind the bar glowing, leaving little pools of soft lights and pockets of shadows. It was a warm and secretive ambience. One where people wouldn't be afraid to share what lived in their hearts. "You could kiss me now."

"I could." And he did. A light press of lips that felt as soft as a feather. She shivered. "And what if I want to do more than kiss you?"

Her breath slipped out, the opposite of a gasp, as if it was being tugged from her lungs. "I think that could be arranged."

She watched him through hooded eyes as he came back around the bar. There was purpose and intent to his gait. God, it was hot. He was hot. And when Donovan flicked open the top buttons of her chef's coat and dipped his fingers into the now-exposed neckline, she shivered again.

"Because I want to do this." He pressed a kiss to the swoop of her collarbone and then drew a line along the ridge with his tongue. Julia felt her legs begin to shake. More wobbly than the perfect panna cotta. "And I want to—" The rest of what he said was drowned out by the roar of lust that filled her ears.

Julia sucked in a loud breath. What had he said? Had it been important? "Hmm?"

But Donovan didn't answer. He nibbled his way down her chest, flicking open more buttons as he went. She had only a thin tank top on underneath her coat, the kitchen too warm for anything heavier. He licked up her chest, into the slight hollow of cleavage, and swirled his tongue in the dip at the base of her throat. Her hands dropped from his head to his shoulders. She clutched him, holding tight to both his body and her heart.

Except she was dearly afraid it was already too late for that. Her heart, her body, her everything, they were all his. No, they weren't. She sucked in another breath. They were hers. And she was sharing them with him only temporarily.

"Donovan?" Now it was her voice that shook like panna cotta.

As though he knew exactly what thoughts were spinning through her head, as though he knew she was on the verge of tumbling, he moved forward one last step so that he was nestled between her legs. A support beam, strong and tall and unmoving. He didn't say anything. Didn't ask why her voice had shaken or why she was clinging to him as though he was a lifeline.

He just let her hang on. Let her know that whatever this was, it was okay with him. She couldn't have been more grateful.

Finally, when Julia was sure her voice was under control and her legs were no longer quivering, she cleared her throat. "What were you going to say?"

He tilted his head back to look at her. "I want you to come to a party at my parents' place next week."

"To cater?" Julia's mind made the most obvious connection. They'd loved her food and they owned the restaurant. It would make sense. Plus, it would be another opportunity to get her name and food into the brains and mouths of people in the industry. People who would talk about her and the restaurant and make sure that tonight's full dining room wasn't an anomaly.

"Not to cater." A small smile made the corners of his eyes lift up. "As my date."

His date? Julia blinked and then swallowed. She shoved those earlier, dangerous thoughts out of her head. This wasn't going to last forever. They were just enjoying each other for now. "Don't you think that's getting a little serious?" They'd been clear on this, hadn't they? That she needed to focus on the restaurant, keep things between them from getting too deep. But he only stared at her, and what she saw in his eyes frightened her. "Donovan?"

"It is serious, Julia. We both know that."

She could hear the thundering of her heart. He hadn't needed to tell her. She already knew. Still, she did her best to hold strong. To pretend that her newly reawakened sex life was just a casual thing—and besides, they'd been together only a few weeks. Not long enough to know. Not long enough to love. "Do we?"

He frowned. "Don't belittle this. Us. I care for you."

She was glad he didn't say *love*. She didn't know what she would have done if he had. Run away? Thanked him? Thrown herself more fully into his embrace and told him to take her to bed or lose her forever? Okay, she really needed to stop watching '80s Tom Cruise movies. "I care for you, too."

"I know. So come with me."

She wanted to say yes. She really did. But the restaurant, her reputation, her—

"Please. It would mean a lot to me."

And how was she supposed to say no to that? She wasn't made of stone. And it wasn't as if she and Donovan were going to start making out in the middle of the living room. She didn't think. She looked at him. He looked back and her stomach did one of those low swoops. Oh, God.

The word came out in a whisper before she even had time to consider the implications. "Yes."

CHAPTER ELEVEN

"WE NEED TO talk about Owen."

Donovan looked up from his computer to find Mal already making herself comfortable in one of his guest chairs. "What is with this family and the barging in lately? Whatever happened to social niceties?"

Mal leaned back as though she owned the place, which, in a way, she did. They all did. "Don't consider this a change of subject, but fine." She widened her eyes and gave him a fake smile. "Hello, brother dear. How are you?"

"Brother dear?"

"You wanted niceties." Mal shrugged. "And now my niceties aren't good enough. Maybe Owen is right about you."

Donovan snorted. "First time for everything." He turned back to his computer, hunting and pecking away. It might be Friday afternoon, but that didn't mean the end of the workweek. Like all of their bar and restaurant staff, Donovan worked into the evenings and through the weekend. "So." His eyes stayed on the line items in his spreadsheet. "To what do I owe the pleasure of this visit and why were you and Owen discussing me?"

When Mal didn't answer, Donovan was forced to turn away from his computer screen. Which wasn't much of a trial, since even he didn't find capital expenses and inventory reports fascinating.

She smirked. "Family secret."

"Oh?" Donovan lifted an eyebrow. "Are we keeping those now?"

"If we're not, we should. Anyway, Owen."

Donovan had known it would be difficult to budge Mal's focus, but he'd felt the need to try. Older-brother privilege and all that. He folded his hands on the desk and gave his sister his complete attention. "What about him?"

"We need to talk about him."

"Which we were just doing."

"A different talk." She pinned him with her best don't-mess-with-me stare. "I think he should take over management at La Petite Bouchée."

Donovan felt a slow trickle of unease work its way down the back of his neck. He wasn't sure he liked this idea. Wasn't sure at all. "Do you?"

"Yes. He's been running Elephants for five months now."

Donovan blinked. Had it really been five months? He was surprised to count off in his head and discover it had been. But still. It was five months of work against years of playing. As far as Donovan was concerned, Owen was still a long way from proving himself. "Five months isn't very long in the big picture."

"No, it's not." He hadn't expected her to agree, which meant she had more to her pitch. Of course she did. She was Mallory Ford. She didn't come in with one lone suggestion. She came in with a detailed list, all with reports to back it up and a plan ready for implementation. Donovan should know. He'd taught her those tricks. "But he's good, Donovan. Have you looked at the latest returns and the profit projections for next year?"

He had and he'd been pleased, even a little impressed. But still. "Elephants has always been a moneymaker." Their first and finest. They could count on Elephants to offset start-up costs and other downward cycles in business in their other locations. Chalking up the wine bar's success to Owen's management as though it was sudden or some sort of turnaround felt disingenuous.

"You wouldn't say that if Owen were a new hire. You'd promote him." Mal leaned forward. "He's ready."

Donovan didn't know if that was true. He didn't know that it was false, either. But to gift Owen with La Petite Bouchée? When it had barely reopened? And was still finding its rhythm? Donovan shook his head.

It was entirely possible that Owen was ready for the extra responsibility and would shine in a new role. And it was also entirely possible that he'd get bored or decide the work was too hard or find something more exciting or any number of possibilities that would pull him in another direction. "He's not reliable. We've all seen that."

Which was why Owen had been given Elephants to oversee. With Jeannie in place and an already-solid customer base, it was a role that was impossible to mess up.

"He's been more than reliable since Dad's heart attack."

Donovan exhaled. "He has, but what about when Dad comes back?"

"What about it?"

"Who's to say that Owen won't revert to his old ways? With enough of us to pick up the slack, I can't say I feel confident that he'll maintain his current attitude." Donovan glanced at the budget, which had not crunched itself in the few minutes they'd been talking. "Look, why don't we give it a trial run. Dad's planning to return to the office in the next couple of weeks. We'll see how that goes. If you still think Owen is ready once Dad's been back for a month, then maybe we can give it a shot."

"I don't think we should wait that long."

"That long? It's not going to be more than six

weeks. And we certainly waited long enough for Owen to show some initiative."

Mal frowned. "They need someone at La Petite Bouchée now." That was true. Julia had mentioned just the other day that they were understaffed for the amount of business now walking through the door. "Why don't we give Owen the position as the trial run. He's done a great job at Elephants."

"Elephants is a bar."

"It's the same industry," Mal retorted. "And they need someone immediately, not in six weeks after a series of interviews and reference checks. He already gets along well with Julia. Why don't you ask her?"

Donovan clenched his hands more tightly. "Maybe I will." Yeah, once he actually told her they were keeping the restaurant in the family.

"Oh, hell, no," Mal said as if she'd plucked the words right out of his brain. "You haven't told her that the sale is a no-go yet?"

He didn't like being chastised by his younger sister. Well, anyone really, but especially not Mal, who used to look up at him with those hero-worship eyes. "I haven't found the right time." But he was making progress. He'd set up an appointment with the lawyer for Monday, and he saw no reason that they couldn't have a contract drawn up before the end of next week. "I've got it under control."

"No, you don't. You so don't." Mal blew out a

breath. The ends of her hair fluttered in the breeze she created. "The longer this goes on, the more difficult it will be. Just tell her."

"I will." He sounded whiny. He hated sounding whiny. "I have a plan, but not all the pieces are in place yet. It's going to have to wait until after Mom and Dad's party." Which was happening on Sunday and already had things out of whack. Evelyn had insisted all three of her children arrive early to greet guests and fix any last-minute problems. Like Gus sneaking an unapproved beer.

"Nothing like putting it off another three days."

"Give it a rest, Mal. I said I'll handle it." Perhaps not only with a stellar contract but with a good bottle of red wine and chicken parmigiana, which was his go-to meal. The one his mother had insisted he learn so that he wouldn't embarrass himself, being in the food industry and unable to cook. A little wining and dining so Julia would be more open and amenable to the idea. He flicked a look at his sister. "And I don't see you being forthcoming about your life."

"We weren't talking about me." She sat back and crossed her legs. Her body language was clearly telling him to back off. But Donovan was tired of that.

"We weren't talking about me, either." Because what was good for her was good for him. "But maybe we should. Since you presume to comment on my personal life, I'm going to ask you. What's going on with Travis?"

"Nothing." But she pressed her lips together so tightly that they turned white. And her eyes seemed full of stories held at bay.

"Really? So you just decided to stop wearing his ring?" Donovan noted the flick of her hand to her throat, as though the physical movement might capture any words that tried to spill out. "What happened in Aruba last month?"

Her eyes grew darker. "I told you—nothing."

"And I don't believe you." They were both silent for a moment, only the low hum of office technology in the room.

Mal wasn't happy. That much was evident. But exactly how unhappy Donovan couldn't be sure. She showed up to work, was polite to the staff and was always well-groomed. But he was pretty sure her social life was on a ventilator. And whatever had happened with Travis was the cause.

He exhaled. He wasn't trying to be a dick, even if Mal might not see it that way. "It might help to talk."

"I know." Her voice snapped through the air. "But forgive me if I don't feel like talking about my sex life to my brother."

"Whoa, whoa." Donovan held up his hands to ward off any future sexually related information.

"I just want to know that you're okay. As far as I'm concerned, you're still a virgin."

She sent him a withering look, but there was a hint of a smile behind it. Donovan knew that look. "Remember Max Thibodeau?"

"No, I do not." He did. The son of one of their father's friends. Spoiled and a little wild. Last Donovan had heard, Max had two baby mamas and was living in Australia.

"Well, the summer I was sixteen—"

"You win." Donovan knew when to concede. Mal was more stubborn than he was, and if he didn't want to be scarred for life, he needed to stop this tale of...well, tail immediately. "No more discussing our personal lives."

"Good." She nodded as if she'd just won. Which she had. "So back to Owen and how you're going to ask him to manage La Petite Bouchée as well as Elephants."

"Seriously. Like a dog with a bone."

"Did you just call me a dog?" Mal narrowed her eyes. "Don't forget, I know where your skeletons are buried. And I have friends in the media. Who would only be too happy to run a story on you with family photos."

"Would you really do that to your favorite brother?"

"Of course not. Besides, Owen hasn't done anything to piss me off in a while." She flashed him a cheeky grin. And even though it was putting him in his place, Donovan was glad to see it. Glad to see any flash of the Mal he knew.

"All right. I'll consider the suggestion. Now, get out of here. And stop talking about your sex life."

"I will." She pushed herself out of the chair and moved toward the door. "But only because I don't have one to speak of."

"Still talking." Donovan closed his eyes, as if that might also close his ears to anything else she had to say, and didn't open them until he heard her laugh trailing down the hall, back to her own office.

He let out the breath he'd been holding. Seriously, he was a saint. A bloody saint. Well, except for the fact that he still had to tell Julia that her dream of owning La Petite Bouchée had taken a serious hit. His stomach muscles cramped. But at least he was working on a plan.

Still, even with the plan, guilt suffused his body. He should never have let it go on this long. He was taking her as his date to his parents' party. He wanted to introduce her as his girlfriend. He wanted to be the only man in her life. And, oh, by the way, he wanted her to be just fine with the fact that he was stripping away her chance at owning the restaurant she thought of as hers.

He forced himself to relax. It would still be practically hers. None of them had any intention of limiting her role or lessening her leadership. The restaurant would still look the way she wanted. Would still serve the food she wanted. Would still have her name on the window by the front door. She just wouldn't have to deal with all the headaches that came with being an actual owner. So maybe this was a good thing.

And with the right ambience, the right mood, the right wine, maybe everything would work out.

CHAPTER TWELVE

THIS WAS SO not how today was supposed to go.

Julia ran around the kitchen at La Petite Bouchée wondering just where and when things had gone wrong. Really, it was a comedy of errors here today. She'd been in early to do prep for the evening service since she was going to be at the Fords' party instead of the restaurant. But her chopping had come to a halt around noon when one of her suppliers had called to tell her that they weren't able to fill her weekly delivery tomorrow but would try to swing by on Thursday instead. Which, yeah, not so much. She needed that product to feed her customers on Tuesday and Wednesday.

After phoning around, calling in favors and threatening to change suppliers entirely, Julia had gotten him to agree to provide an extremely thinned-down order. Which was better than nothing. So along with prep, she'd needed to come up with an appealing nightly special that would convince diners to order it instead of off the menu. Then two of her sous chefs had called in sick. Though she suspected it was less 24-hour bug and more "out too late last night and don't feel like getting out of bed," which was tantamount to quitting in the restaurant industry. She'd already made some calls and had Sasha do the same to try to fill the positions as quickly as possible with employees who could be counted on. And if that weren't enough, her acting floor manager had quit, stating that the job was more stressful than he wanted and he'd decided to go find himself in a Buddhist monastery. Which was good for him, but did he have to wait until they were two hours from opening to tell her?

She'd almost called Donovan then, explained the situation and why she couldn't go to the party, but Sasha refused to hear of it. "Hells, no. You're finally getting a little something-something. I'm not about to let you blow that."

"He'll understand." Julia chopped more quickly and checked the burner under her saucepan.

"I won't. It's almost like you think *I* can't handle it. I'll have you know that I'm perfectly capable of holding down the kitchen. In fact, I do it every night you're off." Sasha poured some wine into a different pan, which sizzled and spat.

Julia knew that was true. But she hadn't taken a night off since La Petite Bouchée's reopening and she didn't feel right leaving Sasha in the weeds. No, this couldn't even be classified as the weeds. It was more like a jungle that required a machete to get out of. Or a really excellent chef knife. "I know you can handle it. But this isn't a normal night. You need all hands on deck."

"No. I need you to get out of here, go home, get into a sexy dress and have a good night. You deserve it."

"Sash…"

"Don't make me threaten to tell the staff that the reason you're so calm even while things are crazy in here is because you're finally getting properly rogered."

"Rogered?" Julia looked up from her sauce.

"Shagged, smushed, played hide the salami."

"Please stop."

"I will." Sasha winked. "When you leave."

But Julia had stayed another two hours, until service actually began, before letting Sasha shoo her out the door. She'd called Donovan to let him know that she'd be late and she'd find her own way to his parents' house.

After a shower that might have set land speed records and putting on her five-minute face, which she'd learned in Paris from a gorgeous model, she climbed into a cab and gave the driver the Fords' address.

The good thing about being so busy was that she hadn't had time to think about the party. But by the time her cab pulled up in front of Gus and Evelyn's house, her stomach was in full roil mode. Maybe because it was more of a mansion than a house.

Julia swallowed the nerves that rose up the back of her throat. There was no reason to feel anxious, no need to feel scattered. If the kitchen hadn't undone her, a simple house party should be nothing. And yet, her legs felt wobbly as she got out of the cab and stared up at the house.

A young man in a red blazer stepped forward to shut the cab's door and point her up the steps to the front door. She blinked at him. A valet? They actually had valets tonight? Another man in the same red blazer walked up the driveway, keys jingling in his hand. Yep, most definitely valets. She'd never been to a private home that had valets before. But then, she generally didn't attend parties that took place in mansions.

She tried to shove the nerves aside. The Fords weren't the old-money, snobby, nose-and-pinkie-in-the-air types she'd run into in Europe. They weren't the trashy nouveau types, either, always bragging about brand-name this and designer-label that, who liked to think they ran Vancouver's social scene. They were a loving and hardworking family who'd simply used good business sense and made smart decisions to turn their effort into a lot of money.

Yes, the Fords were wealthy. But she already knew that, had known before she'd even met them.

They were also perfectly lovely and down-to-earth. And if they had valets, Julia knew it was to make the lives of their guests easier, not to brag or show off.

The house was gorgeous, all stone and glass, a slightly less glossy version of the decor in all their wine bars. It suited the landscape, the warm and welcoming glow of interior lights shining through the windows. It made her feel a little less uncomfortable. And she knew she looked the part, though her shoes pinched her feet.

Julia was used to the discomfort that came from standing for hours at a time. She just didn't usually do it wearing a cocktail dress and three-inch heels. But jeans and flats weren't appropriate for this party, and despite the fact that this wasn't her normal attire, she felt good in it. She'd splurged on the classic dress when she'd lived in Paris. It had eaten up half her food budget for the month, but she'd been unable to return it to the rack after seeing it on her body. And nothing had changed since that first time she'd tried it on.

She took a breath as she walked up the short flight of stone steps that led to the front door. Everything would be fine. Donovan would be happy to see her and there would be plenty of other non-mansion owners in attendance. Donovan had told her the party was for all their friends, the major-

ity of whom were in the restaurant business, and
their staff.

Still, she wished tonight hadn't gone so off the
rails and that she'd been able to arrive with Donovan as planned. But some of her anxiety eased
when Evelyn opened the front doors herself.

"Julia." Her hug was warm, as it always was.
"I'm so glad you made it." Evelyn showed Julia
around the house already filled with laughing people, most with wineglasses in one hand and appetizer plates in the other. And beyond the glossy
heels and expensive jewelry, Julia saw the touches
that made the large house a home.

The throw pillows in bright colors, the family photos taken at the beach with wind whipping
through their hair and everyone moving instead of
sitting in a stilted formal pose. The furniture, while
tasteful and clearly of good quality, also looked
sturdy, as if it could hold up to a spill or people
putting their feet on it. Much like a good restaurant or bar, the space had been designed to move
people easily through the space and would be quick
to clean up with a mop and some elbow grease.

She accepted a glass of wine but passed on the
food, claiming that she'd eaten at the restaurant.
The truth was, she still felt a little too keyed up
to eat. She sipped the wine, taking everything in.
The beautiful room, the more beautiful food and
the incredibly beautiful people.

It was crowded, making it difficult to find any-one, but she recognized some faces. Chefs who'd been featured in international foodie magazines and on TV. A few local actors who seemed to turn up in every other movie as Businesswoman #2 or Architect #3. People who'd been at her event in Whistler and La Petite Bouchée. They greeted her with smiles and polite how-are-yous, and the jagged edge of her nerves began to wear off. She was building a reputation. In fact, maybe she'd already built one. Exactly how long did it take for a reputation to take hold, anyway?

She was almost starting to feel at home, com-fortable and okay that aside from Evelyn she hadn't seen any of the other Fords. She took a sip of wine. Maybe she'd try one of the delectable-looking canapés. The shrimp on toast smelled divine. She caught a whiff of the tarragon as it passed. Or a scallop wrapped in bacon because everything was better with bacon.

But she didn't get the chance. Or she did. She just didn't think she'd be able to stomach it.

Because standing across the room, looking hot as hell and twice as sexy, was Donovan. With the blonde woman he'd been squiring around in January practically inserting herself into his front pocket.

What. The. Hell.

Julia felt the hot burn of anger flare. She wasn't upset that he was standing with the other woman.

It was a party—people mingled and she certainly didn't expect him to cause a scene and storm away. But then again, she didn't expect him to smile at the woman while she pressed her skinny body against his. Julia's fingers tightened around the stem of her glass.

"You could always go slap some sense into him." Owen's voice startled her and she whirled around to find him at her elbow. "I, for one, would pay to see that."

Julia forced a casual shrug and turned away. She didn't need to watch that. To view her humiliation in living color. "I'm fine."

"That death grip you have on your glass would say otherwise."

She glanced down to find her fingers still wrapped tightly around the stem of the glass. She loosened her grip. "I'm fine."

And maybe if she kept repeating it like some sort of mantra, it might become true. It was better than thinking about tossing the contents of her glass in his face. Besides, he was only standing with the woman.

"Right." Owen's tone told her she wasn't fooling him. "So then it wouldn't bother you to know that the woman he's talking to, the one who can't keep her hands off him, is an ex?"

"Not at all." But she felt the unforgiving nature of the glass as her fingers curled around it again.

Owen patted her on the shoulder. "He doesn't want her."

"I know." Julia did know. Donovan was the one who'd insisted she come to the party as his date. He'd even offered to pick her up when she'd called to let him know she was going to be late. And yet—she darted a glance over her shoulder to see that the blonde had now placed a second hand on Donovan's arm—he didn't have to look as if he was enjoying himself quite so much.

"You sure you don't want to slap him? It would do something to liven up this party."

"I'm sure." She looked away from Donovan, thinking maybe if she didn't watch, it wouldn't bother her. "And there's nothing wrong with this party."

"Nothing a little slap wouldn't solve."

"Then you slap him."

"I would." Owen grinned at her. "But my mother would kill me."

"And she wouldn't kill me?" Evelyn wasn't tall, but height didn't equal power.

"Consider it taking one for the team."

Julia laughed and some of her aggravation floated away. "Thanks, but I'll pass."

"Pass on what?" Mal joined them, looking tall

and sleek. But Julia thought Mal's dress hung a shade too loosely, as if it had been purchased about fifteen pounds ago.

"Your brother is causing trouble."

Mal smiled. "What else is new?"

"Excuse me." Owen pasted on a hurt expression. "Shouldn't you be asking which brother instead of assuming it's me?"

"Fine." Mal made a show of turning to Julia and widening her eyes as she placed a hand on Owen's arm. "You couldn't possibly be referring to this bastion of appropriate and polite behavior, could you?"

"I can be appropriate," Owen defended himself.

"When?"

"When I feel like it."

"Which is…"

"Never." The corners of his eyes crinkled.

Julia laughed and her eyes caught Donovan's across the room. Her heart thumped, and for a moment, it was only them. Then she saw that the blonde's hand was still on his arm and her other hand had snaked its way onto his shoulder.

She raised an eyebrow at him, and then slowly and without any attempt at subtlety, she turned away.

DONOVAN FELT HIS pleasure at seeing Julia turn to confusion. What was that about? And as he watched, she turned back, but she didn't return his smile. Instead, she tossed her hair and showed him her back. Oh, hell. Had she heard about their plans for La Petite Bouchée? Did she know they weren't going to sell? Damn it. He had an appointment with the lawyer tomorrow to discuss her new contract, but nothing had been finalized.

"Donovan?" He glanced at Tatiana, a furrow on her usually smooth brow. "Is everything okay?"

He noticed that she now had both hands on him. One on his arm and the other dangerously close to his front pants pocket. Awkward. "Will you excuse me, Tatiana?"

Her fingers curled around his arm when he moved to leave. "Only if you promise to come back."

"Of course." He had no intention of doing so, but he said it with a smile so she might not realize that. His mother hadn't raised a fool.

He'd underestimated Tatiana's understanding, though. She held her grip. "I'm not letting you slip away this easily. I'd really like to talk."

"Maybe later." Donovan could see Julia had glanced back, was eyeing him again with her lips pressed into a tight seam.

"Donovan?"

He didn't take his eyes off Julia. Tatiana was a stunning woman. Smart, charming, gorgeous. But all he cared about was that she wasn't Julia.

"If you'll excuse me," he repeated, already shifting away, moving toward Julia, who slipped between his siblings and disappeared into the crowd.

But he didn't find her when he arrived at Owen's side. No, the only thing he found there was Owen's annoying know-it-all smirk. Donovan swallowed his aggravation. He and Owen had been getting along better these past couple of weeks. They still weren't best friends, but they were coming to find a mutual acceptance. "Where's Julia?"

But he needn't have bothered asking. Like a moth to a flame, his eyes found Julia exiting the main room. He didn't say anything else to his brother, simply headed off in pursuit. If she'd heard about the restaurant, he needed to explain.

By the time he maneuvered through the crowd, he wasn't sure where she'd gone. She wasn't in any of the downstairs rooms, including the washrooms, which he knew because he waited until the occupants came out to make sure. Which meant she could only have gone upstairs. Unless she'd left. But Donovan didn't want to consider that yet.

He'd just reached the top landing when the door to the bathroom he and Owen had shared as kids flew open, revealing her. His relief that she was still there was almost as overwhelming as his need to touch her.

Her face turned stony when she saw him. "Yes?"

Donovan didn't answer, just took her hand and

held it. She wasn't getting away. Not until they talked. He stroked the soft skin on her wrists. "You ran away from me."

She scowled and tugged her hand free. His heart sank. She'd heard about the restaurant. Damn it. Who had opened their big mouth? Owen? He'd been whispering to her earlier. See? It was instances like these that made it clear his brother wasn't ready for a larger role in the company. Donovan brushed off the fact that he'd known about the change of plans for La Petite Bouchée for a while and should have long since shared that information with Julia.

But he wasn't going to let her run off. Not like this. "Let me explain."

"What's to explain? I saw you with your ex. Letting her paw at you in front of everyone." His ex? Pawing? But at his puzzled look, she only scowled more deeply. "Did you think I wouldn't notice? My God, Donovan. She was practically wearing you."

Had she not heard about the restaurant? A flicker of hope leaped to life. "You're upset because of Tatiana?" He didn't exhale until she nodded sharply.

"I didn't like it."

"Neither did I."

She sniffed. "You looked like you were enjoying yourself. Not that I care." The effort she put into acting as if she didn't mind only underlined just how much she did mind. "In fact, you can do whatever you want with whoever you want." She moved to go around him.

"Julia." He reached out, drew a hand along her bare arm and saw her shiver. "The only person I want is you." He heard the catch of her breath and waited for her to turn to face him. When she did, he took a step toward her so their bodies were in full contact.

"I don't believe you."

He could feel how tightly she was holding herself. "It's true."

"Then why were you letting that woman paw you?"

He paused for a long beat. Muted party sounds swirled up the stairs, but for all intents and purposes, they were alone. "*Pawing* is such an ugly term."

"Then maybe you should have stopped her," Julia sniped.

She was right. He should have. He'd been trying to keep an eye out for her, though clearly he'd missed her entrance and had been paying only half attention while Tatiana jabbered at him about whatever was going on in her life and apparently pawing him. "I'm sorry."

He felt some of the stiffness leave her. "It's a start."

"What can I do to make it up to you?"

"Not let strange women paw you." She was leaning into him now.

"Done." He brushed a hand along her neck, feeling the fluttery, feathery ends of her hair slide through his fingers. "Although, I'm not sure it was pawing."

That snapped Julia back to attention. "Oh, yes, she was."

"I don't recall." He moved his hand up her neck, pulled her forward so their foreheads were touching. "Maybe you'd better show me. So I can keep an eye out for it in future."

She narrowed her eyes at him. "You think there's going to be a future pawing?"

Donovan nudged her backward, piloted her through the still-open door of the bathroom, so they wouldn't be interrupted. "I'm certainly hoping." And shut the door with a firm click.

Julia watched him, her eyes big, a light flush creeping up her chest.

Donovan toyed with the neckline of her dress, wanting to see all the glories it covered. "You're looking a little overheated."

"Really? Because I wasn't the one getting pawed."

"Then allow me to remedy that."

"Donovan." His name was a gasp on her lips as he lifted her onto the cool white counter and slid his hand up her thighs.

He loved the way she said his name. Wanted to hear her say it again. His fingers crept higher, closer to the heat between her legs.

"Donovan. We are not having sex in the bathroom at your parents' house." But he noticed she didn't try to squeeze her legs together or push him away.

"What if we call it pawing?" He ran a finger along the edge of her underwear, stroking the silky material and her skin beneath it. "I'm only trying to get a sense of what is and isn't allowed."

He saw her shiver. The flush rose to her cheeks.

"What about this?" He played with the elastic edging of her underwear. "Is this pawing?"

"It might be." Her voice still held that breathless tone. "Maybe you should demonstrate further."

Donovan was happy to oblige.

BY THE TIME Julia and Donovan made it back downstairs and the crowd began to dwindle, it was late. Restaurant workers were used to long hours, so Julia didn't feel sleepy, but she was looking forward to taking off her heels and changing into a pair of comfy pants.

"You can't leave yet," Evelyn said when Julia and Donovan attempted to say their goodbyes. "The family has some news."

Julia instinctively stiffened and glanced at Donovan. He was family. She was not. "I'll wait for you—"

"Nonsense." Evelyn linked her arm through Julia's and proceeded to walk her away from the door. "This affects you, too."

Julia turned a raised eyebrow at Donovan, but he shrugged as he caught up with them. He slid a warm arm around her waist. "I would have told you if I'd known."

Evelyn opened a set of double doors and led them into a large and comfortable sitting room.

Julia would have known it as Gus's enclave even before she saw him sitting in a large, over-stuffed chair at what was effectively the heart of the room. It just looked like him. Full of rich reds and warm browns, the room was furnished with seats that looked as if you would sink into them, curling your feet beneath you. There was a large fireplace on one wall with a mahogany mantel covered in elegant statues and a silver-framed family photo.

Owen and Mal were already there, looking as out of the loop as Donovan, judging from the questioning glances they shot his way. Mal sat on a couch to the right of their father while Owen lounged against the mantel on the left with a glass dangling from his fingertips. It might look like vodka or gin, but Julia bet it was water, which was the only thing she'd seen Owen drink.

"I promise we won't keep you long," Evelyn said and gave Julia's arm a light pat. She moved to join her husband while Donovan and Julia took the matched chairs in front of the fireplace. She could hear the clink of ice cubes whenever Owen moved his glass.

"Finally," Mal said, turning her attention back to their father. "Now maybe Dad can explain what all this is about?"

"All in good time." Gus folded his hands across his stomach and leaned against the back of the chair.

"How much time?" Mal wanted to know. "Some of us have to work early tomorrow." But there was a lilt of humor in her tone.

Julia suspected the family was pleased to see how well Gus looked after the long and high-energy party. His health had continued to improve with no signs of a relapse, but she knew they all watched him carefully, anxious to ensure there were no signs that he'd pushed too hard or set back his recovery.

"Mallory." Gus's voice filled the room. "This is an important moment in our family's history and you're undermining it."

Owen snorted. "Yeah, Mal. Don't you know Dad's got the conch?"

"Wolves and ingrates." But Gus couldn't stop his smile from peeking out.

Julia saw that, rather than engaging in the lighthearted family banter, Donovan watched her. A blast of heat tore through her and she glanced around to be certain no one had gotten singed or noticed the overheated look.

"Now that you're all here, I have some news." Gus made a point of looking at each person in the room, including her.

Julia was filled with a quieter warmth then. One born of kindness and inclusion. She wasn't a Ford, but none of them ever made her feel that way. She saw out of the corner of her eye that Donovan had turned to face his father, but his hand sneaked out to rest on the arm of her chair. She hesitated only a moment before placing her hand atop his.

"Your mother and I have discussed some things and we've come to a decision." He looked completely at ease and relaxed. As did Evelyn, who was standing just behind Gus's chair. Her hand rested on his shoulder. "I've decided not to return to work."

The announcement was met with stunned silence, which lasted for about 2.3 seconds before a trio of voices exploded.

"What?"

"Dad!"

"Are you okay?"

Donovan spoke last, more quietly and so more noticeable.

"I'm fine." Gus nodded, a gesture of reassurance that only quelled the storm instead of calmed it. "In fact, the doctor was very pleased at my last checkup. Good thing, too. I wouldn't want to be eating all that green stuff for nothing."

Evelyn gave his shoulder a hard squeeze.

"Fine, fine," Gus said. "I love that green stuff. Happy?"

Julia pressed her lips together, attempting to tuck her grin away. Even so, it didn't go unnoticed.

"See?" Gus inclined his head toward her. "Julia understands. Although if she were to cook for me every night, I might find myself enjoying whatever it is you're feeding me."

"There's always an open table for you." Even though they were solidly booked these days, there were ways of finding space for VIP guests. Julia figured the owner counted as one. And even if Gus hadn't owned La Petite Bouchée, Julia never turned away people she loved.

"I might take you up on that." Evelyn's fingers squeezed again. "Or not. That's not important. What's important is that I'm retiring. Permanently." Julia couldn't help noticing that although he looked at all four of the under-fifties in the room, the primary focus of his gaze was Donovan.

"What does that mean for the company?" Donovan's voice was low and calm, full of the control needed to take on the leadership of the family company. She squeezed his hand.

"I'd like to suggest that Owen take over running La Petite Bouchée."

There was another silence, one that didn't explode with voices.

"But, of course, that's up to all of you." Gus looked at each of his children in turn. "You'll be in charge now, and while I'll always be here to offer advice, you don't have to run anything past me for approval."

Julia couldn't hear anything over the agonized scream that seemed to come straight from her heart. La Petite Bouchée was hers. Or so she'd thought.

The rest of the family made happy sounds, talking about a future with the restaurant. But all Julia could think was that La Petite Bouchée wouldn't be hers. Not ever. And she wondered if she'd been an idiot to think it could be, to believe Donovan when he'd said he had no interest in the place and that he'd wanted to sell to her.

She pulled her hand from his.

"Julia." Donovan's voice was quiet, rolling beneath the bright chatter coming from everyone else. She only shook her head. She couldn't do this here, in front of everyone. Couldn't announce her hurt and betrayal with everyone watching.

She blinked and turned her face as tears threatened to spill, and managed to take enough deep breaths to maintain her facade.

Julia didn't say anything until they escaped the confines of the house and they were out of earshot. Even then she kept her voice low, in keeping with the still darkness of night that surrounded them. "How long have you known?"

She appreciated that he didn't play dumb. He sighed. "A month. After the day you cooked lunch for everyone at the restaurant."

Somehow that little tidbit made it worse. While she'd been thinking about how much she liked them, he'd been cutting her out of the restaurant.

"I didn't intend for this to happen, but when I pitched the idea of selling again, my father said he wanted to take over instead." He reached for her, but she pulled away, glad for the cool March air that slowed the growing fury in her chest.

A month. He'd known for a month. "Before Whistler, then." It wasn't a question. She could do the math. People were often surprised to find out just how good at numbers chefs were. But keeping track of inventory was often the difference between being in the black or running in the red. Or keeping track of the moment the man you'd thought you were falling in love with chose to shatter your heart.

"Julia."

"No." Julia didn't move, afraid that she might

break, might crumple before him, so overwhelming was the sense of betrayal. "I don't understand. We discussed this. I was going to put in a fair offer, a good offer. For God's sake, Donovan, you said you didn't want the space."

"I know."

"So what happened?" What had changed to cause the family to want to keep it?

"My father. You saw how he feels about the place. He's nostalgic, and since his heart attack… well, it's important to him."

She understood that; she really did. But what about her? What about her ties to La Petite Bouchée? "It's important to me, too."

"I know."

She risked a glance at him, and the sympathy on his face almost undid her. Almost.

"But I'm not family." She tasted the bitterness on her tongue and didn't care.

"That's not what this is about."

No, that was exactly what this was about, but she couldn't say anything. Her chest felt tight and she struggled for breath.

"I don't want you to leave." He ran a hand through his hair. Had it really been only hours earlier that she'd run her own hands through it? It seemed like decades. "I've got an appointment set up with the lawyer tomorrow to discuss your contract."

She barked out a laugh. "Why? What else are you going to try to take from me?"

"Nothing." He reached for her again, but she stepped back and held up a hand to ward him off. "I'm not going to take anything. I want to offer you more. Listen, I know this is a shock and I'm not happy about the way this came out."

That was probably true, but she had to wonder if he'd ever planned to tell her at all. Or was he just going to let her stay in the kitchen, believing that one day she'd be able to buy the restaurant when he had no intention of ever putting it up for sale?

"But nothing has to change. All the renovation choices, the way things run, the staff, the food. Those are all you." He sounded desperate. But not as desperate as she felt. "And I know Owen has no interest in having a hands-on role, so it'll be like you own the place."

Only, she wouldn't own it. "You have no idea what kind of role Owen wants," she told him. But she had a feeling she did. And it wasn't hands-off.

"Julia, try to understand. This isn't just my decision."

It wasn't. "But it was your decision to keep it a secret." He'd had plenty of opportunity to tell her, to work something out before now.

"Julia." It sounded as if his heart was breaking. She ignored the pang in her own chest.

"It's not enough, Donovan." Acting as the owner wasn't the same as being the owner. And to her it was a big difference.

"Why?"

"Because." She couldn't have explained even if she wanted to.

"Julia." He called out as she turned to go.

She didn't look back. "Don't, Donovan. Just don't. I remember what you said. Business is for family." She moved off, away from him, away from everything. "I'll find my own way home."

And she didn't cry. Not even once she got to her own apartment, locked the door, turned off her phone and closed the blinds. Instead, she just sat in the dark, wondering what she was going to do with the rest of her life and praying that she wouldn't always feel as hopeless as she did now.

"MR. FORD?" BAILEY'S voice carried over the line. "Mr. Ford is here to see you."

Donovan still felt sick about what had happened last night. Sick in the gut, sick in the head, sick in the heart. Julia hadn't answered his calls, and even when he'd convinced one of her neighbors to buzz him in, she wouldn't answer his knocks on her door. He'd finally left when a different neighbor had threatened to call the cops if he didn't stop banging.

He'd gone through the meeting with the lawyer this morning, even knowing that the contract would be unnecessary. Julia had sent a resignation email this morning to all five members of the Ford family. She hadn't explicitly stated that it was because of him, but they had to know. He cursed himself for not acting sooner, not telling her immediately and then suggesting they work together to find a compromise that would keep her firmly in place as the executive chef at La Petite Bouchée.

And now he had to face his father and explain just how and why he'd so royally screwed up. Great.

Except it wasn't his father who walked through the door to his office, but Owen. Donovan stiffened when he saw his brother. "Not today, Owen."

"Yes today." Owen took a seat, making himself comfortable in the clear chair. He was wearing a suit, every crease in alignment, every pleat perfect. With sneakers. "What the hell happened?"

"I don't want to talk about it." Couldn't talk about it. He was angry at his father for making a private announcement so public, but really he was mad at himself. He was the dumbass who'd sat on the information for a month, waiting for the right time. Even when Mal had advised him otherwise. So he knew the blame lay squarely on his own shoulders. But that didn't really help.

"Mal said you told Julia you were going to sell her the restaurant?"

"Because we were." The words burst out of him. "Dad wasn't well enough to come back to work, and Mal and I were swamped handling everything."

"What about me?"

"What about you?" Donovan didn't feel like having this conversation now. "You weren't ready for that level of responsibility."

"You're wrong."

Donovan glanced back at his computer screen. Although Owen might be inclined to have this little chat, Donovan didn't have time. There was still work to be done. Lots of work. "Fine. I was wrong. Now that I've admitted it, can I get back to business?"

"That's not why I'm here." Owen didn't raise his voice, didn't get his back up. Just remained where he was, his gaze calm. "I came to find out how to fix it."

The bleakness Donovan had been trying to fend off swelled through him again. "See, that's the thing, Owen. I don't know if we can." God knew he'd racked his brain all night trying to think of a way. In between dialing Julia's cell phone like a stalker. He hadn't stopped calling even when all he got was the mechanized recording telling him her voice mail was full.

"Then we'll have to think of something."

"Like what?" Donovan looked at his brother and for the first time he wondered if maybe Owen did have some good ideas hidden in that head of his. But if Owen had been enlightened, he wasn't sharing.

"I think that's something you'll need to figure out. I just wanted to come in and tell you not to give up on her. She's special."

"I know." But he didn't know how to tell her that when she wouldn't answer her phone.

"She's worth fighting for."

"I know."

"And I'm not taking over La Petite Bouchée."

Donovan didn't even blink, so inured to the bad news flying his way over the past twelve hours. "Okay."

"Because I think we need Julia. Give her shares in the restaurant."

"Owen, it's not about that."

"No, Donovan." Owen stopped him. "It is about that. You just need to open your eyes and see it."

Donovan thought about it. Really thought about it. Opening up the family company to someone else. Letting them in, allowing them a voice to shape and determine their future. It could work. There were plenty of companies that did just that. But they weren't his family company. And he wasn't ready to put all his hard work, all his father's and Mal's hard work, at risk.

He shook his head. "No." The business had always been for family only. When Mal and Travis had wanted to open their own restaurant, it hadn't been under the Ford Group umbrella. It had been separate. That hadn't changed.

Owen didn't say anything, just stared at him for a moment. Then he shook his head, too, and Donovan was almost certain there was disgust in the movement. Which only proved how little Owen understood the business. "I can see you've still got your head up your ass about this. When you're ready to consider other options, I'm willing to help." He stood up. "Now, if you'll excuse me, I'm due at Elephants."

And Donovan could only sit and watch while his brother headed off to take care of business while he sat in his chair and pondered exactly what he was doing with his life.

CHAPTER THIRTEEN

THERE WERE NIGHTS Julia missed the Fords almost as much as she missed Donovan. Tonight was one of them. At least she still had Owen. Sweet and loyal Owen, who'd listened to her rant about his brother and agreed the man was an asshat and refused to leave the family business even though Donovan wasn't giving him nearly enough responsibility.

They were sitting at Elephants, enjoying a quiet Tuesday night. Or not so quiet since the wine bar was, as usual, packed. Julia hadn't much felt like going out the past few weeks and she'd tried to refuse when Owen invited her. It wasn't until he assured her that Donovan was out of town and wouldn't be there that she'd finally agreed. She'd pulled on one of her favorite outfits, fitted jeans with a loose white off-the-shoulders shirt and a breastplate-worth of necklaces, and wished she felt as bright and jingly as her jewelry. But it was better than sitting at home alone. Again.

She hated that every time the door opened, her

eyes darted over and her heart thumped. Donovan wasn't going to waltz through it.

"I thought you didn't want to see him."

It was as if the man was a mind reader. "I don't." But she scowled as she felt the telltale flush on her cheeks. Obvious if Owen looked closely. Fortunately, it was either too dim in the bar to see or he was too polite to mention it.

"Like I said, he's out of town at a meeting." Owen picked at the label on his bottle of water. He wasn't working this evening, but he'd already handled three different staff and patron issues and that was just since she'd been here.

"Why aren't you with him?"

"Because Donovan still doesn't think I'm ready to run with the big dogs. Although I am allowed to work six nights a week at Elephants." He put the bottle down and smiled, but it was forced. "It's fine. I wouldn't want the additional stress."

Julia could tell that was a fib, one to fool her or himself. Maybe both. She gave his arm a reassuring pat. "You're good at this, Owen. Really good. He'll see that."

"Yeah, maybe by the time I'm ready to retire." Owen shook off his pinched expression as easily as a dog shaking off lake water. "Anyway, I think we should talk about you."

"I'd rather not." Julia didn't feel like delving

into her own emotional bruises. "Let's chat about the weather."

Owen wasn't put off. "Let's chat about you. How's the new job?"

Julia picked up her still-full wineglass and swirled the contents without taking a sip. "It's fine." After quitting La Petite Bouchée, Julia had gotten hired at a little café in the West End near her apartment. The Sun Café was far below the types of places she usually worked. They served a workingman's breakfast and closed at 2:00 p.m. The napkins were paper and the lighting was whatever had been supplied by the previous tenant. But the space was clean, the menu was straightforward and the second she walked out the door, she left work behind. It was nice not having to worry about profit margins and overheads, freeing her up to work on purchasing her own space.

She still felt a lingering sense of guilt, survivor's guilt, that she'd left everyone else at La Petite Bouchée and moved on. But it had to be done. And in time, she knew the guilt would fade. But it had been only three weeks.

She was in touch with her investors on an almost daily basis. She felt confident that they'd find the right spot for their restaurant soon. But for now, she'd be at The Sun Café.

"You can't be serious about staying there." It wasn't the first time Owen had made this pronouncement. In fact, he told her every morning when he came in for a vegetarian egg-white omelet. So he couldn't think the place was that bad.

"I told you. It suits me for now." She needed to heal, to grieve properly for her mother in a way she hadn't had time to before. She felt she'd done a fair bit of that the past few weeks. And while it was hard and there were days she wondered if she'd ever stop missing her, most of the time her memories were now happy ones. The way her mother would have wanted to be remembered. Standing over a stove or bossing people around her kitchen with a smile.

"It's a waste of your talent."

"It's temporary." She wasn't going to stay there forever, just until the time was right to make a move.

Owen sniffed. "Still. If my brother wasn't such a stubborn asshat, we wouldn't be having this conversation."

"True." She smiled, appreciating the verbal support. "But then, I also wouldn't know about your omelet obsession."

"It's not an obsession to pay attention to your health. I have a family history of heart disease, you know." He lifted an affronted eyebrow at her.

"Oh, I'm sorry—was that not you I saw wolfing down two double cheeseburgers last weekend?"

"I was refueling after my run."

Julia grinned. "How is your dad?" She hadn't

seen Gus or Evelyn since the night of their spring party. She'd wanted to drop in for a visit or cook them a meal, but she hadn't felt right. She didn't blame them for what had happened—that was all on Donovan—but she didn't feel ready to put it all behind her, either. If Donovan had just told her what was going on, maybe none of this would have happened. She liked to think she was reasonable, and once she'd gotten over the shock of learning that the restaurant was no longer for sale, she thought she would have at least been willing to listen.

"They're fine." Owen reached out to give her a brotherly punch on the shoulder. "They'd like to see you."

He'd told her this before, too, and Julia responded the way she always did. "Not yet."

And maybe not ever. Because every time she considered it, she remembered they weren't her family, no matter how much they'd all come to care for each other. In the end, they were people she'd known for only weeks as opposed to years. And it was better to cut the ties quickly and firmly before she found herself entangled in a world of hurt, having to pretend she didn't mind hearing about Donovan's new girlfriend or wife or family. Because she would. She totally would.

"I'm thinking of taking a trip to Paris." She wasn't—she was trying to save money wherever and whenever she could—but it seemed a good way to change the subject.

"Are you asking me to join you?" Owen pretended to give the matter serious thought. "Because while I think it's a little romantic for friends, it would piss off my brother to no end. So I'm in."

That actually got a small smile from her. Julia didn't like to think of herself as a petty person, but there were nights she dreamed up revenge fantasies that would leave Donovan as pained as her. Though she and Owen saw each other regularly, she never asked about Donovan. Afraid to hear that he was fine, their breakup a mere blip in his golden life.

Still, she didn't want to encourage further discord between the brothers. "That's sweet of you to offer, but this is a solo trip."

"Sweet, nothing." Owen took a swig of his water. "I'm serious, you know."

Julia could tell from his expression that he was telling the truth. She shook her head. A return to Paris would be full of memories both bitter and sweet, and it was a pilgrimage she needed to make on her own. If she were actually planning to go…

"Enough about me," she said. "How's the dating life? I didn't expect to hear from you on your night off."

Owen shrugged. "You ever heard the term *revirginized*? Well, I left that station a while ago."

She felt her eyebrows pop into the center of her forehead. "I think that term is only for women."

"Are you questioning the legitimacy of my sex status?"

Julia snickered. "No, but I find it hard to believe that you can't find a date."

"I didn't say I couldn't, just that I haven't." Owen shrugged again. "I've been putting in a lot of extra hours at the bar, so I haven't had time." He shook his head as though clearing it. "Wait. Did I just say that? I think I should be checked for sickness. Feel my forehead. Do I have a fever?"

Julia rolled her eyes but did as he asked, laying the back of her hand on his forehead. "No temperature. You're perfectly normal."

Owen caught her wrist. "Check again."

She tilted her head to look at him. Owen was touchy-feely and quick to turn to human contact for comfort, but this was something else. "Owen?" But he was already moving her hand back to his face to cup his cheek instead. "That's not going to tell me if you have a fever," she pointed out.

"No." He wasn't looking at her, his eyes focused on something to her left. "But it'll piss off my brother."

Julia turned to look and found a very scowly Donovan staring at the pair of them. "I thought you said he was out of town."

"He was. I guess he came back."

He certainly had and he was bearing down on them like a man on a mission.

EXACTLY WHAT WAS his brother doing with Julia? Donovan narrowed his eyes though he didn't know why. It wasn't an apparition or a nightmare vision in front of him; it was truth. His brother sitting with Julia, Julia touching him. And he probably shouldn't have been so surprised since both Mal and his mother had told him that Owen and Julia still saw each other.

But hearing about it and actually seeing it in living color were two different things. And though he knew there was nothing more between them than friendship, he couldn't stop his hands from curling into fists or his adrenaline from spiking, preparing to attack and defend what he thought of as his.

He heard the thud of his feet over the music playing in the bar. Saw the flash of bodies as they instinctively shifted out of his way, giving him a direct line to Julia. Felt the squeeze of his lungs as he got closer. Close enough to reach out and touch her, to stroke that velvety-soft skin, smell the light lemon perfume that she always wore.

He didn't. Instead, he glared at his brother, who was still holding Julia's hand. Owen didn't let go. In fact, Donovan watched as he wrapped his fingers more tightly around hers. "Donovan. How was your meeting?"

Donovan didn't want to talk about his meeting and he doubted Owen did, either. Unless it was to whine about the fact that he hadn't been included. His little brother was just trying to wind him up. It pissed him off that it was working.

"Mind if I join you?" He didn't wait for a response but plunked himself down beside Julia. He was pleased when she tugged her hand free of Owen's to smooth her dark hair.

Her scent rolled over him, reminding him of the many things he'd missed about her these past three weeks.

Her laugh, her kindness, her loyalty. The way she curled against him as if she belonged there. She wasn't doing any of that now. Her eyes were trained on the full glass of wine in front of her.

"How have you been?" Donovan wanted to reach out and turn her face toward him so he could see those pretty brown eyes. He didn't.

"Fine." Her tone was terse and she made no eye contact.

Well, he hadn't been fine. Even before his family could come down on him about his not telling her that they'd decided to keep La Petite Bouchée, he'd realized his error. But they'd come down on him anyway. And he'd let them. He deserved their censure. Nothing they said could compare to what he'd already said to himself.

And he'd come to realize that his insistence on keeping it all in the family was foolish. Julia wasn't some random investor looking to make a quick buck at the expense of quality. She loved the place more than he did, probably more than the entire Ford clan combined. It shouldn't have taken her quitting, leaving the restaurant and him behind, to make him realize it.

"Owen." He didn't look at his brother, keeping his focus on Julia, drinking her in. "Give us a minute."

He saw the corners of her mouth tighten, but she didn't say anything.

No, that cheerful refusal was all his brother's. "I'm fine where I am."

Donovan glanced over to see Owen stretching out as though planning to stay in the booth a good long while. His gaze, when he met Donovan's, was challenging, daring him to object.

Had he forgotten that Donovan was perfectly capable of physically removing him if need be? Because Donovan hadn't. "Owen."

But his brother ignored the growl in his tone and proceeded to ask Julia if she thought he should consider going blond for the summer.

Donovan snorted. Loudly. Did Owen think he

was fooling anyone? His moves were about as subtle as dying his hair blond would be.

"What?" Owen barely spared him a glance. "I'm looking to have some fun and you know what they say about blonds."

Donovan snorted again.

"You got something caught in your throat?" Owen asked. "Maybe you should go home and take care of it."

"I'm good." Donovan turned the full impact of the firstborn stare on his brother. "But you should feel free to leave anytime. Now would be good."

"Nope."

"Owen." Donovan heard the tightness in his voice, felt it in his throat and the way his fingers curled toward his palms.

"It's okay, Owen." Julia laid a hand on his forearm. It made Donovan a little jealous. "I can handle him."

Him. As though he was a stranger or an acquaintance whose name she couldn't be bothered to remember.

"You sure?" Owen hadn't moved yet. "He might be older, but he's not bigger than me anymore. And he's sure as hell not wiser."

Since that happened to be true in this particular instance, Donovan kept his mouth shut. But he shot his brother another sour look. Maybe if Owen stopped thinking about everything from his own biased perspective for one second, he'd see that Donovan was trying to fix things.

"I'm fine, Owen." She patted his arm. "Really. Go."

Owen waited another second, giving her the chance to change her mind, Donovan guessed, and then slipped out of the booth.

Donovan watched until he was out of earshot, then looked at Julia. She still wasn't looking back. She looked good, so good. God, he'd missed her. "You never answered my calls."

"I didn't." She didn't look up, just stared at the wineglass in front of her.

He'd stopped calling after the first week, when Owen had informed him that she was going to report him for stalking if he didn't back off. And yet, he couldn't help feeling that was wrong. It was wrong to push her, but it was wrong to back off, too. He felt stuck in a no-man's-land.

An awkward feeling crept up his neck. He rubbed it away, suddenly unsure how to start. He'd spent the past couple of weeks thinking about how to fix everything he'd broken. How he'd come to the realization that if she wanted the restaurant, he'd do his best to make that happen. The family had agreed immediately and without question, which had surprised him. Apparently, he was the only one who'd taken "family business" literally. But blurting all that out in a bar didn't seem right. Yet here he was.

He cleared his throat. "How've you been?"

Julia ran her thumb up and down the stem of her glass and didn't look at him. "Just tell me whatever it is you couldn't say in front of Owen."

"You in a rush?" He'd meant it as a joke, but saw from the tension in her shoulders that it wasn't. She was in a rush. To get away from him. That stung like a surprise punch to the nose.

"I'm not looking to linger." She pushed the glass away.

All right, then. He couldn't blame her. "I want to explain. About what happened." He ached to touch her. "I realized some things."

Finally, she looked up at him. But there wasn't anticipation or hope in her eyes. No, it was more straight-up disillusion. "If this is some 'Come to Jesus' moment you've had, that's great. But I don't want to hear about it." She slid toward the opposite side of the booth.

"Julia." She stopped sliding. Donovan ran a hand through his hair. "Maybe this isn't the right place. Can we go somewhere quieter?" Somewhere that didn't have his brother standing on the other side of the room, watching them like some Papa Bear ready to come to the rescue.

But Julia didn't need rescuing. "No, Donovan. You can tell me now or I'm leaving."

He didn't wait. She was already edging her way

down the booth away from him again. "I want you to come back to La Petite Bouchée."

"I already told you that I'm not interested in being another employee."

"Not just as chef." He took a deep breath. It had taken some time to work out the details, but he had. The truth was that although he'd come to love the restaurant, it was only because of Julia. Without her, the restaurant meant nothing to him. It was a box of brick and mortar. "I want you to have it."

Her eyebrows popped up and she stopped moving. "Have it?"

"Own it."

"What are you talking about?" She peered at him. "Are you drunk?"

"No." He'd never been more sober. "The restaurant is yours. It always has been."

"Not anymore."

Was that true? Donovan didn't think so. She might put on a brave face, but he noted the flicker of hope in her eyes, the hurried intake of breath at his words before her icy mask had fallen back into place. "It is. So how can we make this happen?"

It wasn't exactly the way he'd envisioned this conversation, but then, he hadn't expected to see her tonight, sitting in the bar with her hand on his brother's cheek.

He forced his fingers to uncurl. Owen and Julia

were friends. Nothing more. And it would be just like his brother to have engineered the scene just to get under his skin. To Donovan's consternation, Owen had taken Julia's side in this whole mess and told him on more than one occasion that Donovan was an idiot for letting her go.

Julia swallowed. Her tongue darted out to wet her lips. "This is a bit of a shock." She pushed her hair out of her face, exposing that long, slim neck.

Donovan curled his fingers into his palms, this time to keep from touching her. "But you still want to buy it, right?"

She looked down. "I'm not sure."

Now he was the one experiencing a bit of a shock. After everything, her quitting and breaking up with him, refusing to talk to him because of the restaurant, now she wasn't sure she wanted it? "What's changed?"

Julia shrugged. "Nothing. And everything." She slid the rest of the way out of the booth and stood up.

"You're leaving?" Of all the reactions he'd thought she might have, leaving hadn't been one of them.

She nodded, her dark hair spilling across her shoulders. "I don't see any point in staying."

"But…" He'd thought they'd talk about it, determine options, price and, once he'd made it clear there were no strings attached, he'd ask if he could see her again.

"I have a lot to think about."

He swallowed all his questions, all his thoughts. She was right—she did have a lot to think about. "So you're going to consider it?"

"Yes, but that doesn't mean I'm going to buy it. I'll let you know."

She walked off, stopping only to give Owen a hug before sauntering out without a backward glance. And Donovan knew because he didn't take his eyes off her until she was out of sight.

OH, GOD. JULIA felt as if she couldn't breathe. Had felt that way since Donovan had informed her last night that La Petite Bouchée could be hers if she wanted it.

But that was the million-dollar question: Did she still want it?

She flipped the pancakes on her griddle and checked the crispness of the bacon, her mind on her dilemma. Accept Donovan's offer and whatever that entailed. Oh, sure, he said there was nothing hidden, but she wasn't a fool. They'd be doing business together, which meant contact, and they'd always be linked even if it was just that she'd bought La Petite Bouchée from him.

Or she could turn down the offer. No restaurant. No relationship. But the freedom to start fresh wherever she wanted. She wouldn't even have to stay in the city.

But the thought of leaving Vancouver held limited appeal. Sure, she'd be able to avoid Donovan more easily. But she'd risk losing Sasha and Owen, along with the rest of the team at La Petite Bouchée, whom she planned to scoop once she had her own restaurant. And she'd definitely lose her investors, who were strictly interested in a local purchase.

"Egg Whites is here. Three-egg, vegetarian. No bacon. Whole wheat." The server made a verbal fire rather than entering it into the ticket machine.

Julia knew this was just because they liked razzing her about her fancy friend and his fancy order. When she'd told Owen his nickname in the kitchen, he'd howled with laughter. The Sun Café wasn't the kind of place to have egg whites or anything heart smart on the menu. It was the kind of place you came after a night of drinking to soak up the excess alcohol or to indulge in something fatty and delicious before going on a two-hour run to burn it all off.

"Egg whites," she called back to acknowledge the verbal ticket. She checked her pancakes, turned them onto a prewarmed plate, added the bacon, a dollop of whipped butter and a mint leaf and placed them in the pickup window with a ding of the bell. "Order up."

She always found something satisfying about hitting the bell. A sense of completion of a job well done. And it was just fun to give it a sharp smack on a busy morning.

Julia finished the rest of her orders and then dished up Owen's breakfast and pulled off her apron. He always arrived at the end of her shift so she could sit and visit with him.

She carried the plate and a fresh carafe of coffee, her eyes scanning the room until she found him.

He wasn't alone.

"Donovan." His name felt awkward in her mouth. Or maybe that was just the flush of nerves warming her face. At least she'd have a good excuse if either of them noticed. She had just been standing over a sizzling griddle.

But no one mentioned her cheeks or the spot of pancake batter that dotted her shirt, somehow finding its way past her protective apron. She wished now she'd left it on as a guard against whatever was about to happen.

She set the plate in front of Owen. Cups and saucers were already on the table, and she flipped three over and poured the coffee before sitting down in the chair across from Donovan. She'd selected it with the intention of sitting as far away as she could, but she wondered if that had been an error. Because now she had to look at him.

Her lungs tightened. "I haven't decided any-thing," she told him, hoping he might scuttle off to a business meeting or really anywhere but here.

Donovan nodded. "I hope you don't mind that I'm here. Owen mentioned—"

"He followed me," Owen said. "I didn't invite him."

Donovan frowned at his brother. "I called you to see if we could meet this morning and you said you were coming here."

"You'll note there was no invitation extended, just a factual recitation of my morning plans." Owen shot her an apologetic look.

Julia drank her coffee. Owen had nothing to be sorry about. It was a free country and Dono-van could come into her workplace as a patron if he wanted.

"Regardless—" Donovan's tone made clear that he no longer wanted to discuss how he'd arrived at the diner "—I hoped I might have a word with Julia."

"I think we covered that last night." She put her cup down carefully so it didn't rattle the saucer. And she'd given his offer further thought since then. But it wasn't as simple as it had been three weeks ago. When she'd thought she and Dono-van had something special. When she'd thought she could trust him.

"I have more to say."

The way he looked at her made Julia feel as though there was no one else in the room. No customers chowing down on bacon, eggs and hash browns. No coworkers who were certainly wondering who the guy with Egg Whites was. No Owen watching the subtlety of every move.

Just her and Donovan. The way it had been.

Suddenly, she just wanted to get away, but she feared that would create more problems instead of solving them. So she stayed where she was, back pressed into the nubby material of the chair, and reminded herself to breathe.

But Donovan didn't say anything. He simply sat there sipping his coffee and studying her between glances that were clearly intended to hurry his brother along. Owen, contrary as ever when it came to Donovan, refused to be rushed. He was slow to fork up each bite and made a point of savoring every morsel.

"You've outdone yourself, Jules."

She refrained from rolling her eyes at the over-the-top praise since he was only doing it to support her. "Glad you're enjoying it."

"I am. I so am." And judging from the small smirk in his brother's direction, Owen wasn't only enjoying his egg whites.

But eventually, the egg whites were eaten along with the toast, and the coffee carafe was emptied.

"Done?" Donovan asked. It was the first thing he'd said in fifteen minutes.

"The food." Owen leaned back and patted his stomach. "But I still have to digest. It's not safe to leave on a full stomach."

"That's swimming. You're done."

"I think I'll stay."

But this time Donovan didn't scowl. He faced his brother. "I need to have this conversation with Julia privately."

She heard the plea in his tone and Owen must have, too, because he turned to her and asked, "Okay?"

Julia wasn't certain, but she nodded anyway. Donovan wasn't going to let her go without saying his piece. It was best just to let him say it.

Still, the coffee in her stomach roiled when Owen exited the diner, leaving her alone with Donovan, his offer and the unwanted attraction that still simmered between them.

Well, she wouldn't give in to it. Not even if he begged. The image of Donovan on his knees between her thighs flashed through her head. Okay, maybe if he begged. But she would still have to think about the offer of sale of the restaurant.

She took a slow breath and focused on the reason he was here, the reason she was, too. "I'll just tell you now that I'm still thinking about your offer, but I haven't made a decision. So if this is another high-pressure sales job, we can both go."

His eyes were dark and watchful. She saw his hand flick toward her and then drop back into his lap as though he'd thought better of the situation. "It's not about the restaurant."

That image flashed through her mind again, sent color back into her cheeks. She tried to cover it with a sip of coffee.

"It's about us."

Julia put the cup down, forgetting to think about the clatter, the tremor that rocked through her at his words. "There is no us." She certainly hadn't forgotten that. The easy way he'd chosen business over her.

He didn't argue, just studied her, which was more powerful than any rebuttal could have been. She was glad the cup was safely in its saucer or else she might have been wearing the coffee instead of drinking it.

She wanted to rise up like a powerful goddess of the sea, and walk away, but she felt glued to her seat, to her own indecision and his stare. "What do you want, Donovan?"

"I think we both know the answer to that."

"Actually, we don't. Which is why I'm asking you to clarify."

For a moment, his eyes darkened, filled with that deep heat that had always preceded him lowering his head for a hot kiss or peeling her out of her clothes. She felt the pull of desire, the one that she wished she could snuff out as easily as flicking off the gas flame on a stove. "I want you."

Julia's breath caught. She shook off the inclination to go to him, to touch and hold and allow him to kiss away all her hurts. "I'm not a product available for purchase."

"No, you aren't. But that doesn't mean I don't want you."

She didn't say anything. She wanted to look away, to look at anything but him. Her eyes stayed locked on his.

"If that's not an option, then I want you to have La Petite Bouchée."

Julia swallowed. She really needed a sip of that coffee, but her shaking hands made that impossible. She clasped them together in her lap, digging her fingers into the backs in an attempt to gain hold of her roiling emotions. "I told you I need to think about that."

"Why?" There was no underlying note of whining or irritation in his question. Just simple curiosity.

"Because I do." Because she feared that accepting the offer would be accepting him, too, and she didn't know if she could handle that. He'd burned her once. Could she trust him not to do it again?

"Julia, La Petite Bouchée is your dream."

But was it? She'd been thinking about that, too. Yes, La Petite Bouchée reminded her of her mother, of the loving relationship they'd had. But did she really need the restaurant for that? She had her memories, her photographs, her love of food. All of those were part of her mother's legacy. "You know, I'm not sure that it is." She saw his blink of surprise. "I want to own a restaurant, yes. That dream hasn't changed, but I'm not sure it needs to be La Petite Bouchée."

He scratched the side of his jaw, then shook his head. "I'm not buying it. You love that restaurant."

"Buy whatever you want. I'm not for sale."

"Is that what you think? That I'm trying to buy you?"

She hadn't, not consciously, but now that he'd put it out there, she wondered if that hadn't been hiding in the back of her mind, just waiting for a chance to surge to the forefront. She shrugged. "I don't know what you're trying to do, Donovan. I'm only telling you my own thoughts on the matter."

"If not La Petite Bouchée, then what? You have something else lined up?"

"No." She couldn't bring herself to lie to him. "But I will. My investors are motivated and we're actively looking for the right space."

"I'm offering you the right space." He ran a

hand through his hair. "I don't understand you. A month ago, this was all you wanted."

"A month ago, I thought you trusted me. I thought we were a team."

"We were." His hand moved across the table and this time he didn't stop. She didn't meet him halfway, not even a tenth of the way. She leaned back in her seat, staying out of range unless he were to get up out of his seat and come around. He didn't pull back, just remained in the same position, palms facing up, a silent plea for her. "We could be again."

She steeled her heart. "No, Donovan. We couldn't."

"We could." His eyes caught hers and held. Reminded her of how he'd made her feel like something precious. "I've missed you. I want to fix this. All of this."

Her eyes prickled and she blinked rapidly to prevent tears from rising. "I can't do this, Donovan."

"Do what?"

"This." She waved a hand between them. "All of this. It clouds my judgment. I need to figure out what I want on my own." Maybe if she'd done that in the first place, considered her own wants and needs instead of simply assuming that she needed to follow in her mother's footsteps, she wouldn't be in this situation now.

"You've had almost a month."

She nodded. "I know. But I need more time."

"Julia."

She held her breath, afraid that if he pushed, if he came around the table and took her in his arms, she'd crumble. She'd let those raging emotions—the ones that reminded her she loved him, too, and that people made mistakes and that everything from his body language to his actions showed that he was being sincere—take over.

But he didn't. He simply watched her, his expression so open and transparent that she'd have to actively choose to ignore what was there. "How long?"

It took a moment for his words to sink in and her heart to start beating again. "I don't know." She really didn't. Her mind was so frazzled that she couldn't think. A minute, a day, a decade? "I'm sorry, Donovan. I'd tell you if I knew."

He nodded slowly. "Okay."

But it didn't feel okay. And sitting there, his gaze on her, knowing that all she had to do was reach out to have everything she'd wanted so badly only a few weeks earlier, scared her. Because what if she'd been wrong a month ago? What if his presence, so prominent and potent, had confused her into making the wrong choice?

Suddenly, her flippant remark to Owen about heading to Paris for some R & R didn't seem so crazy. In fact, it was starting to sound pretty good.

True, she was saving up to ensure a larger piece of whatever restaurant she decided to buy, but more important than that was making sure she chose the right restaurant. And with La Petite Bouchée back in the game and Donovan pushing hard, she wasn't sure she could make an unbiased decision. Not in Vancouver, where it was too easy for him to find her.

And although he'd indicated that he'd give her time, Donovan Ford wasn't the type to sit back and let things happen. No, he'd be in there directing and guiding to ensure the outcome he wanted. She knew he would. The same way he'd slowly inserted himself into her life until it seemed he'd always been a part of it. He'd do it again. And she'd let him because she still loved him.

Oh, God. She *loved* him. And he'd betrayed her.

She took a long walk home, wandering along the sidewalks, eyes skipping past the cheery trees springing into bloom, the daffodils bursting from the ground. All she could think was that she still loved him. But she didn't know if she could trust him.

Her legs were tired when she finally walked up to the apartment, but her mind refused to shut down. Spinning and spinning, going over the same things she'd already thought of a thousand times until she felt as if she was caught in some sort of tornado.

And she knew what she needed to do to get her thoughts in order.

It was easy to buy a same-day ticket as a single traveler. Before the sun had even set, Julia had packed a carry-on bag, printed off a ticket, grabbed her passport and headed to Vancouver International Airport. She made two phone calls from the cab. One to The Sun Café to tell them that she wouldn't be in for the rest of the week. And one to Sasha so that someone would know where she was.

She considered calling Owen but decided against it. Yes, he'd been fully supportive of her, but he'd also brought Donovan to her workplace. And she knew Owen wanted her to go back to La Petite Bouchée. But she wasn't ready to make that decision. Not yet.

As she watched the city disappear below, she felt some of her concerns slip away, and by the time they neared Orly airport ten hours later, she almost could believe she'd left them behind in Vancouver along with most of her clothes. And she knew she'd made the right decision to get away from everything in that city, the confusion, the worry, the love, and go back to the place where she'd first found herself.

Paris.

Where she'd learned about herself, found her own personal space in the world and grown as both a chef and person. In Paris, she could just be herself. She could inhale the culture, the language, the food and wine, and those would help her uncover what she needed to move forward.

The plane bumped down, the jolt lurching Julia up and down. Much like life in general. The plane unloaded, dropping her off into a world she well knew and still loved. Julia probably could have called one of her old friends, any number of her former coworkers who still called the City of Light home, and found one who would be happy to put her up for a few days. But she didn't want contact with anybody. Even the well-meaning chatter and questions of people unattached to the business might influence her.

Julia knew this was a decision she needed to make on her own.

She booked herself into a small room in a good hotel in the First Arondissement, in the heart of Paris. Although she'd flown through what was nighttime in Vancouver, she'd been unable to sleep. Probably a good thing, as it was evening in Paris now. The smell of the Seine, the twinkling lights that gave the city its nickname. She needed to go out and live it, reset to European time and lose herself. If only for tonight.

But she'd promised to call Sasha upon her arrival, and even though she didn't feel like chatting, Sasha had always been a good friend to her.

If all she asked was for Julia to check in, then she would. She even tried to fake some good cheer when Sasha answered.

"I'm okay," she told Sasha even though she still didn't feel okay.

"Oh, Jules." Sasha sounded sad and worried. "Are you sure?"

"I'm sure." Her throat was thick with pain and disappointment. Julia feared she might actually drown in her own tears. "I just needed to get away."

"I don't see why you had to go all the way to Paris," Sasha said. Her voice sounded tinny or maybe that was the ringing in Julia's ears. "What's wrong with Seattle? Or Whistler?" Whistler. Where she and Donovan had decided to start fresh. Julia's eyes prickled.

"I wanted space." Almost five thousand miles' worth, please.

"You could have come and stayed with me."

Julia didn't point out that staying with someone else would have been the opposite of space. "I appreciate the offer, but I need to figure this out on my own." Needed to see what her feelings were when uninfluenced by the needs and wants of everyone around her, which she couldn't do when she was surrounded by them. Even if they meant well.

"Jules, I'm worried about you."

Julia was worried about herself, but she pasted on a smile, choosing to believe the theory that it would be audible in her voice. "I'm going to be fine. I just need a few days and then I'll be back." And hopefully she would have everything figured out. Or at least her next step. Which didn't seem too much to ask. "I'll be fine. How are you? Everything still good at the restaurant?"

It hurt to ask about La Petite Bouchée. In fact, she rarely did, but it was one way to get Sasha talking about something other than Julia's tender heart.

"Everything is fine, though we're all still waiting for you to realize you belong here." There was a whiny note to Sasha's voice. She'd been acting as executive chef since Julia's departure, but she had no interest in running her own kitchen. She preferred to be the next person in line, which gave her almost all of the same respect and almost none of the same responsibilities. "Last night was a gong show. An absolute gong show."

There were times Julia wondered if Sasha didn't have the right idea. Sasha never ached for more, worried about the customer base, took work home with her. She came in, cooked her ass off and left. If Sasha were in Paris, she certainly wouldn't be concerned about the restaurant. She'd be out shopping on the boulevards and making friends with the locals. "I'm sure you were fantastic."

"I was. But I didn't want to be. Come back. This is where you're meant to be."

But Julia was no longer sure that was true. "Maybe, maybe not. That's what I'm here to figure out."

Julia reassured Sasha again that she was okay and then hung up. She changed out of the pants and sweater she'd worn on the plane and into something clean. Fitted black leggings, a loose black-and-white-striped T-shirt with a bright blue sweater.

But if she hoped that all her fears and worries would fall away in clean clothes, in a new city, she'd been mistaken. They still weighed down her shoulders, made her steps heavy as she traversed the cobblestone streets and sidewalks. Still, she soldiered on. She hadn't dipped into her tiny and hard-earned nest egg only to mope around the entire time.

Paris at any time of year was gorgeous. It was magical whether dusted with snow in winter, during the heat of summer when everyone grew tanned under the bright sun or in autumn as the land and people prepared for the cooler weather. But Julia had always loved Paris in spring. The blue, blue sky, the tree-lined streets, the glitter from the fountains and ponds that dotted the cityscape as the city and everyone in it seemed to bloom.

And on an early-spring evening, Paris glimmered. Too elegant and classy to shake and shimmy, she simply glowed with vivacity and taste. Like a perfectly cut diamond, well aware of her innate beauty and happy to display it to the world.

In her casual outfit with some dangling silver earrings and a bangle bracelet at her wrist, her hair swept back in a loose knot, Julia decided to enjoy it. The trip didn't have to be solely about deciding her future. She could try out some new restaurants and visit some of her old haunts to see which parts of the menu had changed. She could take a trip to the top of the Eiffel Tower or visit Versailles. Two things she hadn't done when she lived here because they'd seemed too touristy and gauche. But she wasn't trying to impress any local-born colleagues now.

She could take the Metro into Montmartre and let one of the local artists sketch her portrait. Take a dinner-boat tour on the Seine and walk along the Champs-Élysées. Indulge herself for the first time in months and figure out exactly what she wanted from life.

She walked for a few blocks, bypassing cafés and bistros until she got to one of her old favorites. She did want to try new things, but not tonight.

Tonight, she wanted to go somewhere she'd been many times before, a place she could trust when it came to food and drink. It didn't disappoint and she allowed herself to get lost in the flavors. Instead of picking apart each bite, trying to pinpoint each of the ingredients and their ratios, she simply ate.

She lingered over her meal as did the other patrons. In France, people knew how to enjoy their meals, slowly savoring each bite.

It seemed nothing had changed. Nothing except her. But she pushed that thought away and enjoyed her meal and the small decanter of wine she drank with it. She wandered back to her hotel, feeling full if not wholly satisfied. She wanted to feel satisfied, wanted to feel that this had been the right decision, the right place to go. Instead, she fell asleep wondering if she was ever going to feel right again.

CHAPTER FOURTEEN

DONOVAN TRIED CALLING Julia's cell phone before he left the office the next day, but it went straight to voice mail. She'd probably forgotten to charge it again. On the plus side, her inbox wasn't full, so he left a message on the off chance she'd think to check it. He considered calling La Petite Bouchée, but was pretty sure that Sasha would be less than thrilled to hear from him. She might technically be an employee, but she was also Julia's best friend. And Donovan knew which one was more important to her.

When he got home, he changed out of his suit and into jeans and a T-shirt. He could casually drop by her apartment, though really there would be nothing casual about it. And they'd both know that.

Donovan exhaled. He'd told Julia that he'd give her some time, even though it felt like the wrong thing to do. He'd given her time before and he was pretty sure it had made things worse. If they'd talked, maybe he would have realized sooner what an idiot he was being. Maybe she'd already be back heading up the restaurant kitchen, back in his arms.

But he'd said he'd give her some time. And now he didn't know what to do with himself. He didn't want to go back to the office, didn't feel like sitting around at Elephants or one of the other bars, but he didn't want to stay home, either.

He got into his car, and drove to his parents', thinking he could hit them up for a family dinner, but they'd eaten early and were sitting in the backyard waiting for some sort of night plant to bloom. He'd declined the invitation to stay. He was desperate, but not that desperate.

Donovan would never have believed it, but his father actually seemed to like mucking around in the garden. Gus had even started to talk about growing his own lettuce and cucumbers, though there was some sort of disagreement about that with his mother, who claimed that she wasn't giving up the plot where her peonies were located.

He left the two of them discussing it in the backyard and got back on the road. But he still didn't feel like going home. His stomach growled. And he was starving.

He turned the wheel and headed to La Petite Bouchée. He wasn't expecting to see Julia there. As far as he'd been able to discern, she hadn't been back since she quit. He didn't know why that hurt him as much as it did. Maybe because he knew how much she loved the space and felt as though he'd ripped it away from her.

The hostess brightened when he walked through the door. "Mr. Ford. Do you need a table tonight?"

"Thanks, but I'll just grab a seat at the bar."

"Of course. I'll let the kitchen know you're here."

"No, that…" But the perky hostess was already moving toward the kitchen, obviously thinking she was fulfilling her duties. Donovan sighed. She probably was.

The dining room was full, as it was most nights, according to Owen. He dropped in regularly to check on the staff. It was just one more thing he'd taken on of late. Donovan knew Owen was changing—had changed. It was just hard to believe that it would be permanent this time.

He greeted Stef with a nod. But maybe it was time to give Owen a larger role. Not too much, more of a gradual adding of responsibilities, but a larger role than the one he had today.

Donovan found a stool and hunkered down, but didn't feel the satisfaction that normally came from taking what had been his usual spot only a month earlier. Yes, it was still his restaurant, but it felt empty without Julia.

He ordered the special and a beer. He sipped while he waited for his plate to come out, and was surprised when it was hand-delivered by Sasha.

"Donovan." She put the plate in front of him and pulled up a stool. "Julia's not here."

"I know. I'm just here to eat." But he didn't pick up his fork, didn't even glance at the plate of food. "Have you talked to her?"

Sasha nodded.

"And?"

"And she's not here."

Donovan looked at the plate. It was visually perfect, worthy of a magazine ad. He still didn't make a move to taste it. "Is she okay?"

Sasha sighed and laid a hand on his shoulder. "Oh, Donovan."

It surprised him, the easy casualness of her gesture. He'd expected she'd be mad at him, too. Which was one of the reasons he'd avoided the restaurant until now. "You're not mad at me?"

"No, I'm still pissed at you." She smiled, which took the sting out of her words. "But I can tell you're hurting."

He was hurting. Not a quick jab like the kicks Owen used to deliver to his shins when they were kids, but a bone-deep throb that took over his entire body. "Just tell me that she's okay."

Sasha looked back at him with massive green eyes. She was a stunning woman, and one a man would have to be blind not to notice, but Donovan barely spared that a moment's thought. He preferred dark eyes with a thick fringe of lashes that looked up at him in bed. Or down at him, depending on their position. "She's fine. Well, not fine. But you know what I mean."

Donovan did know. Julia was hurting because of him. A level of sickness joined his pain. He hadn't meant to hurt her. He thought he'd been doing the right thing for the business and the family. But maybe he'd gotten too wrapped up in the business. No, there was no *maybe* about it. "I feel like I didn't really explain myself." He'd focused mainly on the business, but that had been a mistake because the important part of all of this was him and Julia. The business was only that.

"Well, I guess you'll have to wait until she's back to tell her that."

"Back? Where did she go?"

Sasha got a panicked look on her face. "I did not say that."

"Yes, you did."

"No. Nothing to see here. Move along." She shooed her hands at him.

"Can I eat first?"

"Fine, fine." She hopped off the stool. "I need to get back to the kitchen."

Donovan watched her go. So Julia was away. Out of town, presumably. He forked up a bite of fish. It was good, though not as good as when Julia had been cooking. Of course, he was a little biased.

He wondered where Julia might have gone. Clearly, Sasha wasn't going to tell, but she wasn't the only person he knew who was close to Julia. If he knew where she'd gone, he might get a hint of her state of mind. Whistler? Maybe she was thinking about him, remembering how much fun they'd had up there. Over to Vancouver Island? She might be sourcing out local suppliers in preparation for accepting his offer. Alaska? Probably planning to freeze him out forever or find a hungry-looking polar bear.

He pulled out his phone and punched in his brother's number.

Owen answered his call with a cheerful greeting that Donovan didn't return. Donovan cut right to the chase. "Did you know Julia was leaving town?"

"What?" Bar sounds came through the phone. Donovan recognized the sounds of Elephants, the low jazz music and the particular jingle of glassware. "She didn't say anything to me about it. Where did she go?"

"I was hoping you could tell me."

The bar sounds quieted as though Owen had walked off the floor and into the manager's office. "Is everything okay?"

"Not really."

"Ah." Donovan heard the satisfaction curl through

his brother's voice. "So you've finally realized that you were an asshat to let her go."

"Better late than never."

"Okay, it ruins all the fun if you just admit it." Owen's tone grew serious. "I'll call her."

"Would you?" Donovan knew it was a lot to ask.

"Of course." Donovan appreciated his brother's honesty and loyalty. Maybe Owen had grown up more than he'd realized. "Don't get me wrong. I still think you're an idiot, but I know you care about her, and God knows why, but she cares about you, too."

"I think Sasha knows where she is."

Owen was quiet for a moment. "She probably won't tell."

"I know."

"A woman thing."

"Yep."

"All right, give me some time and I'll see what I can dig up."

Donovan swallowed the lump that rose in his throat. "Thanks, Owen."

He hung up and went home. Donovan didn't rest, though. He was lying in his bed wide awake, feeling how big and empty it felt when Julia wasn't there with him, when his phone rang. He picked it up from his nightstand and looked at the screen.

But it wasn't Julia's number; it was his brother. He answered. "Yeah?"

"I talked to Sasha. She went to Paris."

"Paris?"

"She caught a flight out last night."

"And Sasha just willingly gave up this information?" Donovan couldn't help but wonder if this was a cover and Julia was really at her apartment, tucked securely into her bed.

"Donovan." Owen's voice was patient, as if he was talking to a young, not particularly bright child. "I'm friends with Julia, too, which Sasha knows. So I only tell you this because I trust you to do the right thing with the information."

"And that is?"

"Get on a plane and bring her back."

Donovan was stunned. "Really?"

"Yes, really. You're both miserable without each other. So go fix it."

He wanted to. Oh, how he wanted to. "I told her I'd give her some time."

"And normally, I'd tell you to honor that, but I think she needs to see you. I think you need to tell her how you feel. No more business, Donovan. Tell her how you feel."

Donovan swallowed. Would she listen? "Do you think it'll be that easy?"

Owen laughed. "I don't think it'll be easy at all. If she doesn't make you work for it, I'll be disappointed. But she's happier with you. I already checked. The earliest flight leaves at two tomorrow afternoon. I've booked you on it."

And if Donovan didn't exactly smile, he felt as if he was on his way to smiling. "I don't say this very often, Owen. But good work."

"Aw, I think I just teared up."

This time, Donovan did smile.

CHAPTER FIFTEEN

JULIA SPENT HER second and third days in Paris
seeing the sights. The air was thick and hot. She
could taste it when she breathed. Her head felt
heavy. She hadn't slept well, plagued by restless
dreams and thoughts of the restaurant.

Officially, it wasn't her restaurant, but still. Her
heart hurt. She hadn't realized just how much letting go of La Petite Bouchée had been eating at
her until now.

She visited the Louvre, then walked through
the Tuileries Garden, eating a baguette sandwich
she bought from one of the food carts. There was
peace in the moment, eating the fresh bread, which
always tasted better in Paris, soaking in the sun
and greenery. Some of her tension lessened.

She found a seat on a bench and watched the
people strolling by. The tourists with their thick-
soled sneakers for a day of walking, phones out
the whole time as they snapped pictures of the
various sights and gushed over the beauty of the
city. The locals in their slick European style, looking effortlessly elegant despite the warm day.

She could live here, Julia realized. She'd been happy here before and she could be again. She still had contacts in the city and two years' experience of running her own kitchen. She could pack up everything she owned and move back.

Her eyes tracked a fiftysomething man, his dark hair graying at the temples, dark eyes focused on the path in front of him as he hurried through the park. He could be her father. As could the man walking in the opposite direction, with the kind smile and wrinkles around his eyes.

It was a game she sometimes played with herself. Wondering if one of the strangers around her might actually be her family. Her mother had claimed her father was a born-and-raised Parisian and Julia had no reason to think she'd lied.

Anger rose in her chest. And now she had no one. Her mother had refused to ever tell her who her father was. Not a name, a description, his age, not even where they'd met. Julia suspected it meant he had another family—one her mother didn't want to upset with the introduction of a new daughter—but that hadn't been fair to Julia.

She had been left with no one. Maybe her father and his family—assuming they even existed— would have welcomed her. Maybe instead of staying at a hotel, she'd be visiting them in their city apartment, tucked under crisp sheets. Cooking them a late supper while they all sipped wine.

Julia could picture the scene and she wanted so much to be a part of it, to be a part of something, that her chest ached. But there was no chance of that dream coming true. She had no way of ever finding her father, and though she thought she'd come to grips with that years ago, it appeared there was a small part of her that hadn't.

She sighed. Great. She hadn't come to Paris to add to her misery, to flounder in being a poor little orphaned girl. And that wasn't entirely fair. She wasn't alone. Not exactly. She had Sasha and the staff at the restaurant. At least, she used to have them.

She pushed herself up and started walking again. She headed in no particular direction, just letting her feet carry her around while her mind whirred. She did have a family. Not a traditional nuclear family made up of a mother and father and siblings. But her team at the restaurant was loyal to her and she to them. They'd come with her to a new place; she knew that.

She'd been their leader and occasionally their maternal figure, advising them on personal decisions and pushing them to reach their full potential. Very few of them had left to take other jobs during the renovation. That was unusual in an industry where high staff turnover was both expected and planned for.

Julia curled her fingers into her palms. She

didn't want to give them up or to let them down. She'd done both. She walked a little faster, the heat making her light dress stick to her back, but she didn't slow down, afraid some of her thoughts might catch up to her.

It took the better part of the afternoon before Julia felt ready to sit down and think. She settled at a sidewalk café away from the touristy areas and ordered a light meal and a glass of wine. There would be no point to her trip if all she did was run away from herself.

It was time to face the facts. Something she'd known when she'd packed a small bag and boarded the plane to Paris. There was no easy answer. No quick solution that would make everything all better. But she needed to make a decision and stick with it.

The starter of fresh buttered bread stuck in her throat and she had to wash it down with a sip of her wine. Donovan claimed that he cared about her, that he wanted her to have La Petite Bouchée. But did he really care about her?

Her heart gave a painful thump. Maybe she was just a convenience. A woman he found enjoyable and attractive but not one worth changing his life for.

She took another sip of wine. It reminded her of the first time she'd tried it. It had been her twelfth birthday, and she'd been sitting in a bistro with her mom on their semiannual trip to France. Suzanne had allowed her a small sip as a special treat. Julia hadn't liked the taste, too sharp and full of tannins, but she'd pretended otherwise, wanting to appear mature and sophisticated, like her mother and the other people around them.

Her mother had thrown back her head and laughed. "It's a taste that grows on you," she'd said, her eyes twinkling.

And Julia had wondered why anyone would want that awful taste to grow on them. But she smiled now, recalling how her mother had leaned over and hugged her, told her how much she loved her and let her order whatever she wanted off the menu.

It had been a good trip. As all their trips to Paris had been. Walking along the river with her mom, ordering her first coffee the summer she was fourteen, the fresh pastries, and visiting the market. Julia exhaled.

The memories of her mother swamped her. Her laugh, the way she'd looked standing over a stove, stirring her pots, teaching Julia how to find the best and freshest product at the market. Her mother was in Paris. And La Petite Bouchée. More important, she was in Julia's heart.

Suzanne would have been disappointed in Julia now. That she'd picked up and left other people to handle the situation.

It wasn't as though she'd been left with nothing when she'd learned that the Fords were keeping La Petite Bouchée. She hadn't been bounced out without a reference or a paycheck. She'd still had a job.

And the cohesive marketing plan that Mal had designed had pushed her name into the minds of people both in and out of the industry. She was a draw, something that had clearly excited her investors, judging from the increased dollar amount they'd decided to put forward. If that was what she decided to do.

A new space. One that would be hers and hers alone. She didn't have to throw everything over and remake herself in a new, strange shape, but she didn't have to remain stuck in the past, either. She could ask the staff to work for her at her new restaurant. Sasha would come. The others would, too. And they could bring the traditions they'd started at La Petite Bouchée with them.

Assuming they wanted to come back. The guilt she'd been working so hard to rationalize since quitting swept through her. They'd been there for her when her mother died, had welcomed her easily, accepted her leadership and become her family in the process. And she'd repaid them by dropping out of their lives as soon as things got hard. She hadn't even called or asked Sasha if everyone was okay.

Julia exhaled again. She wouldn't blame them if they turned her down. A swift and firm "thanks, but no thanks" was probably what she deserved. But that didn't mean she had to give up. She'd thought her heart, her future, was with La Petite Bouchée and the staff there. But maybe it was elsewhere. Some new location that she'd yet to discover. Maybe with a new team that she'd yet to meet. Except for Sasha. Sasha would definitely come with her.

The remorse eased a little. Maybe she'd made a mistake by walking away from the restaurant without a fight, but it didn't have to affect the rest of her life in a negative way.

Just because things weren't working out the way she'd hoped, the way she'd planned, didn't mean her dreams were over.

She tore off another hunk of bread and smeared on a pat of butter, watching how it melted into the warm softness. Maybe it was being back in the place where she'd really come into her own as a chef. Where she'd learned why the way a food was cut was important, why certain flavors worked together, and rather than just parroting what she'd been taught in culinary school, she'd begun to understand and to change.

She could change. Yes, traditions could be great. They were classics for a reason, but that didn't mean there was no merit in something new. She could innovate and in doing so, respect the traditions of the past. In fact, wasn't that what she and Donovan had done at La Petite Bouchée? Blending the old with the new to make something that was both fresh *and* familiar?

Some of the anticipation burbling within her quieted at the thought of Donovan. She didn't know what to think about him. He'd given her so many things. Name recognition, the ability to shape her restaurant, a welcoming family, his body. But what about his heart?

Julia put down the bread she'd been about to finish, her stomach suddenly roiling. That was the problem bit. She didn't have his heart, but he had hers. After all her concerns about keeping their relationship professional, making sure she didn't get her personal life entangled with business, she'd dived in headfirst. Alone.

She rubbed a spot over her right eyebrow. She knew he cared for her. He'd said as much and his actions had backed up his words. But when it was crunch time, when things really mattered, he'd backed away. Left her without a safety net when all he had to do was reach out a hand.

Her breath grew shaky. Maybe it was better to know now, to realize that they were heading in very different directions. He'd go on to run a wildly successful family business and she would continue to grow the name and reputation of her restaurant, whether that was La Petite Bouchée or somewhere else.

She sipped her wine, let the liquid roll around on her palate before swallowing. It was the way of things in Paris. To sip and savor, to make every moment, every breath, count. Julia thought about her life the past two years. Leaving Europe to return to Vancouver, watching her mother die, taking over the restaurant and struggling to keep it afloat before Donovan and his family had come along.

There was a low throb in her stomach, the same mix of pain and pleasure as her life had been. And she realized that maybe she hadn't come to Paris to figure out her professional life but her personal one.

Any man she was going to be with had to be the kind of man she could count on, one who would do whatever he could to support her as she would support him in return. Not the kind who would tell her that it was just business and let her dreams crumble.

"Julia." She didn't turn when she heard her name. There was no reason to think anyone was calling her. She was traveling alone and no one other than Sasha knew she was here. But when the call came again, she swiveled her head.

And for just a moment, everything stopped.

Donovan Ford. In Paris. And coming straight for her.

CHAPTER SIXTEEN

DONOVAN COULDN'T BELIEVE he'd found her. In a city of over two million with who knew how many tourists roaming about, he'd found her. Julia.

Thanks to Owen—via Sasha—he knew where she was staying and the hotel proprietor had been more than happy to book him into a room on the same floor as Ms. Laurent. The cheerful little man had even recalled what Julia had been wearing when she left that morning.

Not that Donovan saw anything but her face when she turned to look at him, surprise registering in her eyes. She half rose to greet him, then seemed to stall, the surprise morphing into confusion.

He was filled with gratitude to be here. Glad she was only a few feet away and grateful he'd have her in his arms in less than a minute.

The restaurant bustled around them, people waving their hands as they talked, taking small, delicate bites of food, swilling wine and water in equal measures. Donovan ducked through the crowd, avoiding determined servers.

"Donovan? What are you doing here?"

"What does it look like?" He wrapped his arms around Julia, lifted her to a standing position and held on tight. "Thank God." Her body tensed and then relaxed into his. Donovan gripped her more tightly, inhaling her scent, feeling the whisper of her hair against his neck, the press of her chest to his. "Thank God I found you."

She cleared her throat. "I wasn't lost."

He disagreed. Maybe she hadn't been lost in the traditional sense, but she'd felt lost to him. "I wasn't going to let you get away again."

She pulled back to look at him, a small frown creating a line between her eyes. "Weren't you?"

How could she even ask that? Of course he wasn't. "No."

"I just needed some time, some space." But Donovan noticed she made no move to step out of his embrace. Good thing, too, because he wasn't letting go. "I had to figure things out."

"I thought you'd go for a walk around the Seawall or Stanley Park, not hop a flight to Europe."

A smile ghosted over her lips. It gave him hope. That there was still a chance for them. He'd done a lot of thinking on the flight. Had nothing else to do while he winged over North America and then the Atlantic.

"You never answered my question about why you came here," she said.

She shifted then, leaned back, but Donovan held on for one more squeeze before letting her go. When she sat, he did, too, and took hold of her hand, unwilling to lose contact. "I came to find you."

"I told you, I wasn't lost." That ghost of a smile again. Donovan smiled back.

He reached out to stroke her hair, then the shoulder of her dress, the pale peach material as delicate as gossamer. "Well, no. Not now that I've found you."

Hope lit her eyes and then dimmed. "Donovan." But she didn't finish her thought. She glanced away for a moment and then back to him. "How did you know where to find me?"

"Owen told me."

"Owen?" Her brow wrinkled. "I didn't tell Owen where I was."

"It doesn't matter. I'm here now." He clasped her hand in his. "And I have something else to say. Something that has nothing to do with the restaurant."

Donovan shuffled his chair closer to her and tugged her hand so she would lean in, would hear everything he had to say. The time was right, the warm evening, the spill of French around them, the scent of good food and the love in his heart so expansive that he couldn't keep it to himself any longer. When their heads were mere centimeters apart, he reached out to cup her cheek, running a thumb along her smooth, soft skin.

"I love you."

"Donovan." Her voice was a breath, a barely heard breath, and although she didn't respond in kind, he knew. By the darkening of her eyes, the way her mouth opened just slightly, her body turning more fully toward him. She loved him, too. Even after everything that had happened, she still loved him, too. Thank God.

He kissed her then. A light touch of lips that held a promise of more. Of later. Not just tonight, but every night. Because that was what he wanted with Julia. Everything. From this day forward.

"I love you and I want to make a life together."

She reached out a hand to touch his leg. He loved the way she touched him, firm and strong, the same way she gripped her chef's knife or hefted a pot from the stove. Julia wasn't a tall woman and despite the labor of her job, her arms didn't bulge with muscles, but she was strong. Inside and out.

He didn't know how many people could do what she'd done. Pick up and move to another continent, make a full life there and then come back to care for a dying parent. To hold a restaurant together while doing so and to keep pushing forward, keep dreaming no matter what happened.

His own father's heart attack had scared the

hell out of him. Donovan could well remember the fear that had climbed up his throat, choking him as they'd waited for the ambulance to arrive. Holding everything together to race over to his mother's house and pick her up since she'd been in no shape to drive herself to the hospital. And in the waiting room, those long hours ticking by at a snail's pace while the doctors rushed to save Gus, to keep his heart beating, while Donovan stayed strong, refusing to let his own worries and panic show while the rest of the family crumbled around him.

But they'd had each other. Had worse come to worst, which even now he didn't like to think about, they'd still have each other. A mother, a brother, a sister, aunts, uncles, cousins scattered around the city and the country who all would have come in their time of need.

But Julia? She'd had no one except the restaurant staff.

"Donovan," she started. Her fingers pressed hard into his leg as though she was gearing up for something. But her words stalled when the waiter came by and asked if *monsieur* was going to be eating, as well. Donovan nodded. He was starving. They'd fed him on the flight, but the meals were small and with the travel and time change, he felt as if he hadn't eaten in days.

Julia rattled off instructions in what sounded

like flawless French. Donovan could only assume they were since the waiter merely nodded and walked away.

Man, that was sexy. His gorgeous woman, in her beautiful dress, in a restaurant in Paris, speaking French with her hand still on his thigh. If Donovan hadn't already fallen, that continued connection would have done the trick because it told him everything he needed to know.

She looked at him. "This doesn't change anything."

"Yes, it does." He lifted her hand, linking their fingers together. "See?"

She pulled her hand free. "I still need to think. And I can't have you hovering over me, making me all confused."

He kissed her again. "Would it help if I admitted I've been an idiot?" Or what was the term Owen had used? "An asshat?"

A smile peeked out on her face. "It wouldn't hurt."

JULIA'S BRAIN WAS SPINNING. Donovan. In Paris. For her.

She turned her head to look at him as they walked down the long hall of the hotel to the closet-size bedrooms. "How did you know where I was staying?"

"Lucky guess."

"And you just happened to get a room on the same floor?"

"No, that was pure planning. I charmed the hotelier with my winning smile." He flashed it at her.

She pretended not to be affected. "And what would you have done if there hadn't been any rooms available? Set up a tent in the courtyard?"

He tilted his head. "I'd have considered it. Or I'd have asked if you might find it in your heart to share your room."

She didn't want to be won over by him. But it was hard—really hard. "Donovan."

"I love it when you say my name." He bent to give her a kiss on the side of the neck.

"Stop that." But she didn't step away or insist he do the same. Still, she wouldn't let him in her room when he would have followed. Not even when he gave her the sad eyes. She was stronger than Sasha, who had clearly sold her out. But she wasn't mad. "I'll see you in the morning," she told Donovan and then closed the door before her heart could soften.

He'd proved something to her. But Julia wasn't sure what to do about it. Could she trust him? Or had he already shown her that he didn't deserve her trust? She didn't know. People could change. They could learn from their mistakes. But had he?

Her room was small and sparse, but large enough

for one. She changed into a T-shirt and some sleep pants, but her mind refused to shut down. Not even when she counted sheep. In French. Up to one hundred.

When the knock came at her door, she almost wondered if she'd been expecting it because there had been no jolt of surprise, no wondering who might be there or what they might want. She knew.

Julia crossed the room and flipped the lock, opening the door to let Donovan inside. Just before she kissed him she said, "This doesn't change anything."

And after he'd kissed her back for a solid minute, he pulled his head back and said, "Yes, it does."

She kissed him again, not wanting to talk, just wanting to feel. The smallness of the room became more evident with Donovan in there with her, but it didn't feel cramped. It was cozy, pressing them closer and closer together, the fresh scent of linens on her bed and lemon cleaning products.

Donovan walked her farther into the room, his hands on her waist as he kissed his way along her collarbone. "I missed you."

"You said that before." But her argument came out muffled because he was kissing her again and wouldn't stop. Not to take off his shirt, not to slip her sleeping T-shirt over her head. Not to unbuckle his belt or take off his shoes. No, he managed to do all of that and kiss her breathless. The man had moves.

He didn't stop even when he lowered her onto the cool white sheets of her bed. Her entire body felt sensitized, each kiss lighting a flame in a different location. The sizzle worked its way from her toes out to her fingers. She rolled against him, reveling in the feel of skin on skin.

She'd missed him, too. Though she wasn't ready to admit out loud that she loved him.

Julia had thought she'd been in love before. The handsome Italian Paolo and his soft eyes; Guillaume, a French winemaker who used to take her down into the cellars and undress her with quiet endearments; Chris, her high school sweetheart. But there was something more to what she had with Donovan. Something deeper and scarier, which hooked into the quietest part of her.

She ran her hands up his back, caressing the bared skin and pressing his body more closely to hers. She wanted to feel him, every part of him against her, inside her. Her hand slid up the back of his neck to cup his head, pull his mouth to hers.

He tasted like wine and the chocolate mousse they'd shared for dessert at the restaurant. She shivered and pressed her tongue against his, tangling them together. As their lives were.

Julia felt a pull through her center. She ached

to be completely naked, to strip off the gold silk underwear she still wore, but that would mean letting go of Donovan. As much as she wanted the lingerie to join her clothes somewhere on the floor, she wanted to touch Donovan more.

The ripple of his abs against her stomach as he rocked into her, the crisp curly hairs on his legs as he settled between her thighs, and the smooth, polished feel of his shoulders.

"You taste like summer." Donovan's words whispered against her ear before he caught the lobe between his teeth.

"Coconut and lemonade?" she asked as she stretched, letting her muscles loosen.

"French summer." He kissed her again, his tongue dipping past her lips for a taste. "Crisp white wine, sunshine and heat." He bent his head to the crook of her neck and inhaled. "And you smell like lemons."

Julia shuddered under his ministrations, her body already warming under his touch, aching to let go. She slid the soles of her feet up the backs of his legs and back down. But Donovan didn't speed up. He didn't slow down, either, just kept up his steady, systematic pace that was sure to bring her a great deal of pleasure.

And she wanted that pleasure, to lose herself with him, on him, above him and deal with everything else later.

He slid one hand between her thighs. The thin material of her panties did little to prevent the transfer of heat and touch. "I meant what I said earlier."

"Oh?" She lifted her hips. "What's that?"

"I love you."

She blinked and gasped when he slid his hand back up her body to focus on her nipple, rubbing slowly and rhythmically. She arched her back, silently asking for more as her temperature increased. He lowered his head. She could feel his breath drift across her skin and make her other nipple pebble with need. "That's a pretty big declaration."

He lifted his head to look at her. "It's a pretty big feeling." He sucked her nipple into his mouth then, his eyes still watching her.

Julia gasped again. He loved her. He wanted her. And yet…she couldn't bring herself to say the same, even if she felt it deep in her heart. She ran her fingers through his hair, loving the silky strands as they spilled through her fingers. "Donovan."

"I want to start our lives now." He hovered over her, placed his hand on her heart. "Okay?"

She couldn't speak, couldn't even nod. He smiled a slow sexy smile that made her stomach flip and her limbs weaken. She reached for him, grabbing his biceps, pulling him to her, kissing his mouth, his neck, his chest.

He let her, keeping up a steady exploration of her body while she rained kisses all over him. Stroked her hands up and down his back, sliding beneath the waistband of his boxers and over the smooth globes of his ass.

Donovan rolled his hips into hers. His hard length pressed against her, making her want to strip her panties off herself and open her body to him. But he placed one hand on her hip, holding her still while he ran his tongue down the slope of her breast and sucked her nipple into his mouth.

Julia clutched his shoulders, holding on while he worshipped her.

"I want you." His words were quiet since his mouth was still pressed against her skin. "I want all of you."

"Donovan."

He hooked his thumbs in the sides of her underwear. And drew the expensive material over her hips.

He'd seen her naked before. Plenty of times, in fact, but this time felt different. As if he was seeing more, as if she was letting him. She lifted her hips off the mattress, brought her legs together so her underwear could join the rest of her clothing on the floor, and then let him nudge her knees open.

Julia saw the heat in his gaze, felt it as his eyes traveled up her legs, over her stomach, along her breasts to her face. He kissed her gently, taking his time, sucking on her lower lip and then letting it go. Dipping his tongue inside her mouth while he stroked the outside of her hip, occasionally running a hand across her stomach.

Desire bloomed. She wanted him to touch her, ached for him to slip a finger between her thighs and stroke the warm wetness there. But he didn't, concentrating on other, less obvious areas of her body.

The sensitive skin on the backs of her knees, the outside of her thighs, the spot between her breasts. Places that rarely felt the swipe of a tongue or the caress of a finger. Places that longed for such care, making her feel as though the blood in her veins had reduced to a thick, sweet caramel.

"Donovan, please." She dug her fingers into his scalp, moving restlessly beneath him. But he only smiled and kept up his relentless touching.

When he finally deigned to slide his hands to the sides of her breasts, push them together and run his tongue across her nipples, she almost came from relief. Seriously, she was going to burst, going to pop right open.

She spread her legs, tried to urge him to give her more, but he continued his assault on her breasts. First one nipple, then the other. And back again.

Julia moaned, felt her body soften further, readying itself for him. He sucked one nipple into his mouth and cupped her sex. She bucked her hips against his palm. He didn't move, waiting until she stilled, then slipped one finger inside her.

It wasn't enough. But it was good.

She moaned again, his name this time. Begging with her voice and her body. "Don't stop."

"Never." A second finger joined the first, curled up and pressed. Tiny darts of need shot through her, swelled when he slid down her body and added his tongue to the mix. He pumped his fingers in and out while his mouth circled the tiny button of pleasure at the apex of her thighs.

Julia squeezed her eyes shut, straining for what he offered, what was so close to being taken. She spread her legs wider, touched her own breasts, capturing the nipples and rolling them back and forth.

Her breath came faster, harder. She opened her eyes, looked down at him. His mouth buried against her, the shift and pull of his shoulder as he moved his fingers. And his eyes, watching, taking pleasure from her pleasure.

"Donovan." She came on his name, crying her release, her legs clamping around his head as the shaking took hold, took over, filling her with something much greater than desire or lust. An emotion deeper than need.

He slowed his pace gradually, eking out every bit of bliss. Careful not to push too far, to turn the pleasure into pain. Julia swore she saw stars. Sparkly fireworks that exploded on the backs of her eyelids, and the ceiling of the room.

She wanted to return the favor, to rub her body against him and give him the same gratification. But she couldn't move, not until she caught her breath and felt the control return to her limbs.

Donovan moved up her body, cupped the side of her face. "That was good for me." He pressed his lips to hers. "Was it good for you?"

She laughed, still a little breathless. "I'm not sure *good* covers it, but yes."

He laughed, too, gathered her up in his arms and rolled, carrying her with him so she was on top. She laid her head on his chest, listening as her pulse slowed.

"I might even show you just how good," she told him, toying with his nipple. "Just as soon as I can move without shaking." What was she playing at here? But every time she told herself to pull away, she looked at him and told herself that it was only for tonight. Just one more night.

She rolled off Donovan and onto her side. "Sit up," she told him, maneuvering him into place against the headboard. He let her do it, leaning back and allowing her to shift him into the position she wanted, pulling off his boxers and tossing them over her shoulder.

She straddled his hips and reached down to stroke his cock. It twitched, seeming to leap toward her. He'd been so patient, so good. She stroked him again, then slithered down his legs to roll her tongue around the head.

"Julia." Her name escaped from his lips. She rolled her tongue again and sucked him into the wet heat of her mouth, pressing the flat of her tongue against his length. His hands tangled in her hair and he exhaled. A long, low moan of satisfaction.

She took him deeper and deeper into her mouth, using her tongue and lips to give him greater pleasure. He put his hands on her head, gently at first, then gripping, his fingers catching in her hair, tensing as she hit her stride and found his ideal pace.

"Julia. I'm going to…"

She bobbed faster, felt the clench of his hands and knew she was right. He'd said he wanted all of her. Well, she wanted all of him, too. All of him and then some.

He swelled in her mouth and she sucked harder, not stopping or slowing until he came. Until he shuddered out his pleasure. She swallowed, but didn't move, letting her mouth continue to warm him, letting him come down slowly. His hands relaxed, one sliding around to rub the back of her neck.

Julia lifted her head then. "Well? Good for you?"

Donovan didn't answer, simply grasped her arms and hauled her against him, chest to chest, her legs around his while he kissed her hard. She felt him harden against her, his body rising to the occasion.

"And you said you weren't sixteen," she teased.

"I also said I wasn't dead." He kissed her again, harder, their mouths opening, tongues dancing together. His hands roamed across her back, pulling her closer while she ground herself against him.

God, she was crazy about him. And crazy to want more of him. She clutched at his shoulders, pressing as close to him as she could, feeling the roll of his body as he rocked toward her. "Do you have—"

"In my pants."

Julia looked over the edge of the bed, saw them lying there. He moved with her as she shifted to pick them up, one arm wrapped around her waist, pushing her hair off the back of her neck while he kissed her and she fished the foil packet from his pocket.

Donovan took it from her, settled back against the headboard while he ripped the package open and rolled the condom on. Julia felt her nipples tighten, watching the way he stroked himself, seeing how he grew in his hand.

"Come here." He grabbed her hand, hauled her on top of him, eagerness in every touch. Julia felt the same. She wanted to feel him inside her, his body sunk deep in hers. She gripped his shoulders and rose up. He sucked her breast into his mouth. Her hips rolled, an involuntary movement of need.

And then he was inside her, and her mouth was on his, sucking and licking. Kissing and moaning. He caught her bottom lip with his, dragged his teeth across it. Julia jerked against him, rocked faster, their bodies slapping together. She still wanted more.

She wrapped her arm around his back, gripped his hair in her hand. His fingers bit into her hips, urging her up and down, setting their pace faster and faster.

Julia leaned her head back to look at him, to see the look in his eyes while he pumped inside her. It was a mix of need and lust and something softer, something that made her slow.

"Julia?" Donovan's voice was quiet.

She shook off the feeling and tried to return to their previous pace. "It's fine. I'm fine." But now he slowed, his fingers spasming, then relaxing.

"You sure?"

She looked into his eyes, saw that softness there

again and knew it for what it was. Love. "I'm sure." She rose up and pressed down, slowly now.

He exhaled, cupped the back of her head and brought her mouth toward his. He kissed her more slowly now, too, longer and more intense. She shuddered and he leaned back. "I love you, Julia."

He did, too. She could see it in his eyes, feel it in the way he held her as if she was something fragile and precious. She didn't say anything. They rocked together, each stroke deeper than the last, more meaningful. Their foreheads pressed together as they looked into each other's eyes. She stroked up the side of his neck, ran a finger along his lips. He pressed a hand into her lower back, protecting and supporting.

And when they came, it was quiet. No shouts of release or groans as they finally let go. They came together, at almost the same time, each ripple drawing them closer, merging them more completely. Still looking into each other's eyes.

And then she asked him to leave.

"What the hell?"

Julia rolled off him and tugged the sheets up to cover herself. "I told you nothing had changed."

"Like hell it didn't." He loomed over her, all delightful manly nakedness. "I love you and I know you love me. You can't fake that."

"Actually—"

"No." He cut her off. "Don't make a joke about it. This is serious."

Julia pressed her lips together and swallowed. He was right. She might not be sure of her decision, of which feelings to trust, but that didn't mean she should belittle his. "You're right. Which is why I asked for some time."

"I'll give you time." He sat back. "I'll give you whatever you need."

"Oh? Is that why you kept calling and coming to my home? Why you barged in here?"

"I didn't barge." He stopped and ran a hand through his hair. "Did I seem like a stalker?"

Actually, he hadn't. "No, but it's been a month. And suddenly you reappear and want me to act like we're all good, like the past month never happened. I can't do that."

"I don't want you to pretend the past month never happened." His voice was low and serious. "I want to talk about it."

"About what?" She gathered the sheets more tightly around her, as if the thin material could protect her.

"I followed you here because I want to be with you." He reached out and ran a finger down her cheek. Julia shivered. "I want you to be happy. I needed to show you that."

He'd definitely shown her something. "Donovan." She reached out a hand to touch his shoulder.

He was still warm from their lovemaking. "I understand. I do. But you have to let me figure this out on my own."

He nodded, a short bob of his head. "About us, you mean."

"About everything. You, the restaurant, the future." Everything was too tangled up right now—her thoughts, her wants, her legs with Donovan's.

"I love you."

Her throat ached to say the words back. She didn't.

CHAPTER SEVENTEEN

IT HURT THAT Julia didn't say she loved him. But Donovan didn't push. It wouldn't be meaningful if he pushed.

Instead, he tugged lightly on the sheet she'd tucked under her arms to get her attention. "Julia." She leaned back against the headboard, closing her eyes. But Donovan wasn't so easily denied. He'd flown more than half a day to get here, so a pair of closed eyes wasn't going to stop him.

He knew he could keep pushing, could insist that she tell him what was going through her head, her concerns and fears, and then explain that he could help her with all of that. Or he could try a different tactic.

He ran a hand up and down her arm. He never grew tired of touching her skin. Must be all the hours she spent in a hot, humid kitchen that kept it so soft. He captured her wrist and drew it toward him so he could kiss the inside of her elbow.

"I thought you wanted to talk."

"This is a form of talking." He licked the soft

skin this time. She always tasted sugary, as though she spent her days working in a bakery. "So sweet," he murmured.

"I splashed chocolate affogato on myself." Her voice was gentle in the quiet room. The curtains were still open, the soft glow of streetlamps illuminating the bed.

He kissed the spot again, ran his tongue along the delicate folds to lap up any missed spots. "What is that?"

"A dollop of vanilla ice cream drowned in hot chocolate."

Donovan hummed his approval. He could do a lot with chocolate. And the idea of drowning portions of her body in it, where he would gallantly come to the rescue, sounded incredibly appealing. And tasty.

He pressed another kiss to her skin. "Maybe you should put it on the menu."

"Donovan. Stop." She rolled away. "Don't distract me. You can't stay here."

"Do you want me to leave?"

He wanted her to say yes, to point at the door. She sighed. "I don't know. I'm confused." She glared at him. "You confuse me."

"I love you." Because in his opinion, that was the most important thing. "That means I'll do whatever I can to make you happy. You don't have to decide about the restaurant tonight." He lifted both hands to offer surrender. "But I want you to know that I'm serious. About you and the restaurant."

"What does that mean?" She watched him warily now.

"Just what I said. I want to be with you."

"And the restaurant?"

"If you want to buy it, it's yours. It was always more yours than mine. More yours than any of ours."

She nodded. "I appreciate that. Really. But I'm not ready to make that decision."

"Is it because of me? What if Owen were the one to make this offer?"

"Owen wouldn't be naked in bed with me."

She flipped over to face him. Her nipples brushed against his chest, peaking at the gentle touch. He'd have thought she was trying to distract him again, but her expression was serious. "I'm not refusing. But this would be easier if I didn't—" She halted.

"Didn't what?"

She tilted her face down and away. "If I didn't love you."

Donovan released the breath caught in his lungs. She loved him. In his world, that made everything okay. Or pretty close. He reached out and put a finger under her chin, raising it up until their eyes met. "I'm going to need to hear that again."

She scowled. "Maybe I don't want to say it again."

He waited, patiently, smiling until she blinked.

Then he leaned forward, pressed his lips to hers. Their eyelashes practically touched. "I love you."

He felt her intake of breath, a pulse, almost a hiccup, saw her eyes soften. "I love you."

He reveled in the admission for a moment until she poked him in the chest, and this time not with her nipples.

"Stop looking smug."

"I love you. You love me. What's not to feel smug about?" He gathered her so close that their bodies pressed together. "Since we're admitting what's in our hearts, you want to tell me what's holding you back about the restaurant?"

She stiffened, but he didn't let go. He ran a hand up and down her back in a slow, smooth rhythm until he felt her muscles slacken. Then he rubbed some more.

"I thought you wanted the restaurant."

"I did." She let her chin fall to her chest again and exhaled, her breath brushing across his pecs. "I do."

"Then what's bothering you?"

"I did a lot of thinking over the past month." She kept her face averted. "And I convinced myself that I didn't need the restaurant to feel fulfilled or happy. That it wasn't La Petite Bouchée I wanted. I could be equally happy owning any restaurant."

"Even the diner?"

She flicked a glance at him. "Let's not talk crazy." She lowered her eyes again. "And now you're back in my life and you're offering everything I want and I want to say yes."

"But?" he asked helpfully.

"But I don't know which feeling is real. Do I really want a brand-new space with no memories or does it just feel safer, less scary because if it failed, it wasn't really mine yet?"

Donovan considered that. "Did I ever tell you about my first foray into the industry?"

She glanced up. "If you tell me how it was scary, but it ended up being a big success and—"

"That's not what happened. I failed. Miserably. We shut down after only a year and after bleeding my trust fund dry. So I understand the fear of losing something you really want to succeed." He reached up to stroke her hair. "But that doesn't mean you stop trying."

"No, but I don't have to put my heart on the line, either. Maybe it's better to leave the restaurant with you. You're the one with experience and support from other properties."

"But you're the one who loves it."

"I do." She nodded. "But it would kill me to see it close down. After how hard we worked."

He could understand that. "Would it be easier to see someone else take it over? See someone else in your kitchen? Changing your menu?" He could tell by the way her lips tightened that it wouldn't. "So maybe we consider something else."

"Like?"

"Maybe you don't buy it, you buy *in*. Shares, part ownership." He'd thought through this eventuality, had found it more appealing than he'd expected.

She tilted her head to the side. "But I'm not part of your family."

His hands stopped. Did she really not see it?

"I know that's important to you." And Donovan recognized the thick tone of her voice, the emotion so strong that it infused every word. "It was one of the first things you ever said to me when we talked about the restaurant. The business is only for family."

He had said that. He still believed it. Family was still important to him and so was the family business. He'd fight for both of them. Julia clearly understood that, but she didn't understand one other very important thing.

"Julia." Now it was his voice thick with emotion. He looked down at her. "Haven't you realized yet? You are part of my family."

BUT WAS SHE REALLY?

Julia couldn't quite decide. Donovan was certainly acting as if he believed it. He'd respected her wishes and given her some space in Paris. But after the first day of touring the sights alone, eating by herself and sleeping solo, knowing he was just down the hall, that he'd be by her side in a minute if she asked, Julia had been forced to admit that she missed him. That she didn't want that space. So she'd called, a sense of relief filling her chest as soon as she'd heard his voice on the phone, and he'd spent the remainder of their nights in Paris in her hotel room, even moving his toothbrush to her bathroom.

They'd talked about the restaurant only once. When he'd brought it up over dinner, reaffirming that La Petite Bouchée was hers if she wanted it and even producing a contract from his suitcase stating as much. But she'd told him she still had some thinking to do and she'd let him know when she was ready to discuss terms or conditions or anything at all to do with his offer.

Part of her wondered why she didn't just accept his offer. Ten percent ownership, with an option to increase to twenty-five. All she had to do was agree and go back to doing what she loved best: cooking.

But she still felt uncertain about their situation. Sure, they'd spent most nights together since they'd returned from Paris. But that had been only a couple of weeks. He said he loved her, but they had no official ties. Did he see a lifetime with her? Or was this something more transient? Because suddenly, that felt just as important as any shares.

Julia exhaled and stared at the wall in her apartment. They'd flown home two days ago, but she still hadn't been able to make up her mind.

She didn't want a minimal stake in anything and she didn't want pity shares. And that was what this felt like. She exhaled again. Except Donovan said it wasn't. He said she could turn down the offer. He encouraged her to meet with a lawyer and ask for other concessions. But Julia wasn't sure she wanted that.

She didn't want a business relationship. And that was holding her back. She felt as though the business was tied to their relationship and she didn't want it to be. She exhaled once again and let her head fall back against the gray chair that had been her mother's favorite.

She'd gone back to The Sun Café this morning and surprised herself by quitting. But the relief in her heart told her it was the right thing to do. She might not be sure where her career was heading, but she knew it didn't include coming home with the scent of home fries and sausage clinging to her hair.

Then she'd had lunch with Sasha. Her best

friend still wasn't enjoying her new position as executive chef and told Julia she'd better figure out her plans quickly so that she could hire Sasha away from her current drudgery. Julia only pointed out that Sasha deserved a lifetime of drudgery after breaking the best-friend code and telling Donovan where she'd gone. But she couldn't be too mad, since Sasha had had only her best interests at heart.

Plus, Sasha had told Owen, not Donovan. So really it was Owen who deserved her censure.

They talked about Julia's trip and reconciliation with Donovan and Sasha's hellish night of service last Friday. And Julia pretended everything was fine, that her heart didn't ache whenever she thought of the restaurant, that she didn't miss the long hours and the laughs with staff. That it didn't kill her to listen to Sasha talk about it. The good and the bad and occasionally the ugly, like the server who'd walked out in the middle of service because he was "looking for something a little less stressful."

But it bothered her. She wanted to handle the hellish night of service. She wanted to hire the new server to make sure they were the right fit for La Petite Bouchée. But she couldn't bring herself to sign that contract. She plucked at the hem of her peach dress and brooded.

She was still brooding when Donovan arrived at her apartment that evening.

"Hello, beautiful." He kissed her, and when he did, she forgot about all those worries. With his arms around her, she felt sure. But was she? "You ready?"

Julia forced a smile to her lips and the disconcerting thoughts out of her head. "Yes. Where are we going?" She turned to look at Donovan, who'd only told her to wear something nice as he was taking her out for dinner. She'd accessorized her summery peach dress with her mother's pearls. They felt warm against her skin. She lifted a finger to touch them as they exited her building and headed toward his car.

"You'll see."

She wished he'd just tell her, but he seemed to enjoy the little secret and she enjoyed letting him have it. She resolved to sit back and enjoy the ride. And she did. Right up until Donovan turned the car toward Granville Island.

Her eyes shot toward him, her body tense. But he remained relaxed, hands easy on the wheel as he steered the car through the heavy throngs of summer crowd and pulled up in front of La Petite Bouchée.

Julia balked. She hadn't been back since quitting. Not once. She feared it would be too easy to fall into the rhythms she'd built and created, to take up as executive chef once more. Her hands fisted.

"Donovan?" She glanced at him. True to his word, the restaurant was still part of the Ford Group. Even though she happened to know that he'd received three offers on the property in the past month, each one more generous than the last. "What are we doing here?"

"It's time to come back." He climbed out of the car, came around to the passenger side to help her out.

Julia didn't move, didn't even unbuckle her seat belt. She stared at the hand Donovan held out to her. She wasn't ready to come back.

Her flowing peach dress felt constricting, as though the straps were going to reach up and wrap themselves around her throat, and the gold belt seemed to cut into her waist. Even her strappy gold shoes, which she had to buckle on the last hole to fit her narrow feet, felt tight, as if everything was biting into her.

"I know you've missed it."

His voice was gentle and warm. It rained down on her like a summer drizzle. "It's time to face the kitchen."

She smiled and some of the panic abated. She had missed it. Desperately. She put her hand in his and climbed out of the car.

The air, cooler near the water, eased some of

the tightness in her throat. She heard the familiar call of seagulls scavenging for food on the pier just off the market, smelled the briny scent of the ocean and felt it ease a little more. She'd missed this. Not just the cooking and the people, but the place and the location. She probably shouldn't have stayed away.

She took strength from Donovan, absorbing it the way her pans absorbed heat from the stove. "I have missed it." And she let him lead her down the walkway to the window beside the front door, still emblazoned with her name.

La Petite Bouchée
Executive Chef: Julia Laurent

She didn't say he should change that. She didn't mention it at all. But her eyes stole back to the gold script as they walked through the door. Her name. Her restaurant.

The hostess blinked when she saw her. "Chef."

"Just Julia now," she said, though it made her heart hurt. But it was true. Her name might be on the door, but she was no longer the chef here and the staff shouldn't refer to her as such. She forced a smile.

The hostess nodded. "The rest of your party is already here." She led them out of the small entry and into the main dining room. Julia was pleased to see the place was hopping.

La Petite Bouchée might not be hers right now,

but it was still her hard work that had helped make it a success. Her opinion that had gotten the beautiful walnut bar instead of the glossy white one Donovan had wanted. Her food on the menu.

Her smile grew in size and sincerity when she saw who made up the party waiting for them. She turned to look at Donovan. "What's all this for?"

"You'll see." He merely guided her toward a table at the back. She tensed when she saw who was waiting for them. His parents, Owen and Mal. She was half thrilled, half panicked and sent him a questioning look.

"They missed you, too." His hand was warm on the small of her back. "Almost as much as I did."

Julia wanted to say something. To him, to them. But she couldn't get anything past the lump in her throat.

"Where have you been hiding yourself?" Gus rose to pull her into a warm bear hug. His arms were strong and protective. "Tell my son to stop hogging you to himself."

"Can you blame me?" Donovan moved to tug her back, but Gus spun them away.

"I'm not done with her yet." He gave her another hug then a stern look. "I'm not very happy that you haven't been to see us, young lady."

And Julia felt the lump become a boulder. Maybe she should have gone to see Gus and Evelyn. Should have looked past her own hurt, sucked up her fear and knocked on their door. "Sorry."

"No need to apologize." He smiled, and the boulder shrank to a pebble. "Just make sure it doesn't happen again."

Because they missed her and they wanted to see her. The affection they shared with her wasn't wholly based on her relationship with Donovan. Julia realized she was accepted and it was the greatest feeling in the world. "Yes, sir."

"And don't call me sir. Makes me feel old."

Owen cleared his throat noisily.

"That's enough out of you," Gus told his younger son. He turned Julia back to the table. "Did you hear I've taken up gardening?" He looked awfully pleased with himself, which surprised her, given his less-than-enthusiastic response to foods that were green.

She nodded as pleasure spiraled through her. It was as though she'd never been apart from them at all. But maybe that was how it was with family. "I heard you've got quite the green thumb. How's that going?"

"Why don't you come by and see for yourself."

"Dad." Donovan took Julia's hand back. "Now you're the one hogging her."

"I'm just making up for lost time."

"Gus." Evelyn rose and put a hand on her husband's arm. "Let the rest of us say hello, too."

"Fine, fine," Gus grumbled, but he sent Julia a wink over his wife's head. A private communication between the two of them. Like an inside joke that could be shared only between loved ones.

And for the first time, it really became clear what she'd missed by letting go of them. The support, the cheer, just knowing they'd be there for her.

She wanted to bury her face in Evelyn's shoulder, the way she might have as a child with her mother. She didn't, but Evelyn seemed to sense what she needed anyway.

"It's good to have you back, dear." And though her hug wasn't as strong or bone-crunching as Gus's had been, it was just as powerful. She stroked the back of Julia's head. "Just give it a minute."

And when Julia felt the prickling behind her eyes subside, she gave Evelyn another squeeze. "Thank you."

"Anytime. You're family now."

Not *like* family. Family. Julia darted a look at Donovan. It was the same thing he'd said.

"Told you," he mouthed.

"Did you tell them to say that?" she whispered in his ear a minute later when she finally let go of Evelyn.

"Have you met my parents? No one tells them to do anything."

Julia received a hug from Mal, too, which was just as warm if less effusive.

"My turn." Owen, the only one she hadn't let go because he refused to be dropped, horned his way in.

"I don't think I'm talking to you," Julia told him. "Since you can't keep a secret."

"I didn't tell your secret. Sasha told your secret." He pulled her into a hug. "It's good to see you. And if my brother blows it with you again, I'd like to state for the record that a) he didn't come to me for advice and b) I'm available to travel."

"She's not going anywhere with you," Donovan said. But there was a smile in his voice and on his face.

As they settled into their seats and conversation, Julia's heart grew full. This was how family should be. Loving, welcoming, supportive. She'd missed it. And them.

The food was good, though her chicken was just a shade overdone. Not enough that most people would notice and nowhere near the point of dry. But verging on it. She wouldn't have let it out of her kitchen. *The* kitchen, she reminded herself. No matter that her name was still on the door. No matter that it looked good there. This was no longer her restaurant or kitchen. But she made a mental note to talk to Sasha about it.

Just because La Petite Bouchée was no longer hers didn't mean she wanted it to fail.

They laughed and talked, enjoying their meals and dessert, and as the night wore on, Julia felt some of her fears slide away. She was happy here. She looked around the room, taking it in as a customer instead of a chef. It was classy and comfortable. She and Donovan had done a good job. An amazing job.

And she wasn't the only one enjoying it. The Fords were, too, along with everyone else in the restaurant. Julia felt a niggle of loss. That she'd let this go and walked away. She missed it. Maybe she always would.

But that was her issue to deal with.

A round of coffee had just been poured when Donovan stood up, drawing the attention of everyone at the table. "I think now is a good time."

A good time for what? But when Julia glanced around the table, no one else seemed surprised by the announcement. The Fords didn't seem to think anything was odd or amiss. They all watched Donovan with the occasional eye flick to her. She looked back to Donovan, intending to ask what was happening, but she didn't get her chance.

"As many of you know, I didn't want to buy this restaurant."

Julia wondered where he was going with this. They'd been back only a week, and during that time, he'd promised to let her figure things out on her own. Of course, he'd also forced her to come to La Petite Bouchée.

"And as I've told Julia, I've come to realize the error of my ways."

"Donovan." She tried to interrupt. Other people were beginning to notice him standing in the middle of the room making a speech. "What are you doing?"

"I'm making a speech." He winked and plowed ahead as though she hadn't warned him at all. "Some of you may know that I've been trying to work out ownership terms with my lovely and talented chef." Julia opened her mouth to tell him that she wasn't the chef here anymore, but he just kept talking. "But no matter what I offer, she turns me down. It seems I might have said something during our initial meeting about keeping all ownership in the family."

"You did say that," Julia felt obligated to point out. She could feel the eyes on her now. Her face felt hot and she shifted uncomfortably. She didn't want to talk about this. Not here and not in front of his family.

"I did." Donovan looked only at her. "And I've thought of a solution."

Julia caught movement by the kitchen door, saw Sasha and some of the other staff come through. What was going on? Were they all going to try to convince her? And would she be able to keep up the pretense with all of them watching her, urging her to admit what was in her heart? That she was afraid, but she still wanted the restaurant more than she could say.

"Julia Suzanne Laurent."

She whipped her head around and saw that Donovan had gotten down on one knee.

"Donovan." Julia's voice was a whisper now. "What are you doing?" But she didn't need to ask. It was pretty obvious when he got down on one knee and pulled out a black velvet box and flipped the lid to reveal a stunning ring. A single square diamond surrounded by a circle of sparkling diamonds.

"It was my grandmother's ring that I had re-purposed. A little bit of tradition and a little bit of innovation. Just like us."

Her chest felt full—too full. "When did you do this?"

"I called my mom from Paris, asked her to take it to a good jeweler."

She swallowed and looked at the ring again. It wasn't at all what she would have picked herself, but now that she'd seen it, she couldn't imagine anything else. "Pretty sure of yourself, weren't you?"

"Hopeful."

Owen cough-talked into his hand. "Desperate."

Julia bit her lip to keep from laughing.

Donovan shot a glare at his brother and continued. "I had a special chain made, one with hooks where you can attach the ring, so you don't have to worry about it when you're working. So I'd like to know—will you marry me?"

Julia looked at him, then the ring, then him. He was offering her everything. His heart, his name, his family. All she had to do was accept. All she had to do was believe. Believe that he meant what he said. That he loved her. She looked into his eyes and saw there was only one possible answer.

"Yes." And the band, when he slid it on her finger, felt warm and comforting. The people at their table began to clap, as did the rest of the restaurant.

Donovan rose and gathered her into his arms. "I love you."

"I love you more."

He laughed quietly, the sound rumbling against her ear. "I love hearing you say that. Tell me again."

She obliged twice before Sasha interrupted them, demanding a hug from the soon-to-be bride, then Mal, Owen, Gus and Evelyn, and Julia found herself surrounded by friends and family, those she loved and who loved her in return. It felt good.

Sasha pulled her aside for another hug as the rest of the staff filed back into the kitchen. "Donovan was so sweet. Do you know he came by and asked for my permission?"

"He did?" Julia glanced over her shoulder at Donovan. At her fiancé. More love than she'd thought existed filled her up. Her mother was gone and she didn't know who her father was, but Donovan had still given her the traditions she needed in the only way possible. She wiped at her suddenly wet eyes.

"Yes. And once I was assured that he could be trusted with your heart, I told him I'd be thrilled."

Julia wiped her eyes a little harder. "Does this mean you're planning to give me away?" She sniffled as she thought of her mom and of the family she was about to join. "Because I sort of thought you'd be my maid of honor."

Sasha flung her arms around her. "I can do both. I'm so happy for you."

Julia sniffled some more.

"Do not get snot on my chef jacket. Food safety."

Julia gave a watery laugh. "Then you'd better stop hugging me." But she was grateful that Sasha didn't. She was grateful for everything right now.

Sasha had to go back to the kitchen and invited

Julia to come with her, to say hello to those who hadn't come out and show off her ring. Julia's initial instinct was to decline. Actually, no. That wasn't true. Her first instinct was to fly back there to greet everyone with a big hug and make sure they were taking care of her kitchen.

"I don't want to interrupt service."

Sasha's eyebrows lifted. "And why not? Too good for the likes of us now that you're an owner?"

Julia glanced over at the swinging door that led to the kitchen and, at one time, her salvation.

"They'll be pissed if they hear you were here and didn't pop in." Sasha laid a warm hand on her shoulder. "Come on, chef."

Julia's throat tightened. Chef. She hadn't been called that since she left La Petite Bouchée.

"Don't you want to check and make sure nothing has burned down? I'd tell you everything is fine, but there was that one pan. The one you used for veggies and, well… *Poof.* But it led a good life."

"You burned my veggie pan?" That had been her favorite pan.

"See? We need you."

They needed her, just as she needed them. She swallowed. Maybe it was time to make her decision. One way or the other, she needed to step out of limbo and into her future. Possibility rose in her chest, made her pulse flutter.

As much as she'd appreciated the easiness of the brunch gig, it hadn't even provided enough satisfaction in the short-term. Eggs and waffles, bacon and sausage weren't why she'd attended culinary school, weren't why she'd spent six years in France studying under the toughest and best chefs she could find.

She needed her own kitchen again.

The image of her name on the door flashed through her head again.

"Hey." Donovan put a hand on her shoulder. "You ready to come back to the table? We have champagne."

"In a minute. There's something I need to do." She kissed him, took a bracing breath and looked at Sasha. "Let's go."

She needn't have worried about her kitchen. It was just as she'd left it. Including her veggie pan. She sent Sasha a pointed look when she saw it, with nary a scorch mark, being used to sauté the holy trinity—onions, bell peppers and celery. The crew swarmed her when she stepped up to the pass and called out the next order. They wanted to know she was okay, wanted to know when she was coming back and wanted to know if, since she was marrying the owner—word traveled fast in the kitchen—she'd put in a good word to get them all a raise. She laughed and joked and even handled a couple of orders as easily as if she'd never been away.

She couldn't stop smiling when she got back to the table.

Donovan leaned over to put his hand on her leg. He did that a lot, always looking for ways to touch her, as though assuring himself that she was still here. She liked it.

She put her hand on top of his, feeling the pressure of the new ring around her finger.

She looked down at her hand. The engagement ring felt different—not heavy or ungainly, just different. There was something where she'd been used to having nothing. She tilted her hand from side to side so the diamond caught the light and sparkled. He'd even bought her a special-made chain so she could wear it at work.

Donovan leaned over and kissed her on the cheek. "It suits you."

"You suit me." She pressed more closely against him.

Owen popped the cork on the champagne and poured a row of flutes. The liquid bubbled up but never over the top. He pressed a glass into everyone's hands.

They toasted and tasted, and after another round of hugging, everyone sat down. Donovan leaned closer. "I do have one more bit of news."

His hand slid up her thigh, making her shudder. "Donovan, your family." But when she darted a glance around the table, no one seemed to be paying much attention. Still, as welcoming and easygoing as Gus and Evelyn were, Julia didn't think they'd appreciate it if she and Donovan started making out.

"Not that." But his hand slid a little higher.

Julia put her hand on top of his. Not to remove it, but just to keep him from pushing farther.

Donovan chuckled, the sound sending another warm shiver through her. He raised his voice, garnering the notice of everyone else. "I think it's time for her engagement gift." He gave her a brief squeeze before sitting up straight. "This is something from all of us."

From all of them? Julia looked from face to face, seeing friendly and accepting stares. From all of them. Because she was one of them, or pretty darn close. They loved her, and Donovan loved her. She felt impossibly full, as though rainbows and canaries were going to explode out of her in a sparkly shower of joy. "I don't need an engagement gift." She already felt spoiled.

Impossibly spoiled. Luckiest-girl-in-the-world spoiled.

"We'd like to give you shares in the restaurant."

Julia's breath caught. What? But, but... Her

thoughts devolved into a jumble of yes and she'd start tomorrow and had the Fords read her mind or was she just that obvious? She focused. Tonight had made what she wanted so blatantly obvious. All she had to do was say yes. But she'd already made her decision.

"No." The word was drawn out, long and slow and full of the thoughts still bounding around in her brain.

A circle of surprised faces looked back at her.

"I mean," she hurried to clarify, "that I won't simply take shares. I'll earn them."

Donovan leaned toward her, whispered in her ear, "I have a few ideas I'd like to propose."

"You're lucky you're cute." He grinned and kissed her and it felt good. Better than that, it felt right. This all did.

She took a breath and looked back at the table. "I want to come back as chef. If that's what you had in mind."

They were all nodding as if that should have been obvious. "There was a reason we haven't changed the signage."

In her mind's eye, Julia saw her name in that beautiful font beside the front door. "Okay. Good. And I'll work for those shares. I have some money saved, too."

"Julia." Donovan put his arm around her. "This is a gift. You're family now."

She hesitated and looked around at the Fords' smiling faces. She realized that was true. She was part of their family, had been becoming one of them for weeks now. She saw the smiles of the servers who were nearby, those who'd obviously overheard Donovan's announcement, and she realized they were still part of her family, too. Even if she hadn't seen them in weeks, they still wanted her to be happy, were happy for her.

"Say yes, Julia. He won't give up." Owen raised his glass from across the table. "When Donovan gets something in his head, it's not easy to change his mind. I should know. It took months for me to convince him to believe I'm a capable manager."

"I could still change my mind," Donovan joked, but there was no tension in his voice, and Julia saw the look that passed between the brothers. It was one of appreciation and newfound acceptance.

This was the family she was joining, the family she was part of. A family that loved, that was open to change and always supportive.

She thought about the kitchen that was just waiting for her to come back and the family she'd found both in and out of the restaurant that wanted her to say yes. And when the guilt crept up, she beat it back. Maybe it had been a mistake to leave. Maybe it hadn't. But what mattered now was how she moved forward. Was she going to stay stuck in the past, wallowing in old decisions, or lift her chin and step into the future? She thought about her mom, how proud she'd be to know that Julia wasn't just running the kitchen, but owned a stake in it. So what was she holding back for?

"Yes."

She could return to her condition later. This was a conversation that didn't need to be had here and now. It probably wouldn't have been heard over all the celebrating and glass clinking and smothering hugs anyway.

Julia waited until they were in Donovan's bed, warm and sated from food and sex, to bring it up. She rolled onto her side to face him and put a hand on his chest. "Donovan?"

"Yes?" He opened his eyes and looked at her, trapped her hand against his chest. She could feel the steady thump of his heart.

"About the restaurant."

He yawned. "You already said you'd take ownership. You can't take it back now. We have a verbal contract."

She laughed. "I'm not taking it back, but I want to do something for you." She pressed a kiss to his lips—her fiancé's lips—and felt a shiver of pleasure. Reminded herself to stay on track.

He opened his eyes and looked at her. "You've done plenty. Remember, I'm not sixteen anymore."

"Do you ever think about anything else?"

"You're naked in my bed. So, no."

"Seriously, Donovan? I'm trying to have a meaningful conversation here."

"Then quit rubbing up against me." But he held her in place when she started to move away. "No, I take that back. You're perfect right where you are."

She settled against him, since she liked exactly where she was, too. "Tell me about the pub."

"The wine bars are fine. Better than fine, actually. Owen's made some inspired changes."

"Not the bars." Though she'd love to take the opportunity to talk up Owen, this wasn't the time. "The upscale gastropub. Are you still moving forward with it?"

He looked surprised. "Yes, but what does that have to do with the restaurant?"

"I told you that I wasn't going to just accept the shares. I meant that. I'm going to earn them. I want you to cut my salary, and whatever you'd sell the shares at, and put that money toward your gastropub." It was only fair. He'd given her everything she wanted, so she would do what she could to assist him.

Donovan's eyes softened. "Julia, the company has more than enough money to pursue both options. You don't have to do that."

Julia thought about it for half a second. "I want

to." She didn't think it was enough, but it was a start. A way of showing him that she truly was part of the family. That she would sweat and labor and do whatever was necessary not just for her own happiness but for theirs, as well.

"I'm not cutting your salary. In fact, now would be a good time to ask me for a raise."

"Put it toward my shares." She snuggled closer to him. "And I want to do whatever I can to help get it ready for opening. Create the menu, hire your kitchen staff."

"And run La Petite Bouchée?"

"They managed just fine without me these last couple of months." She could ease off a little to help Donovan.

"Actually, they haven't."

Julia wasn't sure that was true, but it was nice to hear her presence had been missed. "I can do both." She already had some ideas for a more casual menu, thoughts that had risen to the surface as she'd sat in the restaurant, in *her* restaurant. She still got a little thrill when she thought about it. And hiring wasn't an issue. In fact, she already could think of a few staff members who might be a good fit. Those who were ready for more responsibility and who she knew could be trusted to take care of Donovan's dream.

Donovan kissed her. "I don't know what we did without you."

She smiled. "You survived."

"Barely. We need you. I need you."

"You've got me." She leaned forward, kissed him softly on the lips. "Forever."

* * * * *

Don't miss Owen's story, coming from Harlequin Superromance in May 2015!

LARGER-PRINT BOOKS!

GET 2 FREE LARGER-PRINT NOVELS PLUS
2 FREE GIFTS!

☰ HARLEQUIN®

Romance

From the Heart, For the Heart

HRLP13R

LARGER-PRINT BOOKS!

HARLEQUIN *Presents*

PASSION
GUARANTEED
SEDUCTION

GET 2 FREE LARGER-PRINT NOVELS PLUS 2 FREE GIFTS!